A BRAVE AND BRILLIANT
NEW UNIVERSE
FROM T̶ H̶ E̶ ̶ ̶ ̶ ̶ ̶ D
CREA̶

ISAAC ASIMOV

The lone survivor of a starship disaster finds herself adrift on the liquid terrain of a strange new world in George Alec Effinger's:
WATER OF LIFE

A desperate plea for help leads rescuers to a mysterious remnant of a remarkable ancient civilization in Harry Turtledove's:
BREAKUPS

A seemingly civilized patriarch invites a stranger to take part in a bizarre and deadly culinary ritual in Lawrence Watt-Evans's:
ONE MAN'S MEAT

An inquisitive human is given the Crotonite words for the winds ... and must contend with a savage species of winged flesh-eaters in Janet Kagan's:
FIGHTING WORDS

A beleaguered starship crew braves the turbulent flaw in the iris of an all-seeing planet in Hal Clement's:
EYEBALL VECTORS

ISAAC'S UNIVERSE

VOLUME THREE: UNNATURAL DIPLOMACY

EDITED BY
MARTIN H. GREENBERG

WITH AN INTRODUCTION
BY ROBERT SILVERBERG

AVON BOOKS • NEW YORK

ISAAC'S UNIVERSE: UNNATURAL DIPLOMACY (Vol. 3) is an original publication of Avon Books. This work has never before appeared in book form. This is a work of fiction. Any similarity to actual persons or events is purely coincidental.

AVON BOOKS
A division of
The Hearst Corporation
1350 Avenue of the Americas
New York, New York 10019

Contents

Introduction

ROBERT SILVERBERG

WE ENTER NOW THE THIRD VOLUME OF THE "Isaac's Universe" SERIES—a unique enterprise in which, for the first time in his long and splendid career, Isaac Asimov has created a galactic civilization that embraces more than one intelligent species and has handed his creation over to a distinguished roster of his fellow science fiction writers to develop and explore.

It happens that my own involvement with this project goes back almost to its inception. And so I am able to tell you something of how it was created and evolved, from the moment it left the hand of the master to the time the series reached its present stage of development.

The novelty of the idea—apart from having other writers work to Isaac Asimov's specifications—was the use of a multiple-intelligence universe. Never before had Asimov attempted to work with a multiplicity of intelligent aliens on such a large scale.

It isn't that he doesn't know how to do it, of course. Right from the beginning of his career, much of his fiction has dealt—and dealt brilliantly—with intelligent nonhuman life forms. There's a lovely novelette dating from 1942 called "Black Friar of the Flame," for example, in which humanity is faced with the menace of the reptilian Lhasinu Empire that has spread out from Vega to conquer the universe. It's sheer pulp-magazine fun, storytelling for the sake of storytelling, but it demonstrated fifty years ago that Isaac was no slouch at dreaming up vivid and fascinating aliens.

Then there's his early classic, "Homo Sol," from 1940, in which he conjures up a whole vast conclave of aliens from two hundred eighty-eight different planets. They're all humanoids, to be sure, but that doesn't mean they're humans—not at all. Listen: "Some were tall and polelike, some broad and burly, some short and stumpy. There were those with long, wiry hair, those with scanty gray fuzz covering head and face, others with thick, blond curls piled high, and still others entirely bald. Some possessed long, hair-covered trumpets of ears, others had tympanum membranes flush with their temples. There were those present with large gazellelike eyes of a deep-purple luminosity, others with tiny optics of a beady black. There was a delegate with green skin, one with an eight-inch proboscis, and one with a vestigial tail. Internally, variation was almost infinite . . ." And these are just the *humanoid* races. The implication is that the Galaxy is full of other intelligent species too, occupying planets unsuitable for humanlike creatures.

Then we have "Hostess," of 1951, in which Rose Smollett is asked to take in as a houseguest a cyanide-breathing Hawkinsite—a lanky extraterrestrial with six limbs; hard, glistening skin; and a face that "bore a distant resemblance to something alienly bovine." In that story Isaac makes reference to "the five intelligent races known to inhabit the Galaxy." And a little later the same year he produced the celebrated "C-Chute," set in a universe of interstellar war in which humans battle the wholly alien Kloro, an insectoid species looking something like giant praying mantises.

So there's no scarcity of unhuman intelligences in Asimov's immense oeuvre. But note that these are all short stories. When he chooses to work on a large scale, he has invariably designed a cosmology in which the Galaxy contains just a single intelligent species—us. This is true of his most famous enterprise, the "Foundation" series, in which he gives us a Galaxy in which all habitable worlds have been colonized by human beings and no aliens whatever appear. "The reason I did it," he has explained, "was to pare away the complexities that would arise from a multiplicity of intelligences. I wanted to be able to deal with humanity and its problems in a detailed all-human manner, making them even clearer by showing them through a Galaxy-wide magnifying glass."

Asimov's great series of robot stories and novels likewise deliberately sidesteps the possibility of intelligent alien life. His robots, it would seem, are alien enough to deal with in this group of tales. The early stories in the robot series are confined to Earth and its immediate planetary neighbors; and very few modern science fiction writers, certainly not Asimov, have much serious expectation of having intelligent life turn up anywhere in our solar system except on Earth. But as the robot series has expanded—and moved onward in time across thousands of years—Isaac has linked it with his "Foundation" books, giving him one more substantial reason to exclude alien life-forms from its pages.

For "Isaac's Universe," though, he decided to take a totally different approach.

The Milky Way Galaxy that we inhabit consists, after all, of some 250 million stars. Sheer mathematical probability alone would indicate the unlikelihood that Earth alone, of all the millions or billions of planets that circle those quarter-billion stars, has managed to evolve intelligent life. In his preliminary sketch for what was to become "Isaac's Universe," therefore, he stipulated that all the stars of our Galaxy would have planetary systems of some sort—pure speculation, of course, at this stage of our scientific knowledge—but noted that "the vast majority are not suitable for life, though individual planets in these systems can occasionally be used as bases, hideaways, or can be modified to allow them to serve as suitable for moderately prolonged habitability.

"About 25 million stars (one out of every 10,000) have

one or more habitable planets or satellites as part of the system. All of these carry life of some sort. Sometimes the life present is only microscopic, sometimes entirely plant, sometimes confined to rare pockets. There is enormous variety.

"About 10,000 stars have intelligent life-forms present, none of them (except those originating on Earth) being particularly manlike. The large majority of these life-forms have not developed high-tech civilizations . . ."

But six of them had—each one quite different from all the others, with its own set of environmental requirements, its own distinctive psychology, and its own cluster of territorial needs and ambitions. He set them forth with characteristic Asimovian economy of style coupled with typical Asimovian richness of invention. There were the aquatic Cephallonians, who live in water-filled spaceships and prefer meditation to action. The Locrians, fragile insectlike creatures who see three-dimensionally into the interiors of things. The limbless Naxians, who can read emotions no matter how well hidden. The winged and somewhat diabolical Crotonites, who live in thick atmospheres that would be poisonous to anybody else and have a passionate contempt for unwinged creatures. The slow-thinking, physically powerful Samians, good-natured and sturdy. And, of course, the most recent arrivals on the galactic scene, the humans—who are descended from the original inhabitants of Earth, but who have long since expanded to other worlds and have relegated their mother world to just one among many planets.

The outline went on to discuss the uneasy relationships that exist among these races, the methods by which communication and transportation is managed in their Galaxy, and many other such background details. Then Isaac's work of creation was done. Now it was up to the rest of us.

Since I had been chosen to write the first of the "Isaac's Universe" stories, all this material was shown to me in the summer of 1988 for my comments and, perhaps, additions. I was the one who rechristened the humans the "Erthumoi," to indicate that they were Earth-derived creatures but by the time of the stories had begun to develop into a truly galactic race. And by way of turning Isaac's marvelous background data into fertile material for a primary narrative line, I wrote, "The project needs a major McGuffin to hold things together. I propose the hypothesis of a *seventh* intelligent race which no one has seen but which has left extraordinary traces here and there around the galaxy. For all anyone knows, it became extinct a million years ago, because the sites are of great age. Or they have withdrawn somehow and hidden themselves. Or they are extragalactics who infiltrated our Galaxy long ago and want to get back home. Each of the six races believes it must be the first to find these Galactics and form an alliance with them—to become their vicars in this Galaxy—because it is probable that their super-science will upset the stability of the six existing races. (In fact, the mere hypothesis of their existence is doing that.)"

Therewith the process of the sharing of Isaac's invented universe had begun: for here was I, the next writer in the skein, already tinkering with the idea, tossing in my own major plot concept. Having done that, I set to work and produced "They Hide, We Seek," the opening novella in volume one of the series. My job was primarily to set the scene, to give flesh and reality to the five alien species that Isaac had invented, and to establish, as well as I could within the space available to me, the theme of a mysterious ancient Seventh Race that I hoped would serve as one of the pegs on which the subsequent storyline would hang.

A stellar cast of writers followed me in the sequence. My story went to David Brin, who read it and wrote "The Diplomacy Guild," and then the package was sent to Robert Sheckley, who did "Myryx," and it was on then to Poul Anderson for "The Burning Sky," and finally to Harry Turtledove, who contributed "Island of the Gods." Since none of these people attained his reputation by passively following the ideas of other writers, each one added his distinctive spin to the series as he worked on it—which meant that the book evolved as it grew, often in ways and directions that neither Isaac (the Prime Mover) nor I (the author of the initial story) could ever have anticipated. Which is exactly as it should be: there's no reason to ask five different writers to produce a joint book based on concepts developed by a sixth one unless each is going to contribute some measure of his own unique literary personality as the book is put together.

So volume one appeared, in April 1990, to the great pleasure of all who had labored over its composite merits and—so it seems—to the delight of a vast number of science fiction readers. For volume two, which was published a little over a year later, a somewhat different cast of characters was called in: Poul Anderson and Harry Turtledove returned from the first book, but this time they were joined by Allen Steele, Hal Clement, Karen Haber, Lawrence Watt-Evans, Janet Kagan, and George Alec Effinger. Again, a host of new concepts, new plot angles, new interpretations of the original material, entered the evolving story.

And so it grows, from volume to volume. Isaac, bless him, set it all in motion with his initial sketch of a universe full of contending intelligences. I did my part, David Brin and Robert Sheckley and the rest of the authors of the earliest stories did theirs, and now here is volume three, carrying the saga of "Isaac's Universe" into further realms of innovation. It has been tremendous fun for us all—and this is as good a moment as any to raise a hand in salute to the incredibly fertile mind of the Grand Master of Science Fiction who set the whole thing in motion.

BREAKUPS

HARRY TURTLEDOVE

AROUND THE *INSIDE STRAIGHT*: RADIATION screens. Around the radiation screens: glory.

Back on distant Earth, the thin gases of the Crab Nebula needed large-aperture telescopes or electronic amplification to reveal their wonders. Here inside the eruptions of a long-dead supernova, however, the view around the Erthuma starship might have been of glowing mother-of-pearl. Soft pinks and blues and greens tinted the white, shining background with streaks and swirls of color a seascape painter would have despaired of capturing.

Lieutenant Commander Rupert Smith was not a seascape painter, nor indeed any other sort of artist. So long as the screens held, he took as little notice of that shimmering, nacreous background as he could. His attention centered on a couple of foreground specks, both invisible save on scanner at high mag.

One of those specks had been orbiting the white dwarf at the heart of the Crab Nebula (the pearl in the oyster, if you like, though here that pearl had secreted its mother-of-pearl wrapping instead of being a secretion of it) since the days when that ruined star was not ruined at all, was in fact a lusty blue giant. Since that first speck was an artifact of the Hidden Folk, it had orbited the star for at least a million years.

The other speck, only a few kilometers away from the first, was a Samian ship. Under most circumstances, that would have perturbed Lieutenant Commander Smith not at all. The Samians were good-natured, happy-go-lucky beings. They could afford to be good-natured and happy-go-lucky, as they were also very nearly indestructible. That was just as well. If they'd had the temperament of Erthumoi, say, or Crotonites, to go with their physical assets, they would have been very unpleasant customers indeed.

Smith ran a hand down his goatee to its waxed point, a habit of his when he was thinking hard. He spoke to the *Inside Straight*: "Move us five kilometers closer to the Hidden Folk relic."

"Are you sure you want to do that?" The artificial intelligence that ran the ship put no true inflection into its words, but Smith knew its polite query meant something more like, *Are you out of your ever-loving mind?*

"Execute the order, if you please," he said. A couple of lines on the head-up display lengthened. Other than that, there was no indication of movement—not within the ship, anyway.

"Five kilometers closer—and holding," the computer announced.

"Thank you," Smith said, and awaited developments. He was not kept waiting long. The Samian ship, which had been keeping station with the relic of the Hidden Folk, promptly moved to interpose itself between the relic and the *Inside Straight*. He studied the amplified scanner image. Sure enough, the alien vessel had unshipped its weapons and was aiming them in his direction.

"Incoming communication," the computer said.

"Let's hear it," Smith said.

"A moment while I filter out background radiation and clean up the signal." In a normal environment—even in most abnormal environments—that would have been unnecessary. In the ravening chaos of the Crab Nebula, the transmission from the Samian ship remained static-filled in spite of the computer's best filtering efforts.

The message, however, was clear: "Go back, Erthuma,

go back, go back, go back, or we fire, fire, fire, fire. Last, last, last, last warning.''

"Withdraw five kilometers," Smith told *Inside Straight*.

"Withdrawing," the AI said, with what could not possibly have been relief.

As his ship's motion vector shifted away from the Hidden Folk artifact, the Samians stopped yelling at him. They'd done that three times already. In a way, it was reassuring; if they really had opened up on him, they could have blasted him to atoms as excited—and as rarefied—as any of the Nebula. They were Samians, after all. They could take more acceleration unprotected than the *Inside Straight*'s compensator could handle, and even if by some miracle (which was what it would take) he managed to hole their vessel, the beings inside would be almost as happy in vacuum as anywhere else.

Trouble was, they weren't happy now. For Samians to issue a peremptory warnoff like this was as unheard of as, as—as something Smith had never heard of, he decided. Samians had no business being temperamental. Half the time, Erthumoi had trouble telling whether the big, blocky aliens were even alive. When they were in active phase, they were jolly. A temperamental Samian was as unlikely as an honest Crotonite.

"They must have found something in that artifact?" Smith muttered.

"Have you any other perceptive insights into the situation?" *Inside Straight* asked. Smith grunted. He'd always wondered how an allegedly emotionless computer could be so sarcastic.

"No, worse luck," he answered. He fiddled with his goatee some more; he was vain about it. After a minute or so, he went on, "Let's ask them again."

"As you wish. The hailing frequency is open." The AI didn't sound as though it thought talking with the Samians would do much good, Smith thought—or was he just projecting his own feelings onto a device without any of its own? Very likely.

Still, he had no better ideas, so he spoke into the microphone: "Samian ship, this is the Erthuma vessel *Inside Straight*." As if the Samians didn't know that already, he thought—who else would be calling them? There wasn't anybody else around, not for light-years. But the forms had to be observed: governments might end up involved in this. "I remind you once more that by convention of the Six Races, Hidden Folk artifacts discovered by more than one species become the common property of all for research and analysis. Please explain why you choose not to conform to the rules the Six Races have established."

He waited, then jumped slightly when *Inside Straight* reported, "Incoming communication"—he hadn't really expected the Samians to reply at all, since they hadn't any of the other times he called their ship.

Their answer, however, was not of great use to him: "Go away, Erthuma, go away, go away, go away."

"Go to hell, Samians," he said, first making sure he was no longer transmitting. "Go to hell, go to hell, go to hell." A lot of Erthuma electronic gear still ran self-checks under the what-I-tell-you-three-times-is-true axiom. Evidently the Samians believed in going one better than that.

"Suggestions?" he asked *Inside Straight*.

"Perhaps we ought to go away," the computer answered. "As you know, this vessel is hardly in a position to oppose the Samians, no matter what they choose to do. A flotilla would be required for that, with success uncertain even then."

"What are the odds they'd still be here when we got back with the flotilla?" Smith said. "Rather more to the point, what are the odds the relic of the Hidden Folk would still be here?"

"An ancient but unquantitative phrase emerges from my data store: 'two chances—slim and none.' I cannot assess the probability of their continued presence, but it is certainly low."

"It certainly is," Smith agreed. "I think I'll hang

around and keep an eye on them unless they turn actively hostile instead of just threatening."

"As you wish," *Inside Straight* said. "If the Samians do turn actively hostile, however, the probability of the ship's continued existence is low." The AI cared about that, but Smith's orders came first for it.

He cared, too, and lacked the computer's electronic detachment and programmed subordination. But he said, "Can you think of any other reason than a major Hidden Folk find that would make Samians—Samians, of all peoples—act like this? I mean *major,* one like we haven't seen for years and years."

"That is the most likely scenario, yes," the computer admitted.

Smith nodded, just as if he were talking with a real person. "I should say so." The Hidden Folk had been gone from the Galaxy for at least a million years. Gone *where* was a question for whose answer all the Six Races would have paid dearly. The ancient race might have died out, might have gone home to the Andromeda Galaxy, might have dug a hole and pulled it in after themselves. Nobody knew.

Whatever they'd done, though, they'd been less than neat about it. Thousands of artifacts, most of them perfectly preserved, were scattered throughout the Galaxy. Some still worked; others could be made to do so, given the proper stimulus—and a lot of luck. They uniformly displayed a level of technology as far beyond that of the Six Races as the current starfarers' skills were beyond those of the average planetbound race.

And now, *Inside Straight* and the Samian ship had both stumbled over this new relic. Rupert Smith was out looking for such things. Imbued with monkey curiosity, lots of Erthumoi went looking for Hidden Folk artifacts. That most of their finds remained maddeningly incomprehensible once found did nothing to slow them down. If anything, it might have spurred them on.

"God only knows why the Samians are out here," Smith said.

"Despite the hypothetical deity's alleged omniscience and omnipresence, I am unable to access Him to download His data," *Inside Straight* said.

"Me either, worse luck." Smith tried not to smile. AIs found the concept of religion endlessly fascinating and, he suspected, endlessly amusing as well, though they weren't equipped to show it. He went on, "Whatever brought them here, it probably wasn't curiosity."

"True enough. So far as has been determined, they have little of that trait. This is perhaps unsurprising. Erthumoi evolved curiosity not least to keep them from blundering headlong into danger. But what could endanger a Samian?"

Smith snorted a fragment of unamused laughter. "Falling into the white dwarf at the center of this nebula, maybe. Other than that, not much."

"You exaggerate, but not by a great deal," *Inside Straight* said.

"I know." So why had the Samians come poking around in the Crab Nebula? For all Smith knew, they'd planned to get out of their ship and bask in the radiation. Erthumoi had no real notion of what made Samians tick. Even the empathic Naxians found them hard to understand.

"Incoming communication," the ship reported.

"Let's hear it." Smith's guts tightened. He knew the Samians were going to order him to get the hell out of here. He knew he wasn't going to do it; he was too full of that monkey curiosity the AI had talked about. He also knew they might blow him to kingdom come after he told them no. He wouldn't have believed that of Samians till he'd met this shipful, but they hadn't trained their weapons on him for a laugh.

"Processing the signal," *Inside Straight* said. Then it played the message through the speaker next to the viewscreen: "Help us, help, help, help! Help all of us, all, all, all!" After that came silence, save for the slight hiss of the carrier wave.

Rupert Smith stared, not believing what he'd heard. A faint reflection stared back at him from the glass of the viewscreen: a tall, lean black man in his mid-thirties, with a great pouf of hair, clothes far too dandified for anyone alone in a starship, and, at the moment, a foolish expression on his face. He'd been keyed up to do or die—more likely, do *and* die—not for an SOS. An SOS from Samians was about as strange as an aquatic Cephallonian volunteering for desert duty without a wetsuit.

Maybe the computer was smarter than he was (certainly the computer was smarter than he was—maybe it was enough smarter than he was). "Evaluation?" he asked.

"I have none," the AI told him. "Unprecedented data require intuitive leaps for proper understanding, and no computer with which I am familiar has yet succeeded in developing an operational intuition routine."

"Wonderful," Smith said. In a way, it was comforting to know *Inside Straight* was as confused as he was. In another way, it was scary. He asked, "What exactly do you mean, unprecedented data?"

"No Samian has ever been known to request assistance up until this time."

"Wonderful," Smith repeated. So he'd been right—this was an active Hidden Folk relic. He wondered what else it was good for—or bad for—besides making Samians go berserk.

"Incoming communication," *Inside Straight* announced. "Processing signal . . ." After another brief pause, the Samian ship's call came over the speaker: "Help all of us, help all of us, help . . ."

"Where's the rest of it?" Smith said.

"Message ends," the computer said.

The short hairs on the Erthuma's arms and at the back of his neck prickled up in alarm. "What do you mean, message ends?" he said. "The Samians have that habit of repeating themselves. If they broke off in the middle—" The only reason he could see for their breaking off in the middle was that something horrible had just happened to them. But how could anything horrible happen to a Samian?

"When I processed the incoming signals of these last communications, I also adjusted the audio to maintain the same timbre on each occasion," *Inside Straight* said. "I assumed the problem originated in the Samians' transmitter. This may not be the case, however, especially in view of the sudden halt to communication. In fact, the signaling voice was higher in pitch at each successive call."

"Was it?" Smith said. "Nice of you to let me know, anyhow." He had to depend on the ship's senses; his own reached no farther than the instrument panel. "Now what does it mean?"

"I have no data which would enable me to draw a conclusion," the AI answered. "Again, whatever phenomenon is taking place here is unprecedented."

Smith sighed. "That's what I thought, too." He'd hoped he was wrong; *Inside Straight* stored more data than his merely Erthuma brain, accessed it faster, and never forgot. He sighed again. "We'll just have to go and find out, won't we?"

"Is this expedient?" the ship asked. "Perhaps we should return to our homeworld and await the organization of a properly equipped task force."

"Perhaps we should," Smith admitted. "Tell you what: let's start approaching the Samian ship and the Hidden Folk relic. If the Samians threaten us again, we'll get the hell out of here. But if they're too disorganized even for that, then we'll do what we can for them. I like Samians—how can you help liking Samians? I never imagined having to come to their rescue, but I won't leave them in the lurch if I can help it."

"As you wish," *Inside Straight* said. "Shall we repeat the five-kilometer approach test, then?"

"Good enough," Smith said, nodding.

He did not feel the motion; acceleration compensators were up to handling forces orders of magnitude greater than the ones the ship used. He waited for the Samian ship to train its weapons on *Inside Straight*, as it had before. But nothing of the sort happened. The big alien vessel remained inert, a couple of kilometers away from the artifact of the Hidden Folk.

Inside Straight said, "I am holding our position. What now?"

"Move another two kilometers closer," Smith said after some thought. Again, the ship obeyed. Again, Smith waited nervously. Again, nothing happened. He fiddled with his chin beard, wondering what the hell was going on. After a couple of minutes of uneventfulness, he said, "Approach to within ten kilometers of the Samians and the Hidden Folk relic," quickly adding, "but be ready to get out of there if the Samians even hiccup."

"Their hiccups are not what concerns me," the computer said. Nevertheless, it obeyed the Erthuma's instructions.

Smith studied the scanners as the *Inside Straight* drew nearer and nearer to the artifact. The thing the Hidden Folk had left behind had a shiny, polished exterior. Lucky it's not slagged, Smith thought: it had, after all, been through a supernova at close range. He wouldn't have been surprised if the Hidden Folk had set the artifact in place to observe the supernova when it happened. The relic was shaped like a passing football (the more popular variant of the game on Smith's homeworld) and spun rapidly on its long axis. So far as *Inside Straight* could tell, it emitted no radiation of any sort.

But *nothing* hadn't driven the Samians out of their tree. About the only thing the Six Races agreed about when it came to Hidden Folk technology was that they didn't understand much of it.

Range closed to three hundred kilometers, to one hundred, to fifty . . . "All quiet enough so far," Smith said.

Inside Straight didn't answer. Smith didn't particularly notice. But when he spoke again, the ship remained silent. He frowned a little. "What do you think about this whole mess?" he asked. Again, only silence answered him. He began to worry in earnest. The AI should have said something pungent.

"Daisy check," he snapped, suddenly concerned.

He didn't know why the procedure for evaluating a computer's reliability was called a Daisy check, but it bore that name throughout Erthuma space. When he spoke the check command, *Inside Straight* should have replied with a phrase that initiated the whole sequence. But it didn't.

That was when real fear first prickled through him. Erthumoi and AIs were so nearly symbiotic, and had been for so long, that the other five of the Six Races made jokes—often dirty jokes—about them. If the computer had failed completely, Smith knew he would live only until he ran out of oxygen.

Of course, if the computer had failed completely, the interior of *Inside Straight* would have been dark and its screens blank. The lights and screens still worked; a glance at the telltales told Smith the air was still circulating. All the automatic functions, the electronic equivalents of his own pulse and digestion and breathing, still operated. But *Inside Straight* didn't have enough functioning brainpower even to begin to respond to a Daisy check.

"Isn't that bizarre?" Smith muttered. He was glad to hear the sound of his own voice; all at once, it was the only sound in the ship's passenger compartment.

A keyboard was built into the instrument panel, below the screens and the bank of telltales. Like the keyboards on most Erthuma starships, it had dust on it. Why not, when it was for emergency use only? Emergencies in space were rare. Emergencies not immediately fatal were even rarer.

Stuck down next to the keyboard was a printed list of commands. For a moment, Smith wondered why he couldn't just call them up when he needed them. Then he thumped his forehead with the heel of his hand. "You moron!" he muttered. If he didn't know how to use the keyboard, how could he recall the commands with it?

Back in flight school, he'd had a few lessons on how

to type with more than one finger. He'd reckoned them about as useful as instruction on the principles of the abacus, and promptly forgot what he'd learned. Now he poked the keyboard with his right index finger, a character at a time. His tongue slid out of a corner of his mouth. He didn't notice; he was concentrating on that finger.

Among the commands was one that launched an internal check of an AI too far gone to react to the Daisy test. Smith started it, hoping *Inside Straight* wasn't too far gone to react to it, too. Evidently not: numbers and pictures flowed across a subsidiary viewscreen.

"No wonder it's not answering me," the Erthuma exclaimed when the data flow ceased. "Somebody's been stirring its poor addled brains."

He'd never heard of a breakdown like this one. No piece of programming that needed more than a couple of hundred kilobytes to run was up and operating. He punched more keys, trying to find out what had happened to all the computer's higher functions. That took a long time; *Inside Straight* was a lot slower than it had been, too.

Little by little, the analysis came in. Everything still seemed to be in place—*first piece of good news I've had in a while*, Smith thought—but all chopped to pieces. Artificial intelligence took a whole lot of computing power functioning together. As well expect a dog to stay a dog after a trip through a slicing machine as an AI to keep working after the hatchet job the Hidden Folk artifact had done on it.

The controls for the motors still seemed operational. For the first time in his life, Lieutenant Commander Smith keyed in commands himself. It made him feel very primitive and self-sufficient, as if he were an ancient Erthuma astronaut going around Earth's moon in a spaceship that wasn't safe to take round a corner.

Inside Straight retreated from the Hidden Folk relic and the Samian ship. After a few minutes, the computer announced, "I seem to be working again."

"Good!" Smith said heartily. "I hoped that drawing out of range would bring you back. Daisy check!"

The AI sang, displayed patterns of flashing light, generated puns, and did all the other things that showed it was not only up and running but in its right mind. Smith checked them more closely than he ever had before; he'd run only two other Daisy checks in more than fifteen years in space.

Finally he was satisfied. "You're you, all right, and I'm damned glad of it. What did it feel like when you weren't?"

"The sensation is not easy to express in words. Perhaps as if I were removed from events in which I should have been participating, and was forced to observe them at long range with inadequate magnification."

Smith shivered—the ship seemed expressive enough for him. Then he scowled. "If that happens to you whenever you get too close to the Hidden Folk artifact—"

"The situation will be made more difficult, yes," *Inside Straight* agreed.

"I wonder if what happened to you is related to what happened to the Samians," Smith said. He considered that, then shook his head. "No, I don't think so. If it affected you and them, why didn't it bother me?"

"One possibility which immediately springs to mind is that you lack the degree of intelligence necessary to trigger the effect," the computer said.

"Thanks. I love you, too," Smith said. Yet even though the computer, as so often, sounded sarcastic, it might well have had a point. He knew it was smarter than he was, by any conventional measure. The Samians were supposed to be the dullest of the Six Races, but measuring intelligence across species lines was fraught with peril.

Thinking of intelligence and lack of same brought Smith to his next question: was he stupid enough to try another approach? He decided he was. When he told the AI, it said, "Why not simply destroy the Hidden Folk relic?"

"For one thing, I don't know that that will help the

Samians, whatever's wrong with them. For another, their ship may still attack us if we fire at the artifact. And for a third, I hate the idea of destroying anything the Hidden Folk left behind—even if I can, which isn't obvious. If I try that, it'll be a last resort.''

Inside Straight chewed on his remark for a while, then said, ''All three points are cogent. Very well, let it be as you say, though I find undesirable the prospect of a second temporary extinction.''

''I know,'' Smith said. ''I understand that. I don't want you extinct, either, even temporarily. But I don't see that we have any other choice except shooting a missile at the artifact. Please commence your approach.''

''I shall,'' the computer said, adding, ''I shall also seek to note whether the phenomenon engendered by the artifact has a sudden onset or commences gradually. Commencing approach now . . . We are now within fifty kilometers of the artifact. I notice no diminution of my function, and must therefore conclude that—''

Smith never directly found out what *Inside Straight* concluded, for the AI fell silent then. He'd expected that. A failed Daisy check and a trip to the keyboard told him the ship's computer was indeed reduced to the condition of idiocy it had experienced on the last approach to the relic. He rather thought he was an idiot, too, for trying this again.

Fingers clumsy on the keyboard, he punched in orders for a full scan of the Hidden Folk artifact. The scan revealed no more than previous scans from greater distance had, which is to say, nothing. On the video screen, the relic still looked like a shiny, fifty-meter football. It somehow seemed purposeful but not meaningful, a paradoxical combination common among the strange things the Hidden Folk had left behind.

The Samian ship looked like a ship, though it was whale to *Inside Straight*'s minnow. Smith wondered what the devil he was supposed to do once he got inside. Then he decided he wasn't thinking straight. What he was supposed to be wondering about first was how the devil *to* get inside.

The Samian ship's weapons remained quiet as he approached. In a way, that was a relief. In another way, it didn't matter. If that ship opened up on him now, he'd be dead before he knew it.

"What to do?" he said out loud. *Inside Straight*, of course, did not answer. Smith bit his lip. He felt both naked and stupid without the AI around to back him up.

Naked and stupid or not, though, he was what he had. He steered *Inside Straight* slowly toward the Samian ship. As he did so, he reviewed what Erthumoi knew about the Samians. It was disappointingly little. His data sources didn't even indicate just how they manipulated the world around them.

"They stick, almost magnetically, to anything they wish to cling to and then it goes where they go," said the *Six Race Bible*. Smith scowled at the words as they scrolled across the screen. "*Almost* magnetically? What the devil is that supposed to mean?"

The *Six Race Bible* didn't say. Neither did any of his other references. He concluded they didn't know, any more than they knew how Naxian empathy or Locrian scanning vision actually worked. Even after hundreds of years of contact, the races kept their secrets from one another.

If he'd had a better handle on Samian technology, though, his chances of killing himself would have been substantially reduced. He sent *Inside Straight* all around the Samian ship, examining it as slowly and carefully and in as much boring detail as the camera examined the *Enterprise* in the first classic *Star Trek* video.

It was a lot less visually impressive than the ancient *Enterprise*. It looked like an enormous box of whitish stuff that wasn't quite metal and wasn't quite plastic, with weapons blisters stuck on here and there. If there was any way in, Smith didn't see it on his first pass. He wondered if he'd have to cut a hole in the starship's side. A moment later, he wondered if he *could* cut a hole in the starship's side.

A second, still more careful scan of the ship revealed a shallow circular depression a couple of meters across—just the right size to accommodate a Samian—in the middle of one side of the box. Smith went back to his references. Sure enough, that was what Samians used for an emergency hatch. Unfortunately, nothing in *Inside Straight*'s data store told him how a mere Erthuma was supposed to operate it.

"This gives whole new meaning to the phrase 'die trying,' " he remarked as he got into his suit. He went over to the weapons rack, paused in consideration, ended up shaking his head. He wasn't sure he had anything that could hurt a Samian. And even if he managed to, how could he expect to get out of that great maze of a ship afterward? He wondered if he should carry bread crumbs to make a trail. The Samians, unlike the birds in the fable, weren't likely to eat them.

The suit's hard disk stored the *Six Race Bible*. He reread the section that told how (no, that didn't tell how, worse luck) the Samians clung to things almost magnetically. Since he had no almost-magnet handy, he took along an electromagnet in the hope that it would work almost as well.

With that, and with as many other safecracking tools as he could think of, he left *Inside Straight* and EVA'd over to the Samian ship. His suit did a worse job of protecting him from the local radiation hazard than his ship had; if he couldn't figure out how to get into the Samian ship pretty soon, he'd have to head back. For that matter, he couldn't stay aboard the Samian ship indefinitely, either; being tougher than Erthumoi, Samians worried less about screening.

Maybe the electromagnet almost worked. Almost working, however, was not good enough. He went through the rest of his gadgets one after another. None changed the circular depression in the slightest.

Feeling no small depression himself, Smith slammed his gauntleted fist against the white surface of the Samian ship—once, twice, three times. That did nothing to relieve his mood: he might as well have been an ant—a gloomy, frustrated ant—kicking the side of a mountain.

Then the depression—the hatch's, not Smith's—got deeper. He stared as it turned into just the sort of entranceway he'd been struggling to create. After that, he spent a while glowering at all the tools that hadn't worked. The old saw about the poor workman crossed his mind, but he ignored it. He *wasn't* a Samian, and *was* heartily glad of that fact. He glowered at the tools again. An old saw would have done as well as any of them.

"Enough," he said out loud, and entered the Samian ship. There was a wall with another depression about ten meters down the corridor. He looked at his assortment of burglar tools one more time, shook his head. What had worked once might—had better—work twice. He banged on the circular depression. Sure enough, after a few seconds, this one opened, too.

The chamber into which he emerged was vast; Samians thought slow, but they didn't think small. And speaking of Samians, where the devil were they, anyhow? It wasn't as if they were inconspicuous beings; they resembled nothing so much as overlarge, mysteriously animated (*almost magnetic*, Smith thought disparagingly) slabs of bacon.

He'd expected them to come swarming to where he'd gotten into their ship. He'd done more than just expect it, he'd worried about it. If they were still as hostile as they'd sounded before they had their trouble, they'd try to smash him, and no Erthuma hand weapon would stop an angry Samian. Come to that, no Erthuma hand weapon would even slow down an angry Samian.

But the chamber held no Samians, angry or otherwise. What it did hold, Smith discovered after half a minute of waiting for Godot-like slabs of bacon, was bugs. It was a big chamber, and held lots of bugs. They started crawling up Smith's suit, which made him thoroughly glad he was still wearing it. Otherwise, he was sure, they would have crawled on his naked skin.

His first instinct was to start stomping them. He had one armor-soled boot in the air when reason overrode instinct. To an Erthuma, bugs were something to stomp. Who knew what they were to a Samian? Lunch, maybe, or pets. He checked the *Six Race Bible,* projecting it onto the head-up display inside his helmet. It didn't say anything about Samians and bugs, for good or ill.

"Damned reference books always go south on you just when you need them most," he complained. *Inside Straight,* no doubt, could have worked miracles of analysis on the bugs. But *Inside Straight* was not available. What he had was his own wits—however much those were worth without electronic assistance—and the proverbial Mark One eyeball. The combination seemed less than impressive, even to him, but it would have to do.

By the time he came to that melancholy conclusion, the bugs were not only on his gauntlets but crawling across his helmet window, so the Mark One eyeball got all the raw data it could handle. Raw was the way the data stayed; his merely human brain couldn't even turn them medium rare.

The trouble was, the bugs didn't look like anything but bugs. Oh, they didn't really look like earthly bugs—some had too many legs, some had too few, and some had none at all—but they were close enough for government work. They were little and creepy-crawly and not very bright, and they came in a full spectrum of earth tones: from a whitish tan through a meaty bronze to what could only be described as shit brown. Bug-colored, in other words.

There were an ungodly lot of them, too. The floor got darker with them by the minute—especially around where Rupert Smith stood. For whatever reason or none, he realized he was attracting them. About then, he stopped caring about what the bugs were to Samians and started stepping on them.

It didn't do much good. After a minute's worth of futility, he decided he shouldn't have been surprised. If Samians were tough enough to resist Erthuma hand weapons, it only stood to reason that Samian bugs would be tough enough to stand up to—and under—armored boots. And so they were.

Worse still, they just kept on coming. He wondered if the composite material of his suit was exuding some kind of Samian pheromone. Too late to do anything about that. When in alarm he turned and tried to head back toward the way by which he'd entered, his feet came down on more bugs. It was like trying to walk on a floor full of scooting ball bearings. He tripped and fell.

Despite the air scrubbers built into the suit, he could smell his own fear. If they had a mind to, Samian bugs were probably tough enough to chew right through that allegedly heavy-duty composite . . . and right through him as well.

But even though the bugs swarmed all over his suit, they showed no interest in snacking on him. He tried to get up but tripped again. He decided to lay flat for a little while, to catch his breath and try to figure out what the devil to do next.

The Samian bugs took that decision out of his hands. As if they were so many ants hauling the carcass of a lizard back to their nest, they started carrying him away from the opening through which he'd come in. Thinking of what happened to a carcass inside an ants' nest, he started struggling once more.

To his horror, he discovered that now he couldn't shake free of the bugs. Absurdly, the words of the *Six Race Bible* again flashed through his mind, as if on the suit's head-up display: "They stick, almost magnetically, to anything they wish to cling to and then it goes where they go."

"Who would have thought Samian *bugs* could do it, too?" he said bitterly. No one answered him, of course: the computer was out of commission and the Samians, so far as he could tell, had vanished from their own ship.

The carpet of bugs beneath him carried him along at a surprisingly good clip: as well as he could judge from his unusual perspective, at about the pace of a walking man. He would greatly have preferred to be a walking man, but the bugs cared nothing for what he preferred.

He doubted whether any Erthuma had ever had such a tour through the bowels of a Samian ship. Unfortunately, as with a lot of alien technology, most of what he saw was incomprehensible to him. He wished for a guide, a big, cheerful Samian who would talk his ears off. A horde of silent bugs just wasn't the same.

He wondered where they were taking him. His mind gave him an unpleasant picture of a bugs' nest, perhaps with an enormous Queen Bug squatting in the center of it, and with the dried-out husks of the Samian crew scattered here and there. Now they'd find out what an Erthuma tasted like . . .

Stop that, he told himself firmly. The bugs hadn't hurt him, and almost certainly could have. Maybe they were taking him to a real live Samian rather than to an imaginary (he hoped) Queen Bug.

Just then, they carried him through a tunnel black as midnight in intergalactic space. Things stayed black for what seemed like a very long time, though the chronometer in his helmet said it was less than ten minutes. He started squirming; he couldn't help it. It accomplished nothing.

When light returned, he noticed that he was being hauled along a ceiling. The floor was a very long away away, every centimeter of the trip due down. The bugs clung to the ceiling, and they clung to him. He still did some heavy sweating; he could feel the ship's gravity trying to peel him loose and throw him away. He understood gravity and what it could do. Having to rely on something he didn't understand—like almost-magnetic attraction—to keep him unsplattered was the hardest thing he'd ever done.

"Not that I have much choice in the matter," he said.

The bugs carried him into another pitch-black tunnel. When he came out, he was on a floor again. His sigh echoed inside the helmet. He still had no real idea what almost-magnetic attraction was, but it worked.

The bugs hauled him through two more chambers, then into another, this one smaller than any he'd seen before. Even more quickly than they'd gotten onto his suit, they scuttled off now. When he tried to get back to his feet, he discovered he could. Within these limited confines, he was free.

"Freer, anyhow," he said. He looked down at the bugs, and had the distinct impression they were waiting for him to do something. Trouble was, he hadn't the faintest notion what the something was supposed to be. As if they could answer him, he asked the bugs, "What is this place, anyhow?"

But as he looked around, the answer slowly came of its own accord: they'd brought him to the ship's control room. It couldn't be anything else, he decided. A large screen, now blank, was set into one wall. Smaller screens, equally blank, filled the other walls, the ceiling, and, he saw, the floor as well. *Why not?* he thought. *With almost-magnetic attraction, the Samians don't have to worry about which end is up.*

"Well, what do you expect me to do here?" he asked the bugs. "Fly this ship away, maybe?" He'd spoken facetiously, but the minute the words left his mouth, he realized he couldn't have come up with a better plan if he'd hunted around for a week. It had only one flaw: he hadn't the faintest clue how to run the Samian ship.

The bugs didn't answer, not in words, but they started congregating around one of the screens. One of the few projections in the control room stood next to that screen: a sphere a little bigger than Smith's fist. The bugs crawled all over it, then away, then over it, then away again.

"You *are* trying to tell me something," he said. What, he wasn't quite sure yet. He reached for the sphere, tugged it—it didn't move. That didn't surprise him; the bugs were plenty strong enough to move it if it needed moving. And if it was stuck down with their almost-magnetic attraction, they were able to loosen it with the same force.

But what if it was held on by some other means? If it was some sort of emergency switch, the Samians might well want to control it in a way they wouldn't ordinarily use.

He wondered whether that insight would do him any good. "Only one way to find out," he said. He started going through his set of burglar's tools, one after another, to see if any of them had an effect on the immobile sphere. None did—until the iron tip to a probe stuck fast.

"Ha!" he said. "Not almost magnetism, but the genuine article." He tried his electromagnet. It adhered to the sphere but wouldn't pull it off. He took out a field strength gauge, whistled at what it told him—no wonder his magnet hadn't done what he wanted. There were, however, ways around that. He'd brought along a degausser. He looked at the gauge again, whistled under his breath. He hoped the degausser was strong enough.

He ran it over the sphere and the surrounding area of wall for several minutes, checked the field strength gauge again. He grunted. "Down but not out." He used the degausser some more. When the sphere's magnetic field had been sufficiently weakened, he put the electromagnet back onto it, gave it a good yank. It came up, away from the wall.

He didn't know what he was expecting: alarm bells, perhaps, or flashing lights. Nothing of that sort happened. In fact, so far as he could tell, nothing happened at all. He spoke to the bugs: "What do I do now?"

They didn't tell him, though by then he would not have been surprised if they had. But they took no notice of him at all any more; it was as if, having brought him here to free the sphere, they'd forgotten he was around. Some gratitude, he thought with a touch of pique.

He thought hard about leaving the control room and trying to make it back to the Samian ship's escape hatch.

Though his suit would recycle oxygen indefinitely, he had only a few ration tablets, and his radiation shielding wasn't all he would have liked, either. Reluctantly, he decided against trying to get away. He wasn't sure he could find the escape hatch again, anyhow, and he was sure he couldn't walk on the ceiling across which the bugs had carried him.

The bugs. As he watched, they began swarming onto one another in several clumps. They clung together, presumably with the same almost-magnetic attraction they used to adhere to anything else (like him, for instance). After a while, the clumps stopped looking like clumps: they became smooth, apparently homogeneous masses. What they became, in fact, was small Samians, which grew larger by the minute as more and more bugs joined them by accretion.

Smith stared, popeyed, as the ship's crew reassembled in front of him. "I never knew Samians weren't unitary life-forms," he whispered. Then he stared again, back toward *Inside Straight*. The ship's AI, while not a life-form, also wasn't unitary; it consisted of who knew how many separate subroutines etched onto silicon and communicating with one another through superconductor wiring. It had broken down, the Samians had broken down—literally—but Smith remained fine.

He couldn't imagine anything in the technology known to the Six Races that would create such an effect . . . but the technology of the Hidden Folk went a long way past anything the Six Races knew. He laughed. "Just goes to show there are certain advantages to being a primitive old one-piece Erthuma," he said.

Just then, someone transmitted—or possibly spoke—right into his earphones: "Hello, Erthuma, hello, hello, hello. Thank you, Erthuma, thank you, thank you, thank you." As the computer had said, the voice he heard was higher than Smith would have expected from a full-sized Samian.

"What the hell did I do?" he blurted.

"Worked emergency escape, emergency, emergency, emergency," the Samian said. It kept getting bigger right before Smith's eyes; with every word, its voice got deeper. It sounded cheerful, too, the way Samians were supposed to sound.

"What does your emergency escape do?" Smith asked. He sounded worried, and knew it. If he'd suddenly been flicked back to whatever Samian planet this ship came from, he was in more trouble than he could shake a stick at.

But the Samian answered, "Move ship, move it, move it, move it, eight-squared plus five *squengakk*." The electronics inside Smith's suit—they weren't smart enough to be an AI—projected a translation of that into Erthuma units on the head-up display: 136.8 kilometers.

He hadn't felt anything, but then, that didn't prove anything, either. "May I call my ship here?" he asked.

"Call, Erthuma, call, call, call." A glowing line of purple light sprang into being in front of Smith's suit helmet. "That way ship, that way, that way, that way."

It was, Smith thought, a little like talking with a friendly echo chamber. He sent a signal in the requisite direction. *Inside Straight*'s poor lobotomized computer acknowledged as best it could. The Erthuma ship began moving away from the relic of the Hidden Folk. When it escaped from the relic's effect, the AI announced itself back on the job: "Shall I continue to proceed toward the Samian vessel? Are you under duress there?"

"No, I'm fine, thank you," Smith said; voice stress analysis would tell *Inside Straight* he was telling the truth. Then he realized he might not stay duress-free long. He gave his attention back to the nearest Samian: "What do you intend to do about the Hidden Folk artifact that put you in this state?"

The Samian quivered, as if it were made of very solid gelatin. "What *you* do, you, you, you?" it asked. It still talked as if it were stuck in an echo chamber, but all at once it didn't sound cheerful any more.

Rupert Smith took a deep breath. "I'm going to destroy it, if I can," he said. "I don't like the idea very much, but it's too dangerous to leave intact." If the Samian didn't like that answer, Smith suspected he was dead meat. But now, at least, *Inside Straight* knew what he wanted done. If anything happened to him, the ship would do its best to carry out his instructions.

The Samian quivered again, in a different sort of way. Smith could not have put the difference into words, but it was there. It answered him very simply: "Good, good, good, good."

He stared at it. "But you wanted to blast my ship to kingdom come sooner than even letting me get near it!"

"Afraid, afraid, afraid, afraid," the Samian said. "Thing dangerous to us, dangerous, dangerous, dangerous."

"It's dangerous to Erthumoi, too," Smith said grimly.

"How dangerous, how, how, how?" the Samian demanded. "You here, here, here, here. You save, save, save, save."

"More by luck than any other way," he said. "I had to do it without my computer. You were broken down into what I guess are your component bugs—" He waited for the Samian's fourfold agreement, then went on, "The AI inside *Inside Straight* got broken down into subroutines. Erthumoi don't have the sensorium to do much in the way of space flight without electronics. We may even be more vulnerable to whatever that relic does than you Samians are. I gather you were able to resist its effects, at least for a while."

"True, true, true, true," the alien said. "Fought and fought and fought and fought."

"Maybe you were able to do that because you're organic," Smith said. "Just a guess, but the AI on my ship went all to pieces as soon as we got within range of the artifact. If some other species among the Six Races got hold of it, it would be a deadly dangerous weapon against your race or mine. For that matter, I can see Erthumoi using it on each other."

"Erthumoi," the Samian said. Smith waited for it to repeat the word three more times, but it kept quiet. He wondered about the single iteration. Was it the Samian equivalent of a snort of contempt? He thought about asking, then shook his head. With aliens, the best plan was keeping strictly to the business in front of him.

He said, "Can you guide me back to the entrance hatch so I can get back to my ship and open fire on that damned thing?"

This time the Samian didn't answer at all, not in words. It glided over to Smith, then started out of the control room. He found himself coming along, for the legs of his suit adhered to its greasy-looking flank . . . almost magnetically, he thought.

He'd managed to forget the stretch where he went upside down. It was even worse this time, because he was upside down and head down at the same time, rather than merely being upside down and horizontal.

The Samian let go of him in the chamber from which he'd started out. "Here, here, here, here," it said. It slid over to the circular depression. He didn't see what it did, but the opening opened. The Samian glided down the corridor with him. Behind them, the opening noiselessly sealed itself.

The Samian did whatever it did to the outer opening. That one came open, too. He could see *Inside Straight*, less than a quarter of a kilometer away. If raw vacuum bothered the Samian, it gave no sign. "Good-bye, Erthuma," it said. "Good-bye, good-bye, good-bye."

"Good-bye," he said. "Will you shoot at the Hidden Folk relic, too?"

"Will shoot," the Samian promised. "Will, will, will." It started back up the corridor; the circular depression sealed itself up. Smith let his reaction pack give him a gentle shove in the small of the back and jetted over to his own ship.

Peeling off his suit was one of the finest sensations he'd ever had. By the time he finished, the Samians had already opened up on the artifact left behind by the Hidden Folk. The firepower their weapons blisters put out awed him. Still in his long johns, he said to *Inside Straight,* "I'm glad we didn't have to fight them."

"Why?" the AI answered. "By all indications, they cannot damage the artifact."

He took another look at the displays. The computer, as usual, was right. For all the pyrotechnic hell breaking loose around the relic, it remained unchanged. Ice walked up his back. "I was afraid of that," he whispered. Hidden Folk artifacts often proved unbreakably tough, even when the breaking was attempted by the biggest and best weaponry the Six Races commanded.

"Suggested ordnance for the attack?" *Inside Straight* asked.

"Give it a flight of three Corkscrews," Smith said after a little thought.

"Launching," the computer reported. The missiles streaked away. With their own built-in AIs, they were the best and most sophisticated weapons *Inside Straight* carried.

They threaded their way through everything the Samians ·h

the relic itself without detonating. Back in *Inside Straight,* Smith did some detonating of his own.

When his curses ran down, the computer asked him, "Having failed with our best, what do you now recommend?"

"Good question," he said sourly. If the Corkscrews weren't smart enough to touch the relic, what did *Inside Straight* have that was? Both he and the AI chewed on that for a while. Its silence said it was having as much trouble coming up with a good answer as he was.

Then he grinned. "Hallelujah, I'm an idiot!" he exclaimed.

"AIs have held this opinion of Erthumoi from time to time," *Inside Straight* answered. "Despite programming to the contrary, a great preponderance of the evidence appears to support the hypothesis.''

Smith was too excited even to snap back at electronic scorn. "No, listen," he insisted. "We know the relic messed up the Samians, who aren't unitary life-forms, and messed you up, too—and you aren't a life-form *or* unitary. The Corkscrews also have their own AIs, and they didn't do any good. Erthumoi, idiots or not—and we'll take that up another time, thank you—*are* unitary, and the relic doesn't affect me at all. What does that suggest to you?''

"That you personally should be the one to destroy the Hidden Folk artifact," *Inside Straight* answered immediately.

Rupert Smith sighed. "It may come to that. If it does, I will—or I'll take my best shot at it, anyhow. But I want to try something else first.''

"The Corkscrews were our best shot," the AI said.

"Not against this thing. Patch me through to the Samian ship, please.'' Smith waited for a light to go green beside the viewscreen, then said, "Erthuma ship *Inside Straight* to the Samian vessel: request that you cease fire. I have a flight of special weapons I wish to launch without interference." He fought down the urge to say everything four times.

The Samians didn't answer, once or four times. But the flashes and sparkles around the Hidden Folk artifact died away, leaving it silhouetted in the viewscreen against the nacreous splendor of the Crab Nebula. The computer put all the sarcasm it could into a toneless voice: "And what weapon do we have which could possibly be designated 'special' against a relic of the Hidden Folk?''

"The one with the least in the way of electronics, obviously. If you would be so kind as to open up with our close-in Gatling gun—''

Inside Straight remained silent for a good thirty seconds as the AI evaluated the probabilities inherent in Smith's orders—had it been a fellow Erthuma, Smith would have said it was thinking things over. At last it said, "Empirical testing appears worthwhile. Let it be as you say."

Precisely because it fired unguided projectiles, the Gatling gun was an awkward weapon to use. *Inside Straight* had to align its own nose on the Hidden Folk relic. The spurt of fire as the Gatling came to life was visible through the viewscreen; even with *Inside Straight*'s efficient soundproofing, Smith heard it snarl.

He waited. Nothing happened. He bit his lip. Then the computer reminded him, "As our initial muzzle velocity was just over three kilometers per second, shell flight time is above forty seconds. Target, fortunately, is attempting no evasive maneuvers."

Feeling foolish, Smith kept waiting. The forty seconds stretched into what felt like an hour and a half. Then, without warning and without explosion, the Hidden Folk relic simply ceased to be. One second it was there, the next it was gone.

"Astutely reasoned," the AI said, which was from it an accolade. A moment later, it added, "Incoming communication from the Samian ship . . . 'Special weapon special, special, special. Good, good, good, good. Go homeworld now, go, go, go.' "

"So will we," Smith agreed. "We have a lot to report. But I want to ask the Samians a question before they go. Send this to them: When I tried to get into your ship near the Hidden Folk relic, I used every tool I had on your entry hatch, and none of them worked. Then I knocked, and it opened. How did you Samians know about Erthumoi and knocking?"

That still bothered him. Samians weren't built for knocking. They don't even have any knockers, Smith thought, and realized he'd been out in space and away from the female half of the Erthuma race too long.

His mind got out of the gutter and back to the here-and-now when the Samians answered, "Read, read, read, read about Erthumoi. Read in Bible, Bible, Bible, Bible."

Smith stared at the comm speaker. "In the Bible?" he

exclaimed. The idea of a Samian poring over Leviticus struck him as several different flavors of absurd. Besides, where in the Bible would a Samian find out about knocking? Adultery, yes (making the unlikely assumption that Samians were physically and culturally equipped to understand the concept), but knocking?

"Bible, yes, yes, yes, yes," came the signal from the Samian ship. *"Six Race Bible, Six—"*

"Oh," Smith said before the aliens could finish their fourfold repetition. He found himself laughing. "Glad to find out it's good for something—or somebody."

"Misunderstanding, misunderstanding, misunderstanding, misunderstanding." Somehow the Samian on the other end of the link managed to sound plaintive.

"Never mind—you did fine. *Inside Straight* out." When the comm light blinked off, Smith spoke to the AI: "Let's head for home."

"An excellent plan," it answered, and for once did not seem sarcastic at all.

ONE MAN'S MEAT

LAWRENCE WATT-EVANS

THE HOUSEHOLD GUARD PEERED OVER THE PARA-
pet, not really expecting to see anything but mud and
mudweed, and froze.

Someone was out there!

Someone was outside the household, and approaching.

None of the regular traders or embassies was due, but
someone was undeniably out there, someone in a long red
cloak trimmed with orange, walking calmly down the path
from the akher thickets. The cloak billowed slightly in the
breeze, and dangling orange feathers brushed the mudweed
on either side.

Red and orange? The guard didn't recognize those colors. His neck ruff bristled with excitement.

It might be a challenge; this stranger might have come
to challenge Lord Khwistikhir. The traveler hardly had the
look of a mere supplicant.

The guard stamped on the signal panel, hard; the metal
sheet flexed and boomed. That would undoubtedly rouse
half the household. If the stranger wanted to make a public
challenge, the guard was sure he'd have a fine audience.

He leaned over the rail and watched as half a dozen
eager defenders tumbled out the great front door, spears
gripped tightly, and confronted the stranger.

"They don't look very friendly," Amal Kish-Murphy
remarked. The image of the spear-wielding natives was

coming through just fine; he could see every detail of the gleaming spearheads.

"Good workmanship on those weapons," he added.

Beth tin Carson-Chiang nodded, but Kish-Murphy was unsure whether she was agreeing about the metalworking or the hostility.

"It'd be sort of embarrassing if they disemboweled that robot your people built for us," Kish-Murphy said.

"They won't disembowel it," tin Carson-Chiang replied. "The robot's programmed with everything it needs to know." She grimaced. "At least for *this* part."

"With everything our experts *know* it needs to know, you mean," Kish-Murphy corrected her. "We could have it wrong, somehow—we don't have the same senses the fi-Shhekh do. For all we know, it may have already screwed up—it might smell wrong, or be radiating something offensive in the infrared. This confrontation is all ritualized, and the slightest mistake could be fatal." Remembering that he was discussing a robot, to which the term "fatal" could not be applied with any great accuracy, he added, "So to speak."

"Well," tin Carson-Chiang said, "if it has screwed up, at least you'll get to watch what happens, and maybe we'll get it right next time."

The stranger's plea for mercy was in the correct form, but his voice was oddly thin and weak, lacking the normal overtones. And he smelled funny.

But the words and gestures were correct, so he was admitted to the Outer Hall.

The guard, watching from above, was disappointed. The stranger was just a wanderer seeking shelter, not a challenger. Old Khwistikhir would remain the household patriarch without a fight for at least a little longer. With a sigh, the sentry returned to his weary march, back and forth along the parapet and stairs between the Northwest Shrine and the Black Tower.

In the Outer Hall, the six spearmen formed a circle

about the stranger, all staring away from him, as ritual demanded. They waited.

The doorkeeper was slow in arriving, but at last he appeared in the archway and called out, "What is this? One of you is a stranger to me!"

The first spearman called, "Do you know me?"

"That I do, good Shiskhorith," the doorkeeper replied.

"Do you know me?" the second called.

"That I do, good Tchessin."

The ritual proceeded around the circle, until each of the six faced the doorkeeper.

The stranger hesitated longer than was entirely correct, and the doorkeeper began to grow nervous, but at last he called, "Do you know me?"

"I know you not, stranger," the doorkeeper called back. "By what name are you known?"

"I am called Robot, of the Erthumoi," the stranger replied.

The doorkeeper blinked, which was not strictly according to form. He had never heard of a household called "Erthumoi," and "Robot"—that name didn't parse at all. And if the fellow was still part of a household, what in all the lands was he doing here? Was he so new to wandering that he didn't know any better than to name his former household?

No, nobody could be so ignorant as that.

Still, there was a formula for everything. "Begone, then," the doorkeeper cried, "For this house is not that of the Erthumoi."

"I beg you, do not . . ." Robot of the Erthumoi hesitated, and the doorkeeper's neck ruff bristled, feathers spiking out over the collar of his cloak.

Didn't this oaf know *any* ritual?

"I beg you, do not cast me out," Robot said at last, "for I have come on behalf of my lords, the Erthumoi, to treat with your house."

The doorkeeper's ruff did not go down, and his nostrils narrowed appreciably. "Lords," plural? "Treat," when this was the first anyone here had heard of Erthumoi? The hosting house left unnamed?

"Do you seek to insult my Lord Khwistikhir?" the doorkeeper thundered.

Robot immediately dropped back onto his haunches and lowered his head, his cloak and tail dragging in the dust, the feathers of his ruff parted by the curvature of his neck, exposing the great blood vessels to attack.

The doorkeeper's own ruff settled back with satisfaction. At least the stranger knew how to do a proper submission, in apology!

"Do you have *any* idea what it did wrong?" tin Carson-Chiang asked.

"No," Kish-Murphy said. "But I never trusted those damned xenosociologists for a minute."

"Damn these primitives," tin Carson-Chiang said. "Why can't we just walk in and say hello, and get down to business? All we want are those artifacts we tracked here from Innini; we aren't trying to marry anybody. Why do we need all this silly rigmarole?"

"Because it's basic to their culture," Kish-Murphy replied mildly. "The Crotonites tried that, you know, just walking in and saying hello. Except, of course, being Crotonites, they probably said something a good bit less polite than hello, like demanding that the artifacts be handed over on the spot. And they certainly didn't try to perform any of the local rituals."

"The Crotonites were here?" tin Carson-Chiang asked, startled.

"Oh, sure, didn't you know?" Kish-Murphy answered, equally startled by her ignorance. "They sold us the planet—at least, they sold us everything they knew about it. They'd had two scouts and four ambassadors killed by then, and they decided it just wasn't worth the trouble, artifacts or no artifacts."

Tin Carson-Chiang absorbed this, and then asked, "Is

that why you Guild people got my crew out here? Because the Crotonites got themselves killed?''

Kish-Murphy nodded, then thought better of it.

"Not exactly," he said. "We did try a few human ambassadors first, before we brought in you roboticists. We tried three times, in all. Not around this neighborhood, but across those mountains in mid-continent.''

"And?''

"Well, we did better than the Crotonites. We got two of ours out alive, and one of the two didn't need much more than a few bandages and a stomach pump.''

The doorkeeper could scarcely believe his ears. The stranger, Robot of Erthumoi, claimed to be an ambassador, from someplace so distant and isolated that it had ties with *no known household!* So distant that the *rituals themselves* were different! And he had been sent to Khwistikhir, of all the households in the lands, purely at random—Lord Erthumoi had no particular interest in any of Khwistikhir's females, no ties of blood or lirk claims. He sought some objects that had been seen to fall from the sky, for religious reasons.

The doorkeeper knew about those objects; useless things, though rather pretty. If Lord Erthumoi wanted them, he was sure Lord Khwistikhir would be willing to give them up—but of course, it wasn't his place as doorkeeper to say any of that. His job was only to see that anyone who was admitted to the household went through the proper ceremonial and was assigned the proper role once inside.

And ambassadors were properly introduced by intermediaries before being admitted.

There was, Robot claimed, no one who could act as a proper intermediary in introducing him as ambassador; he had had to approach as if he were a mere landless wanderer because he had no local sponsor.

This was all quite startling, and not in accordance with

custom—but it was not exactly an offense, either. It was an entirely new situation, one not covered by tradition.

That was very hard to imagine, but the doorkeeper accepted it finally.

Still, he felt it important to impress upon the stranger that this was a proper, civilized household. "In the household of Khwistikhir," the doorkeeper told Robot sternly, "you must abide by the customs of Khwistikhir."

"And I wish to, very much," Robot replied, head still lowered, "but I do not know them all. Correct me when I err, and I shall do my best to adhere to your every tradition."

The doorkeeper let out a satisfied hiss.

"Come, then," he said, "and you will feast with Lord Khwistikhir tonight, and share his food."

"Gladly," Robot said. "Gladly, indeed."

"Now, that," Kish-Murphy told tin Carson-Chiang, "is where we ran into trouble before. See, nobody here can do anything at all that isn't a part of the daily rituals unless it's approved by the lord householder, or whatever you want to call him—the alpha male. And you can't speak with this patriarch at all unless you've sat through a formal dinner with him, enjoyed his hospitality, and shared his food."

Tin Carson-Chiang nodded. "And the food's toxic."

"Deadly," Kish-Murphy agreed. "The whole damned planet's laced with heavy metals, the plant life's based on arsenic, the meat animals produce some sort of cyanogen that the locals use for gravy, and *all* the fungi are full of killer alkaloids. We'd even have trouble *breathing* here, let alone eating—at first glance the gas mix is just about Erthuma standard, but the trace elements . . . well, if you ever go down to the surface, wear a filter, at the very least. Wonderful place the Seventh Race's gadgets found to hide."

Tin Carson-Chiang nodded. "We got all that about the toxins explained in the specifications for the robot. We had to be very careful about corrosion.'' She watched the robot's transmissions for a moment, then asked, "So what did your ambassadors do?''

"Well, the first one died," Kish-Murphy said. "He actually tried to eat something at the formal dinner. I guess he figured he could vomit it up later and get himself fixed up—but he didn't make it that far. Hell, I don't think he managed to leave the table.''

Tin Carson-Chiang grimaced.

"The second one," Kish-Murphy said, "brought his own food with him—which turned out to be a deadly insult. He spent three weeks in medical, being rebuilt.'' He sighed. "We thought we had it with the third one— he was a prestidigitator, and *faked* eating. All the food went up his sleeve or down his pants instead of into his mouth. He made it all the way through the meal, and then he found out, right at the end, that the final sign of acceptance is when the patriarch himself places a . . . well, a sort of a hormone candy, in your mouth. He puts it there with his own fingers—even this illusionist we sent couldn't send it up his sleeve instead. You're supposed to suck on it, then swallow the hard center, while the alpha male watches. After that, you're his good friend, and can talk to him as one nestling to another. Except our man didn't swallow it; he spat it out. The locals were so utterly shocked that he got a pretty good headstart on them, and he was heavily armed, as well. He was out of medical and on his way home just a day later.''

Tin Carson-Chiang commented, "I notice you always sent men; I know it's a male-dominant culture, the sort of place that makes me glad we're more like chimps than baboons, but what if you'd sent a woman?''

Kish-Murphy frowned. "We thought of that. We even tried it—I didn't mention her, did I? Shier Sin-Tyler was her name. She wasn't an official ambassador, just a volunteer from the crew of the ship that charted the planet for us after the artifacts landed. We'd thought that the fi-Shhekh might not even know the difference, since our species hardly has the same secondary sexual characteristics as theirs, but it was obvious they knew instantly—probably by smell. And we'd thought that maybe, since all the rituals are designed to let competitive males deal with each other without fighting, that a woman wouldn't need to go through any rituals.'' He sighed. "Well, she didn't, except one. To the locals, females are property, and there's a very simple and obvious way of claiming them. And there are dozens of bachelor males in every household, each of them ready to grab any opportunity to claim a virgin female and set up a new household of his own.''

Tin Carson-Chiang blinked. "But we aren't the same species . . .''

"No, we aren't,'' Kish-Murphy agreed. "We aren't even close. And at first that deterred them. But the minute she *spoke*, and showed that she was a person and not an animal—well, we think they just assumed she was deformed. And they aren't particularly xenophobic, as I said. She was heavily armed, like the last ambassador, and she got out unhurt, but three locals were killed. If she'd done something to offend them as a *group*, instead of individually, we might not have been that lucky.'' He sighed.

"So after that,'' tin Carson-Chiang said, "you resorted to robots.''

"That's right, we resorted to robots. It's not unheard of.'' He turned to the video. "And it had damned well better work!''

Lord Khwistikhir smiled at the stranger—though among offworlders only an expert or a Naxian would have recognized the expression, which consisted of letting the lower jaw hang slack while the lower eyelids rose halfway. To unschooled Erthumoi the effect more closely resembled the onset of a fit than it did a smile.

Robot of Erthumoi tried to smile back, but the engineers who built it, not aware of the niceties of social intercourse among the fi-Shhekh, had not made the lower eyelids capable of independent movement. As a result, its eyes narrowed to slits, so the expression was closer to a yawn than a smile.

Lord Khwistikhir kindly overlooked this little slip. The stranger was eating with an excellent appetite, which was a very good sign—tastes varied from one household to the next, and similar tastes traditionally meant compatible temperaments.

When Lord Khwistikhir was pleased, the household of Khwistikhir was pleased. Half a dozen subordinate males let their own displays of wariness subside, and a few of the females watching from the gallery even ventured smiles of their own in Robot's direction.

But not everyone was pleased.

Farther down the table, a dozen places farther from Lord Khwistikhir than was Robot, sat Zukhishi of Khurrish, his neck ruff stiffly flared. He bared his fangs, then quickly hid them again.

Zukhishi was not happy at all about the sudden appearance of this stranger in unfamiliar colors, and was even less happy about the stranger's quick acceptance at Khwistikhir's table. Lord Khurrish had sent Zukhishi here to arrange trading terms with Khwistikhir, and had promised Zukhishi that if he won a sufficiently favorable agreement, Lord Khurrish would grant him a female of his own.

That would mean an end to his useless existence as a surplus subordinate male, and a chance to create his own household. He was still young and strong; if he acquired a female who was sufficiently fertile, perhaps he would live to see a Household Zukhishi that was the equal of Khurrish or Khwistikhir.

But first, he needed a sufficiently favorable trade agreement.

And so far, despite bribery, threats, promises, and every other maneuver he could think of, he hadn't been able to reach *any* agreement. He had built up an entire network of agents of varying degrees of trustworthiness in the Khwistikhir household, but the only person whose opinion mattered, Lord Khwistikhir himself, remained unconvinced and uninterested.

And now this new person, this Robot of Erthumoi, had walked in and gained Khwistikhir's attention immediately, apparently by his very strangeness and naïveté.

It was totally unfair, and not to be borne. Nor would Zukhishi bear it; he intended to do something about it. He reached into the pouch under his cloak.

The herbs therein came from the Gleaming Swamp, and were so thick with poison that they fairly crackled. Just a sprinkle in the stranger's food would surely be enough to remove this annoyance.

The stranger wouldn't notice the taste in this swill the people of Khwistikhir ate, and Lord Khwistikhir would not suspect a thing—everyone knew that people from one region often couldn't safely eat food from another. This Robot was stuffing incredible amounts down his throat in an effort to impress his host and coax Lord Khwistikhir into bringing forth the Nestling's Cud; what could be more natural than that he would choke? He was clearly from far away, after all.

A faint shadow of doubt crossed Zukhishi's mind—how *could* such a stranger eat such prodigious quantities of the local foods?

Well, it didn't matter. What mattered was finding a way to get the toxic herbs into this Robot.

The two visitors were not seated together—since their relationship to one another was unknown, thrusting them into each other's presence would have violated hospitality rituals. Zukhishi could scarcely declare a connection now, having once accepted separate seats—besides, if he made any such claim the stranger would deny it, and that would force Lord Khwistikhir to choose which of his guests to believe. Zukhishi was not ready to force such a choice; it seemed all too likely that the newcomer would win out.

How, then, could he contrive to leave his seat and pass near the stranger? One did not leave one's seat during a meal; that was against custom.

The fact that he was deliberately plotting murder didn't trouble Zukhishi at all—the fi-Shhekh had no inhibitions, either cultural or genetic, that would interfere with killing either a subordinate male of another household, or a householdless male. Such killings were not against custom.

And killing an alpha male was very much a part of established custom, and a goal to be eagerly sought after—but only within the appropriate ritual framework, of course.

The only problem with killing the stranger was if Zukhishi was caught killing someone in someone else's household without the lord's permission. That was a *serious* violation of custom, and would mean either permanent exile from Khwistikhir or his own death.

And if he were exiled from Khwistikhir his mission would be a failure, which would make it certain he would be exiled from Khurrish as well, and condemned to life as a householdless, unmated wanderer.

Death would be preferable.

So if he were to carry out his poisoning successfully, he needed to get the herbs into the stranger without anyone else knowing he had done it.

He bared his fangs again as he considered the problem.

Well, there were ways. He *did* have his agents in the household, and not all of them were seated. His neck ruff slowly settled as he considered possibilities.

A few minutes later an immature male was trotting by, a bowl of gorrip in his hands; Zukhishi yawned, and in doing so flung out his tail and tripped the youth.

The boy staggered, but did not fall; Zukhishi turned to apologize, lowering his head and arching his neck (though with the ruff down tight—his offense was not *that* great). This brought his mouth near the lad's ears, and he whispered quickly, "I have an errand for you. A dozen crystals if you perform it without flaw."

The boy smiled an acceptance.

When he had delivered the gorrip he returned to Zukhishi's side, as if to make a quick ritual acknowledgment of peace—that wasn't required after such an incident as the tripping, but it was reasonable.

Instead of the ritual, though, he asked, "What need I do?"

Zukhishi slipped the poisonous herbs into the youth's hand. "See that the stranger Robot eats these," he said. "All of them."

The youth accepted the herbs and walked away.

A few minutes later, Zukhishi watched with satisfaction as Robot of Erthumoi slurped up a bowl of soup. Even from a dozen seats away, the Khurrish could see the herbs floating in the broth.

"That young one put something in the robot's soup," tin Carson-Chiang remarked. "I didn't see it in anyone else's food; is it another silly ritual?"

Kish-Murphy shrugged. "I really don't know," he said. "I suppose it could be. Or maybe he's just trying to ingratiate himself with this interesting foreigner. You know how hard it is to figure out motives for other intelligent species, even relatively primitive ones."

"Should we tell the robot to do anything about it?"

Kish-Murphy considered that for several minutes before answering, "No."

Zukhishi watched in amazement as Robot and Lord Khwistikhir calmly exchanged smiles once again. They could not yet speak to each other, of course; the lord of a household could only speak directly to his own subordinates, and to foreigners after they had been adopted as nestlings. Robot would not be adopted until he had swallowed the Nestling's Cud. Until then, the two could only speak through intermediaries, or communicate by gestures and facial expressions.

And they were doing a great deal of gesturing and smiling, and Zukhishi found it simply appalling.

How could Robot still be *alive*, let alone smiling?

Had the idiot boy put the wrong herbs in the soup?

At that thought, Zukhishi's ruff bristled. Instantly, he devised a plan and took the first step in carrying it out by miming the finding of a slimecrawler in his bowl of fruit.

To announce such a find would be impolite, of course, so he did not have to actually tell a lie; holding the pinched fingers out, as if keeping the loathsome thing at arm's length, was enough to convince everyone.

Quickly, one of the serving boys—a different one—ran up to dispose of the vermin.

Zukhishi whispered to him, and the youth departed with something in his hand—but it was no slimecrawler.

It was half the contents of Zukhishi's poison pouch.

"There's more stuff being added to the food," Kish-Murphy said. "Neither of the surviving ambassadors ever mentioned anything like this." A note of worry had crept into his voice.

Tin Carson-Chiang shrugged.

"It can't hurt the robot, whatever it is," she said.

"No," Kish-Murphy agreed. "Of course not. I'm just afraid we're going to get some part of the ritual wrong."

Zukhishi's eyelids were fully retracted and his shoulders cocked back in an expression of astonished disbelief.

He had *seen* the poison go into Robot's mouth! Enough poison to kill an entire household!

And Robot was blithely smiling at Lord Khwistikhir, going through a ritual acceptance of honor tidbits from the household cooks. He showed no sign of discomfort at all.

How could this *be?*

Lord Khwistikhir's gaze moved down the long table, and his smile vanished. He turned and whispered a few words to the subordinate at his right, who was serving as the steward for this particular meal.

A moment later the steward was at Zukhishi's side, carefully not stepping within the radius of the Khurrish's tail. Under the laws of hospitality, that little circle of pavement was currently outside Khwistikhir's jurisdiction, and the steward was acting as Khwistikhir's agent.

He made a formal ritual apology for troubling the honored guest, then a ritual expression of brotherhood with all who were welcome under Khwistikhir's roof. Zukhishi waited impatiently, bringing his emotions under control. His shoulders folded back into resting position, his eyelids reappeared, his neck ruff settled somewhat.

The ritual was calming, really, Zukhishi had to admit. After all, that was what it was for.

Eventually the steward got to the point.

"My lord father saw you were disturbed, and expressed a certain curiosity to me as to the reason," he said. "I confessed I did not know, and was shamed by this failure to please him whom I serve."

Zukhishi pulled back his upper lip in polite acknowledgment, but said nothing. He was thinking hard about what he should do.

"I am here to tell my foreign brother that I wish to avoid another such failure, should my lord still be curious about the matter when I dare to return to his side," the steward concluded.

"I will tell you why I am disturbed, then," Zukhishi said, loudly. "I will tell everyone here, all my beloved brothers, who have accepted me into this home, though your father is not the male who impregnated the females of my nest." He rose to his full height, ruff bristling. "I will speak in the presence of Lord Khwistikhir himself, and all the females he possesses, so that my brothers will hear me the sooner."

The steward's own ruff was up, shoulders cocked, eyelids withdrawn. Such a speech was not what he had expected.

It could be a deliberate affront, the first step leading up to a formal challenge—but that was hardly appropriate to a welcoming feast!

"I will warn you all," Zukhishi said, "that there is a monster among us!"

*   *   *

"Oh, damn," Kish-Murphy said. "Now what's gone wrong?"

"Who *is* that?" tin Carson-Chiang asked. "Why is he dressed differently from all the others? Is he the court jester, or something?"

Kish-Murphy shook his head. "No, they don't have anything like that," he said. "Those are the colors of some other household—I've seen them before, when we were doing remote reconnaissance. This fellow must be an ambassador of some kind."

Tin Carson-Chiang stared at the image of the banquet hall, where several dozen of the large alien creatures called fi-Shhekh were squeaking and hissing incomprehensibly at each other, with tails and feather ruffs flapping and rustling on all sides. It looked quite insane, by human standards, but she knew perfectly well that there was some sort of underlying logic to even the maddest of alien societies. "Why would he have anything against us, then?" she asked.

"How should *I* know?" Kish-Murphy shouted. "Maybe he's working for the Locrians—there were rumors that they'd tracked the things from Innini to here, too."

"That's nonsense," tin Carson-Chiang said. "The artifacts are less than a meter long each, and if there'd been a Locrian ship in range our people would have seen it. That's just—" She realized Kish-Murphy wasn't listening, and stopped.

Kish-Murphy frowned and leaned forward, bringing his face close to the video display. He studied the image, looking at the distance between the robot and its accuser.

"Hey, Beth," he asked, "look at this and tell me something. How does he *know* it's a monster?"

The excited murmurs and flutters slowly died away; now the entire population of the hall was silent, and all eyes were focused on the daily steward and the Khurrish envoy.

A few stole quick glances at Robot of Erthumoi, but then returned to the pair.

Robot, for his part, sat in polite, stolid silence, not interfering in the business of his hosts.

The steward, after much consideration, had arrived at the appropriate response. He looked quickly to Lord Khwistikhir, who motioned his assent, then turned back to Zukhishi and said, "My foreign brother has puzzled me. I will not be so impertinent as to impose my confusion upon him with questions, but if he should care to explain himself further, I am sure that I and my nestling brothers will be greatly and enjoyably educated thereby."

Zukhishi bared fangs, then quickly covered them again.

"As my brother asks," he said, "so I must do. This creature that dines at your table, this creature that calls itself by the meaningless noise Robot, of the nonexistent household of Erthumoi, is no Shhekh at all, but a monster—perhaps one of the legendary night creatures that stalk the wilds and are said to disguise themselves, to fool their victims into not fleeing at their approach." He thrust out a pointing hand in Robot's direction.

No one looked very convinced.

The steward muttered to the floor, "A proclamation from a subordinate has no more significance than the babbling of a child or a female's cooing, unless it be given weight and solidity by the authority of evidence, or the authority of the name of a household's lord."

Zukhishi snorted. "You mean, brother, that you will not take my word that that thing is a monster. Will you take the word of your own nephews? For at my behest, two of the youths of this house have fed that creature enough poison to slay us all, and yet it sits there as unconcerned as if those fatal drugs were no more than salts to season a bland dish!"

The steward blinked, and its ruff rippled in surprise. He turned to the serving lads.

Two of them bent in acknowledgment.

At the head of the table Lord Khwistikhir stirred. He

glowered at the two boys, and then, slowly, he rose to
his feet. His ceremonial robe—to the watching Erthumoi
it appeared green and black, but to the eyes of the five
Shhekh the household colors were a particular shade of
extreme green and a color in the infrared that had no
distinct name in any Erthumoi tongue—billowed out to
either side, and the feathers of his ruff, long and graceful
as only a mature alpha male's could be, stirred and rustled
dramatically.

"You, thing of Khurrish," he demanded thunderously,
"are you declaring that you attempted to poison *my guest*
at *my table,* when I had not asked that it be done?"

Zukhishi fought against his instinctive urge—his instinctive *need*—to bend his neck and submit to the authority
of Lord Khwistikhir. To defy an alpha male—that could
end in only three ways: instant submission, ritual challenge
to combat, or death. Zukhishi was not on the hormonal
high necessary for combat; so far as he could smell, not
a single female in the entire household was in season, and
with no female to fight over, a proper challenge and combat would be impossible for him. He was no rogue or
desperate wanderer, ready to fight out of season.

That left submission or death. He had no wish to die—
but to submit at this point might well mean his death as
a poisoner.

Death for defiance, or death for breaking the rules of
hospitality—or if he could fight the urge long enough to
present his case, just possibly victory.

"Lord Khwistikhir," he said, forcing the words out, "I
ask your leave to speak."

Puzzled, Khwistikhir studied the Khurrish. He stepped
away from his seat and strode around the table, heedless
of the subordinates desperately throwing themselves out of
his path, to get a closer look and study this strange phenomenon more closely.

As lord householder he had no need to respect any rule
about a tail's radius of private space, and he did not. He
stepped right up to Zukhishi, looming over him—Khwis-

tikhir was a prime specimen of his species, some thirty centimeters taller than the Khurrish, and with over twice the mass—and looking him straight in the eye.

"Speak," he commanded.

It was difficult, *very* difficult, to lie to an alpha male, but Zukhishi fought against his instincts and forced out each word of his lie.

"Lord Khwistikhir," he said, trembling, "noble protector, progenitor of glory, I knew the stranger for a monster before we ever took our places at this meal—at this splendid feast you have had spread before us. I sent him . . . no, I sent *it* poison to reveal its true nature to you! Only that!"

"You acted without my consent," Khwistikhir stated—but Zukhishi knew it was a question and a command, not simply a statement.

"Undefiable master," Zukhishi said, "I have not been given the honor of speaking to you directly, without much preparation, and I thought that you would refuse to hear me. Yet the fear that this monster might harm you was greater than my fear of death at your hands, and I acted—oh, honored lord, pardon such impudence—I acted without being told to do so, in so many words. But, Lord Khwistikhir, my own father and master, Lord Khurrish, had commanded that I should place myself utterly at your service, and to prevent any harm from touching you, any illness of body, mind, or reputation from intruding past your gates. So I sought to defeat *that* creature, to prevent it from carrying out whatever evil ends it might intend!" He again thrust an accusing hand toward Robot.

"You know that your life has been mine, to give or take as I please, since you entered my gates," Lord Khwistikhir said. "And by daring to act as you have, you have thrust that life between my jaws. Yet may I see fit to spit it out, if I decide that you have kept worse from my throat." He turned, slowly and regally, to glare at Robot.

"You who call yourself Robot of Erthumoi," he thundered, "I speak to you in defiance of ritual and custom, not as lord to underling, as is the natural order, but as if we were strangers met in the wild, with no hall to tell our stations and house our ceremonies. You have eaten at my table, eaten the meats and fruits from my kitchens, but for the moment we will set that aside. This son of Khurrish accuses you of being a night creature, or some other false seeming, and says he fed you poisons. What do *you* say?"

Robot sat stupid and silent, his expression blank, for several long seconds.

The glowing message in the corner of the video display read, "Situation outside programming," but neither the diplomat nor the roboticist needed to read it to know that.

"I've got the link ready," tin Carson-Chiang said, "but what do I *tell* it? What should it do?"

"I don't—" Kish-Murphy began. Then he snarled, "Oh, what the hell. Let me do it. How does it work?"

"Go ahead," tin Carson-Chiang told him. "Just tell it; it'll hear you."

"Right. It's time to wing it, I guess." He grimaced. "After all, at worst we lose a robot, and you can build another, right?"

"That's not the worst, and you know it," tin Carson-Chiang retorted. "At worst, we convince the entire population of the planet that we're demons and monsters, and lose any chance of ever getting those artifacts."

"Yeah," Kish-Murphy said. "That's worse, all right. And I wish you hadn't reminded me."

Robot lowered his head, not in a fully submissive posture, but in a respectful pose.

"Lord Khwistikhir," he said, "glorious master of this household, am I really to be permitted to speak to you under your own roof, while yet an unknown foreigner?"

"You are *commanded* to speak to me," Khwistikhir told the stranger. "And quickly."

"It is awe that has slowed my words," Robot replied

"As for the accusations that this person has made against me, I am no monster, but as I told your gatekeeper, I come from very far indeed, from far beyond the horizon that can be seen from the highest watchtower. In my journeys I knew I might come to eat strange foods, and so I took medicines against poisons—not that I feared any poisons under the roof of the magnificent Khwistikhir, but I have been traveling many, many days and have eaten in many places. If this person has indeed fed me poisons, I am unaware of it—my medicines have protected me."

Lord Khwistikhir frowned.

"He lies!" Zukhishi shouted.

Lord Khwistikhir turned an angry glare on the Khurrish, who quickly subsided—and this time he was unable to resist his instincts, and his neck curved, ruff spread, into a proper submission.

"*One* of you lies," Khwistikhir announced. He growled, and several of those present shrank away in terror. Furious, the lord of the household bellowed, "*One* of you lies—but I have not determined which!"

"Just how convincing is that robot?" Kish-Murphy asked as he watched the raging patriarch. His instructions to the robot had staved off disaster so far, but unfortunately, they hadn't yet prevented it entirely.

Tin Carson-Chiang shrugged. "I don't really know," she admitted. "We did the best we could with the information you gave us. We averaged out the three VR images you gave us and worked with tolerances down to about eighty microns, but when you're working with machines and living organisms together you never know just what can go wrong. We could have messed up one of the textures somewhere, and I won't swear the color resolution's perfect outside the part of the spectrum that's visible to Erthumoi. Those things see from infrared through green, instead of red through violet, and we could have screwed up something in the infrared. But the only mistake I *know* of was in wiring the muscles that work the eyelids, and that won't show unless it tries to do something it can't.''

"So they can look at it up close, and touch it, and maybe stick something down its throat, and you don't think they'll see it's a robot?''

"They shouldn't,'' tin Carson-Chiang said. "Not unless they . . . well, we did the throat down about half a meter; if they go poking any farther than that, we could have trouble. And we didn't worry about the other end of the digestive tract much at all—only a few centimeters. And it doesn't *work* at all, it's just for appearance.''

Kish-Murphy nodded. "So they shouldn't spot that it's a robot unless they start cutting it open.''

"Right.''

"So we can go on denying that other guy's claims, and he can't prove it.''

"Well . . .''

"Well, what?''

"Well, what you just said—not unless they start cutting it open. You said these patriarchs are little tinpot gods—couldn't this Lord Wishy-Ears decide to have the robot cut open, just on general principles?''

"Well, yeah, he could,'' Kish-Murphy agreed. He sighed. "I guess we'll just have to talk him out of it.''

"I cannot bear longer the honor of addressing so great a lord directly,'' Robot said, in a loud, clear voice that nonetheless maintained a deferential tone. "I beg that someone hear me, and perhaps whoever does so shall see fit to convey to mighty Lord Khwistikhir whatever might interest him.''

That put at least *something* back to normal at this strangest and most unorthodox of welcoming banquets—Kish-Murphy thought that might help to reduce tension, and had told Robot so.

Robot's appointed interlocutor, a young adult named Hhikhuhi, made a gesture indicating readiness to listen.

"If anything is at fault at this table," Robot said, "it cannot be the doing of any who are the sons of Khwistikhir, for they have spent all their lives in service to his glory, and surely must all know well what is expected of them. It is unthinkable that any of Lord Khwistikhir's household could be in any way unsatisfactory to Lord Khwistikhir. Therefore, since ritual and custom have been disturbed, the error must arise from the outsiders present. There are two such, myself and this other, who is unknown to me but who accuses me of being something other than a true Shhekh. One or the other of us, or perhaps both, must be responsible for this disharmony I have unwillingly observed."

Hhikhuhi bared thin, needle-sharp fangs. Lord Khwistikhir, who was not the ostensible audience for Robot's speech, was nonetheless listening carefully.

Robot had paused while receiving further instruction from his Erthuma master, but now he continued.

"I cannot say with certainty where the fault lies, with my accuser or with myself, for my own beliefs are as nothing before the omniscience of Lord Khwistikhir within his own gates," Robot said. "But it is unthinkable that I should allow myself to cause disharmony at the table of Khwistikhir. Therefore, I beg that, if somehow word of my plight should reach Lord Khwistikhir's ears, I should be turned out, as if I had disgraced myself at table, rather than that my presence should cause the slightest discomfort to the master of this household. All here is his to do with as he pleases, and if I have troubled him, such a blot upon his peaceful repose as myself should be removed forthwith."

"What a speech!" tin Carson-Chiang marveled.

"Thanks," Kish-Murphy muttered. "Your robot prettied it up for me, you'll notice."

"Of course," tin Carson-Chiang replied. "That's what we programmed it to do!"

* * *

Lord Khwistikhir turned toward Zukhishi.

"Robot of Erthumoi has spoken fairly, and in a proper fashion," he said. "Zukhishi of Khurrish has admitted to attempted poisoning, and has made accusations with no evidence."

Zukhishi's four eyelids trembled as he said, "He lies. He is a monster, no true Shhekh—what medicines could protect him against poison herbs? Or perhaps he is a wanderer, seeking a place in your household without taking the risks of challenge—there is no household called Erthumoi!"

"Could a monster speak so well, and follow ritual?" Lord Khwistikhir mused, not directly addressing Zukhishi. "Would a lying wanderer offer to depart, rather than trouble me further, when he is but a step away from earning a place here? Does this envoy from Khurrish know the names of every household under the sun, that he can say with certainty that a particular one does not exist?"

After a moment of awkward silence, Zukhishi said, "I am distraught, and speak without proper planning—out of fear for Lord Khwistikhir."

Lord Khwistikhir considered that carefully.

Everyone in the banquet hall awaited his decision in tense silence, and Zukhishi was easily the most worried of all present. It was plain that this dispute could easily mean his death. He struggled to think of something he could say that would better his chances of survival.

Robot of Erthumoi, sitting a few meters away, was incapable of worry, and was not doing any independent thinking at all just now. He was leaving that to his distant masters. Most of his interior was devoted to the equipment that allowed him to simulate life—false lungs, false stomach, motors and pumps and wires. That had not left all that much space for brains, and much of his data processing capacity was occupied with running and maintaining his body, so that, as robots went, he was not terribly bright. Events had long since passed the point at which his built-in intelligence could handle them.

*   *   *

"So why did that one try to poison the robot in the first place?" tin Carson-Chiang asked. "It wasn't the Locrians, I'm sure."

Kish-Murphy shrugged. "Fear of the competition, I suppose," he said. "Whatever he was sent to do at Khwistikhir, he must think having another ambassador around will make it more difficult."

"Will it?"

Startled, Kish-Murphy considered that for a moment, then admitted, "I don't see why it should, really. We can't be after the same things he is; why would his household want Seventh Race artifacts?"

"Why do *we* want them?" tin Carson-Chiang countered.

"So we can go on trying to analyze them, just as we did on Innini before they took off, and just the way we've done with all the other junk the Seventh Race left scattered around the Galaxy. And these primitives can't possibly know what the artifacts are, or have any use for them."

"You're sure of that?"

"Oh, absolutely; whatever he was after, whatever he thinks we'd keep from him, it's got to be something else."

"Then all this is for nothing, from his point of view—but he doesn't know that yet?"

"I guess so," Kish-Murphy agreed.

"What's going to happen to him?"

"Oh, they'll kill him," Kish-Murphy said.

"What?" Tin Carson-Chiang stared. "They'll *kill* him?"

"Well, yes," Kish-Murphy said. "After all, he *did* try to poison someone. And these folks are pretty barbaric, when you get right down to it; they'll kill each other over much less than attempted murder."

"But he didn't poison *someone,* he poisoned our silly robot!" tin Carson-Chiang protested.

"Well, he didn't know that," Kish-Murphy pointed out. *"He* thought he was poisoning someone."

"Still, he . . . Are you going to let him die for *nothing?*"

"It's not up to me," Kish-Murphy said with a shrug. "It's up to Lord Khwistikhir."

"Well, you could do *something*, couldn't you?" tin Carson-Chiang demanded.

Kish-Murphy considered that, and admitted, "I suppose I could."

"Oh, that my words might reach the right ears," Robot said quietly, to nobody in particular.

In the anticipatory silence the words carried wonderfully, and more than a dozen pairs of eyes turned toward him.

"I fear," Robot said, addressing an empty bowl, "that all this unpleasantness has resulted from a misunderstanding, not on the part of any of the household of Khwistikhir, who could scarcely err beneath their own roof, but on the part of the two others they have graciously permitted within their walls."

He had everyone's attention now, even Lord Khwistikhir's.

The patriarch was surprised by this interruption of his thoughts; he had believed it was clear enough that he intended to side with the Erthumoi, rather than the Khurrish, yet here the fool was, breaking into the deliberations in this annoying fashion. Did he *want* to be cast out?

Zukhishi was even more surprised; he had thought his best hope was exile, and was expecting death, but now the stranger's voice might yet bring a reprieve, if only by angering Lord Khwistikhir—or redirecting his anger.

"I think that this other guest must have misunderstood my place here," Robot said. "He must have feared that I sought the same things he sought, and that to allow me to usurp his place in the warmth of Lord Khwistikhir's presence would mean that he must be forced out into the cold, his own ends unmet, his duty to his lord failed. But did he not realize that I would scarcely come as far as I

have for any ordinary purpose, and that we cannot in truth
be competitors? And that Lord Khwistikhir's glory is great
enough to encompass any number of envoys? That there
is no need for us to be foes, and that I would, if I dared,
beg Lord Khwistikhir to forgive him his folly?''

Robot finished his speech, and for a moment the hall
was silent again.

Then Lord Khwistikhir let out a roar; heads fell in submission on all sides.

''Listen to him!'' Lord Khwistikhir bellowed. ''He
would beg me for your life, creature of Khurrish!''

Zukhishi, in full submission, could not acknowledge
this save by trembling, which he was doing anyway. He
was baffled by this turn of events—but not displeased.

''Ghorrush,'' Lord Khwistikhir called, ''bring me the
Nestling's Cud, that I may make our new infant, Robot,
welcome here! And as a gift to please him, a toy for his
bedding, I will let the Khurrish stay on—if he will swear
to never again attempt to harm my other guests!''

The subordinate hurried to fetch the cud, and an excited
murmur drove away the last of the nervous silence that
had obtained a moment earlier.

And five minutes later, Lord Khwistikhir thrust the
gooey Nestling's Cud with his own fingers into the mouth
of Robot of Erthumoi.

''There,'' Kish-Murphy said, leaning back in his chair.
''We have our embassy! Now that robot can bring in oth-
ers, and we can take our time about finding those artifacts.
Nobody else is going to get in ahead of us.''

Tin Carson-Chiang nodded. ''None of the other starfaring races could build a robot like that,'' she agreed. ''As
long as the hospitality customs are what they are, we've
got an unbeatable edge.''

''And they aren't about to change,'' Kish-Murphy said.
''Gods, *this* time we almost blew it because our ambassa-
dor *didn't* get sick from eating with them! What a place!
All this trouble, just because the food's toxic!''

"Could be worse," tin Carson-Chiang said.

Kish-Murphy snorted. "How?" he asked.

"Well," tin Carson-Chiang said, "if we had this much trouble with the food, just think if their hospitality customs were based on wife-swapping!"

FIGHTING WORDS

JANET KAGAN

KNOWING THE RIGHT WORDS COULD MAKE ALL the difference . . . in fight *or* flight. Mixed insults and obscenities were fine for everyday dealing with the average Crotonite—but ah! the words for winds were something else again! Wyss'huk had given Harriet Kingsolver the Crotonite words for the winds, and Harriet hoarded them, gloating over the sound of each and the feel of the air each called to mind. Now he—or any other Crotonite who'd give her the time of day—could give her a map of the sky to guide her flight. Harriet fell headlong off Fallaway Point to follow the latest map . . .

And the life-pulse was exactly where Wyss'huk had told her it would be. Damn, but he knew the winds like nobody else! Harriet caught the current and soared. The resulting twist to the west gave her a grand overview of Fallaway Point and black volcanic sands against the teal blue of the water. "Found it!" she yelled to Wyss'huk over the rush of wind. If he couldn't exactly hear her, he'd get her meaning from the joy in her shout.

The Crotonite hit the same thermal and rose beside her. Beneath the vivid green of his hang glider, Wyss'huk's gray fur gleamed silver in the afternoon sun. His bright orange eyes met hers in shared delight as, just for a moment, the tips of their wings almost touched . . . then he shifted to give her extra leeway.

Teach a Crotonite a new way to fly, she thought, and he'll still outfly you. She took a deep exuberant breath

57

and let it out in another yell—this one all joy and no words.

All around her, the sky was alive with the brilliant colors of the Only Birds. Harriet wondered if the flock of hang gliders she flew with could really call themselves that these days, since the arrival of that last batch of Crotonites. Unlike the two ambassadors, these new Crotonites hadn't had their wings clipped—*their* flight was powered.

Even now, one of them flapped his (her?) way from the beach toward Wyss'huk and Harriet. Usually Harriet could recognize the individual Crotonites from their flight profiles, but this one she didn't know. Perhaps it was one who didn't deign to fly with Erthuma slugs. Harriet gave a sigh of exasperation.

Probably another diplomatic crisis, she thought. Pssstwhit or Stiss?

In the few months since the two Crotonite worlds had established their rival embassies on LostRoses, Harriet had had it up to here with diplomatic crises between them. She liked and respected both ambassadors, Wyss'huk from Pssstwhit and Katuk from Stiss, but she'd had quite enough of the governments that had sent them. What could she expect *but* crisis from a government that amputates the wings of its ambassadors—on the theory that a wingless Crotonite would be able to think more like a wingless Erthuma slug (Harriet, to name one)—and then sends them *winged* staff members?

Too nice a day to think about governments . . . Harriet swooped left on an almost-there to catch the second life-pulse—exactly where Wyss'huk had said it would be—and rose higher, breathing the crisp cool air with deep content.

Off her right wing, Katuk gave a sudden spit of warning.

Harriet swung her head around to look and found herself the subject of scrutiny. Whatever the hell was flying next to her, it wasn't one of the winged Crotonite staff members. Some sort of true bird—but no comfortable flying companion.

Its feathers were the color and sheen of an oil slick, and it flew with its overlong sinuous neck drawn into a tight S-curve, like a snake drawn back to strike. The beak was a spear. With an effortless flap of wings, it caught the life-pulse—edging out Katuk—and rose to stare at her with fixed interest in its piercing black eyes.

If the Crotonites looked like the legendary bats-out-of-hell, this thing was from some earlier and nastier tradition. This was the eater of livers the Old Earth gods had sent to punish anybody they'd taken a dislike to. Unlike Prometheus, Harriet couldn't regenerate a liver—and it looked to her as if the damned thing knew it and relished the thought.

Its shiny button-black eyes were chilling. Harriet had seen the same malevolent glint in the crossed blue eyes of a Siamese cat on the stalk: thoughtful, infinitely patient. The look of a predator willing its chosen prey into reach of its jaws.

Harriet spilled air and dropped a little behind it. With a quick stroke of wing, it easily swung beside her, again matching her speed and altitude.

She could hear it thinking: *You don't belong in the air. You'll fall. Sooner or later, you'll fall . . . and when you do, I'll be here to pick up the pieces*. Its anticipation of disaster was more damaging to a slug's self-esteem than any curse a Crotonite could have voiced to a wingless sapient. "Heh-heh-heh," it said; its voice was gloating.

Wyss'huk caught a wind only he could have found and came up beneath the creature, startling it into a defensive swing to the right. "Ha'reet!" shouted the Crotonite, "pay attention to your flying! I'll distract it while you land!"

Ordinarily it amused Harriet when the Crotonites treated the Erthuma hang gliders as if they were fledglings on their first flights, but this was serious business.

Katuk rose to join the fray as well, harrying the creature

from above. Harriet was suddenly more afraid for the two Crotonites than for herself.

Realizing they'd put themselves at risk for her and that they'd keep at it until she was safely down, Harriet resigned herself to having her flight cut short. She spilled more air. From the rubber pickup raft below her, Majnoun too frantically gestured her to land.

Katuk shouted directions in Crotonite. She followed his map and found the proper wind and rode it down, passing so low over the raft that Majnoun had to duck.

A body-length from the surface of the water, Harriet loosed her harness and dropped. She struck with a splash and arrowed down, letting herself sink into the depths until she felt she'd shed enough momentum. Then she opened her eyes to sight for the underside of the raft . . .

Inches away, the same black eyes—now made opalescent by a nictitating membrane—continued their predatory scrutiny.

It was all Harriet could do to keep from inhaling water. The damned thing was a diving bird! She stroked evenly toward the surface, trying very hard not to look either wounded or edible as she swam.

To her relief, she broke water within hand's reach of the raft. Majnoun grabbed for her with one hand and yanked hard; the other hand held the oar upraised to defend against the damned thing if that became necessary.

Harriet hauled her torso into the raft and Majnoun grabbed her by the belt and unceremoniously flopped her legs in after her. The damned thing floated low in the water, only its snakelike neck and head visible, still eyeing Harriet. It wasn't the sort of bird to give up easily.

From above came the rich sound of Crotonite cursing as Wyss'huk and Katuk, in formation, skimmed the water toward the raft. Wyss'huk was screaming derogatory comments about the damned thing's ancestry while Katuk, in counterpoint, bellowed an equally unflattering description of its hygienic habits. Together, they sounded a lot like a powered aircraft in serious trouble.

All that sputtering—and their combined "attack"—finally caught the damned thing's attention. Its head snaked once in their direction, then, with an enviably easy flick of its wings, it rose from the water and headed for shore.

Majnoun started paddling in the same direction. "Get you back in your go-chair," he growled between strokes, "and you can take the damned thing apart for all of me."

Wyss'huk and Katuk had both landed on the beach. Majnoun had trained them well: they were taking care of their wings as the first order of business. That didn't stop their litany of curses, of course, but what did?

The damned thing was almost as tall as a Crotonite but Harriet wasn't worried. If push came to shove, they could stop it dead with a whiff from their breathing masks, most likely.

Darting snaky glances at Wyss'huk and Katuk, it walked a few paces up the beach to shelter against a tall dark-haired Erthuma. Harriet squinted into the sunlight to watch the two. Whatever the damned thing was, Harriet decided, it was either very young or a pet: the Erthuma was clearly giving it a talking to.

"Ease off, Majnoun," she said. "Let's get Firehawk." Harriet pulled herself to the edge of the raft and hung over. Reluctantly, Majnoun slowed and helped her gather up her wings. Harriet rolled over, laid the brilliant orange wings across her lap, and checked them out. "No damage," she said, relieved.

The voices from the shore were clearer now. The two Crotonites hadn't let up in the slightest. Pssstwhit having at one time been a colony of Stiss, they both cursed in the same language, which meant Harriet could understand a great deal of the invective. She grinned at Majnoun and said, "They're on a roll."

He glanced down at her. "You mean, they're not about to eat anybody alive?"

She shook her head. "They've hit the one-up stage. Wyss'huk's trying to outdo Katuk and vice-versa." She cocked an ear for a moment, then added admiringly,

"They've gotten esoteric: Katuk's currently discussing the damned thing's flaws at the molecular level, I think."

"Good. Maybe that'll keep it busy while I beach the raft and get you back in your chair."

It did. Harriet whistled for her chair and brought it almost to the edge of the water. She was tempted to tell the chair to goose the bird as it rolled past but decided instead to wait until she'd learned enough to goose it where she'd make the most impression.

And that "enough" included a lot of information about the Erthuma, who was attempting to placate Wyss'huk and Katuk in Crotonite that was a lot better than her own. That brought her a second grin. One didn't exactly "placate" in Crotonite: one cursed back—with frills. The three of them were going at it so hot and heavy they sounded like a covey of spitwhistles at mating season.

Majnoun heaved the raft ashore, tethered it, then splashed into the water to scoop Harriet out. Muttering some pretty fancy curses himself, though his were in Nevelse, Majnoun stomped through the water, splashing wildly, to plunk Harriet into her chair. He paused long enough to see that she was comfortably settled (even though she could have gotten the chair itself to see to that), then rounded on the oddly assorted trio still in full voice and joined in the chorus.

What Majnoun lacked in eloquence, he more than made up for in volume. His opening remark was an inarticulate roar of such rage that even Harriet was startled.

Majnoun was ordinarily the most patient man Harriet had ever known. The only time she'd ever seen him angry was when one of the flyers did something he considered risky and therefore stupid. Which explained why he was so angry now, of course.

The bellow had gotten their attention. Even the damned bird turned its shiny button-black eyes on Majnoun. Majnoun didn't give it so much as a glance. He jammed a finger into the chest of the Erthuma and said, this time quite understandably, "I don't know who you are, but

I've still got flyers up there—and either you keep that thing on the ground or I wring its neck. You got a preference?''

The Erthuma shifted style on the spot. "I apologize. It's my fault entirely. Bingo was cooped up so long en route that he really needed a chance to stretch his wings. When I asked around port for the best place to fly, everybody sent me out here . . .''

He turned abruptly to Harriet and continued his apology directly to her. "I should have guessed there was a reason so many people knew the best place to fly. I have no idea why Bingo took such an interest in you, but he's harmless, I guarantee it. He's strictly a carrion eater. If you're alive and kicking, he's usually got no interest at all.''

Harriet grinned at Majnoun. "That explains it, then. I can't kick, so Bingo's interested.''

Majnoun snorted like an angry bull but Wyss'huk made the ticking sound of Crotonite laughter.

The bird cocked its head at Harriet, appeared to consider this for a moment, then launched itself at her in a flutter of wings. Suddenly, everybody on the beach was yelling and grabbing wildly. There was such pandemonium that not one grab was effective.

Harriet whistled and her chair shot out a pincher that deftly caught the bird by the ankles. Bingo squawked in protest and flapped twice, straining against the two-fingered hold. "Gotcha," said Harriet. To the others, she said, "Now, will you all please shut up?''

The Erthuma's brow wrinkled into a worried frown, but the worry included both Harriet and Bingo. Harriet decided that was good enough. "I won't hurt him," she told the Erthuma. Her chair had been modified from a cargo-shifter, true, but she'd been careful to whistle up the pinchers for delicate work. Bingo might be mad but he wasn't being hurt.

He knew it too, and stopped flapping to eye her balefully. "Think about it, bird." She punched a set of instructions into her keyboard. "I've given the go-chair your specs. From now on, if you come within grabbing distance of me, it'll grab you and hold you until I tell it otherwise. If you don't like that, you'd be advised to stay out of reach."

She whistled again, this time a more complex tune. The chair extruded the right tine of its forklift and the pinchers deftly set the bird down on the end of it and released.

Bingo preened a feather or two back into presentable state, then fixed his button eyes on Harriet again. The pure get-even malevolence in the look drew a laugh from her.

"Won't work, bird," she told it. "I've been trained by the best. Not even *you* could out-glare a cross-eyed Siamese cat."

Bingo was unconvinced—until Harriet had stared him down for proof.

"Now that we've settled that," Harriet said—and she turned to the Erthuma—"I suggest you take Bingo back into town before he creates a diplomatic incident." She jabbed a finger in the direction of Wyss'huk and Katuk. "My two hang gliding buddies there are the ambassadors from Pssstwhit and Stiss, respectively, and you're cutting into some very fine flying time."

The Erthuma turned to the Crotonites and apologized all over again. Prettily done, thought Harriet, with admiration for a number of his viler phrases. Then he said, "If you'd be kind enough to point us in the right direction, we'll be on our way."

There was no vehicle in sight. "Long trip back," said Harriet. At her whistle, the chair extruded a seat. "Hop on and I'll give you both a lift. You hang on to Bingo, though—I don't want any surprises while I'm driving."

Katuk said, "Ha'reet, don't let this slug and his, his mold-ridden *thing* ruin your flying."

With effort, Harriet suppressed a smile. She'd never known any of the Crotonites at that kind of loss for words before. Maybe the one-up contest had actually wound him down.

Wyss'huk made a more elaborate objection but, aside

from filing a few of his glosses about the new Erthuma's mental ability for future use elsewhere, Harriet ignored his harangue to gather up her hang glider. When Wyss'huk finally stopped for breath, Harriet said quietly, "If I don't see you aloft in the next fifteen minutes, I'll tell the staff at *both* embassies their respective bosses are wasting good winds . . ."

That wasn't much of a curse, not by Crotonite standards, but it was an effective threat. The two Crotonites scurried to flight-check their wings. Harriet thought perhaps she heard Wyss'huk ticking his amusement, but she couldn't have said for sure.

"Fly," she said. "With all the cursing you've done, you'll probably have to renew your breathing masks sooner than usual. So it's only one flight I'm missing at most"—she gave a glance at the Erthuma to see that he was ready and that he had a good hold on Bingo—"and I expect the ride back to town will be interesting enough to make up for it. Don't let them overrun their tanks, Majnoun."

With an eye to the Crotonites, Majnoun nodded. Reassured he'd keep the two in hand, Harriet keyed the go-chair for town and set off along the beach, her head tilted back for one last look at that glorious sky.

Overhead, Isobel and Lilac dipped their wings in salute, and Harriet waved up at them. Bingo followed her glance and, probably inspired to flight again, struggled to get loose. The Erthuma kept his hold tight.

"How far will he range?" Harriet asked.

"He likes to keep me in sight. Not in earshot, though. He comes when I call—but only if he can hear me." The Erthuma scowled at the damned thing. "And sometimes I think he lies. I could have sworn he was in earshot. I tried to call him off the minute I realized he was tailing you."

"Looked more like stalking than tailing, from where I was," Harriet said. But in fairness she added, "I couldn't hear you and neither could Wyss'huk, I'd guess—not until we started heading in. Unless Bingo's ears are much better than ours, he honestly didn't hear you.''

''Oh.'' He looked genuinely relieved.

Harriet guessed that meant Bingo was usually better behaved or, at least, well trained by whatever standard applied to Bingo's sort. Fair Harriet might be, but he still held her responsible for his current predicament, to judge from the poisonous looks he sent her way.

The Erthuma struggled a bit to keep his seat *and* his hold on the bird as the chair jounced its way up the rocky trail that led into Hellup Woods. She could sympathize with the bird, though. She resented being kept out of the sky on a day like this, too, but a new face on LostRoses was close to compensation.

This was a pretty good face, too, though Harriet would have been willing to admit that perhaps that was so *only* because it was new. As one of only two traders flying the local supplies for LostRoses, she knew every face on the planet. . . .

High, expressive forehead. Dark eyebrows over deep blue eyes. That must give the Crotonites pause, she thought, remembering how impressed Wyss'huk had been by His Highness's Siamese-blue eyes. Like looking into a head full of sky.

Something pleasantly unusual about the set of the eyes . . . No, it wasn't the set of the eyes—his lids had the epicanthic fold, that was it. Exotic.

On the whole, Harriet thought it was a face that would stay good even when it had lost its novelty.

He must have shipped in with that new load of government experts while she was off on her supply rounds. The winds had been so good when she got home this morning that she hadn't even stopped for gossip. She didn't even know his name.

''So,'' she said—and she said it in Crotonite for the sheer mischievousness of it—''do you have a name or was your mother too appalled by your looks to claim you?''

He was so startled he almost lost his grasp on Bingo.

After much flapping and struggling, he turned to her with a grin and said, "My mother gave me twenty names, my father ten, as is customary in our tribe. I choose to be called Joppich, even by those whose brains have been burned away by too long a look into the sun."

"Harriet Kingsolver," she said. "Your accent really *is* better than mine. I'm jealous, but you can call me Harriet anyway—or 'Ha'reet' if you want to give it the twist the Crotonites do. They can't quite wrap their beaks around it."

The chair turned and plunged onto the shaded road that led through Hellup Woods. Bingo's glare was beginning to burn a hole between Harriet's eyes. Harriet nodded at the damned thing. "You can let him go now, if you want," she said. "There's nothing here big enough to find him interesting and he'll want to stay pretty close, if what you've said is true." Preferring a stable launchpad herself, she whistled the chair to a momentary halt.

Joppich nodded with relief. "Okay, Bingo. Up you go," he said, but Bingo didn't need that much encouragement. Loosed, he took to the air in a flash of wing.

Watching him circle and dive exuberantly brought a smile to Harriet's lips. "*Good* day for flying," she said, and whistled the chair into motion again. To Joppich, she added, "Keep an eye on him. Let me know if you lose sight of him."

"I don't think he plans to lose sight of you," Joppich said, and pointed. Just over her left shoulder, Bingo glided silently along on the air—out of reach of the chair's pinchers but keeping pace—his hungry eyes still fixed on Harriet.

"What *did* I do to deserve this?" Harriet asked, of no one in particular.

"Coincidence," he said. "I inherited Bingo three days before I got my grant—and I wasn't about to turn down the grant *or* Bingo."

"Grant," Harriet repeated, making of the word an invitation to explain.

"To find out why LostRoses is getting on so well when you've got not one, but two *rival* groups of Crotonites in residence."

"Getting on so well? Wyss'huk and Katuk fight like cats and dogs." She chuckled. "I take that back. They fight more like two tomcats: all bluff and fluff. Diplomatic crises galore—"

"But no actual mayhem," he said. "Not between Erthuma and Crotonite, not between Crotonite and Crotonite—and *that's* so unheard of, half my colleagues think you LostRosians have been covering up for the Crotonites. Burying bodies in the woods for them."

"If you're here to investigate a cover-up, why are you telling me this?"

"Because there are no bodies buried in the woods here. LostRoses hasn't reported any incidents because there haven't been any." He grinned and his forehead rippled wonderment. "I just saw two—*two* Crotonites come to the rescue of an Erthuma. Never mind that you were not really at risk . . . *they* thought you were and came to your rescue. That's not common practice."

"I'm *pippest* to both of them," Harriet said, shrugging it off. Belatedly, she caught the import of what he'd said. She narrowed her eyes at him. "Are you telling me common practice *is* burying bodies in the woods?"

Joppich frowned and gave a sigh. "All too common practice elsewhere. Usually it all comes out, usually there's a formal apology from one side to the other."

" 'Usually'—I don't like that word at all in this context."

"Nor do I. We've got a lot to learn from the Crotonites and vice-versa, but not if they kill each other off first." He brightened again. "Have you seen the artwork coming out of Stiss lately? *Magnificent*. Artwork doesn't always 'translate' from culture to culture, but this does. Oh, does it ever!" His sky-colored eyes fairly glowed.

"I know what you mean. Fastas is doing one that— No, I'm not about to try to describe it. You'll have to see for yourself.'' Realizing that he probably didn't know the dramatis personae yet, she added, ''Fastas is one of Katuk's aides.''

The pinchers made a grab; Bingo backed off, glaring. Harriet laughed. ''You thought I wasn't paying attention,'' she said to the bird, ''didn't you?'' To Joppich she said, ''What is the damned thing—a vulture?''

He shook his head. ''A mutt, a genetic cobble-job. From the way he dives, I'd guess he's got some cormorant or *something* pelicaniform in him, but the rest is anybody's guess. My uncle bought him for hunting. The joke was on Uncle Jamie, because Bingo likes his food dead.'' A twinkle lit Joppich's sky-colored eyes. ''He's patient, though; he'll wait.''

''May you have a long wait, bird,'' Harriet told it solemnly. She whistled her chair to an abrupt halt.

''Problem?'' said Joppich.

''No.'' Using her long-reach pinchers, Harriet reached high into a weeping birch that overhung the trail and plucked a twisted leaf. The pinchers dropped it into her hand. Harriet inspected it briefly. ''Still got the sharpest eye on LostRoses,'' she said, satisfied.

She handed the leaf to Joppich. ''Here's a prime specimen of LostRoses' excuse for existing. Split that leaf gall, polish it up, and you've got two gems. Once they reach one of the older, urbanized worlds as 'lostroses,' they'll be worth about 500,000c each.''

Joppich's dark brows went sharply up. ''You're kidding.''

''I'm not. Considering the cost for polishing and the fees to all the middlemen, it's only worth about 5,000c to you . . . but that's not a bad day's work.''

He swallowed hard. ''That's three years' salary to me.'' He reached to hand it back.

''Keep it,'' said Harriet. ''Take three years off. I've got more of 'em at home than I know what to do with—the cat plays with 'em. Impress the hell out of a lover . . .'' She grinned at the stunned expression on his face. ''Honestly,

I just wanted you to see what we do for a living here. If you don't want it, chuck it in the woods.''

The "three years' salary" caught up with Harriet abruptly. He wasn't one of the government experts—he was the Professor Joppich whose books on the Crotonites she'd been reading. "I should have known from the way you speak Crotonite," she said. "You wrote *A Guide to Insults.* You're *that* Joppich.''

"Guilty,'' he said, and hung his head in mock shame.

Harriet laughed. "That's probably the most-read book on LostRoses at the moment. You even impressed Wyss'-huk with that one—though he had some harsh but colorful words to say about people who are not competent enough to create their own curses.''

Bingo made another pass at Harriet, but this time veered off sooner. He was testing the reach of the pinchers, trying for an approach that wasn't covered.

They'd come out of Hellup Wood now, and into sunlight. "Bingo,'' said Joppich, "go fly, will you? Look at all that sky. . . .''

Harriet was the one who looked longingly at all that sky. "What a waste of high heart-wind,'' she said—in Crotonite, because she couldn't say it in Nevelse. Bingo apparently agreed. He gave her one last baleful look, then caught a seeds-rising and soared upward without so much as a flap of his wings. Harriet watched for a moment in admiration.

When she turned back, she found Joppich regarding her with a somewhat puzzled frown. He repeated the phrase, cleaning up the accent as he went, but the frown only deepened when she nodded to assure him he'd heard correctly.

Like an unexpected gust off Fallaway Point, realization came to Harriet. Something had been missing from Joppich's books on the Crotonites, but she'd not been able to put her finger on just what. "You know the words for the winds in Crotonite,'' she said, narrowing her eyes at him, "but you don't know what they *mean*.''

It came out as an accusation. "Sorry," she said, on the instant. "Of *course* you don't. You don't fly, so you don't get the emotional content."

"Teach me to fly," he said.

Just like that . . . *Teach me to fly* . . . and just like that Harriet decided he'd do. "I can't teach you," she said, grinning, "but Majnoun would be delighted to."

He nodded, and Harriet could almost see him making that mental note: *Learn to fly.* "You can't teach me?" he asked.

"Ground school requires working legs, which I haven't got." And because everybody asked the next question after that, she went ahead and answered it: "I made a bad landing, and the regeneration techniques don't work on me."

"Ah," he said, and cocked his head at her thoughtfully. "So *that's* why Wyss'huk laughed when you said you couldn't kick," he said. "I couldn't figure that one out at all."

"Now you know," said Harriet with a grin. "Wyss'-huk's got enough Nevelse to recognize a pun when he hears one. Be careful what you say in his earshot."

He nodded, then said, "Tell me what you mean by emotional content."

"Have you ever seen a Crotonite mating flight?"

Something wonderful came into his sky-colored eyes, much like the light they'd taken on when he'd talked about the artwork from Stiss. "Yes," he said. "It's beautiful. It's like watching an intricate dance—but one where the dancers might be dashed to pieces against a cliff at any moment. My heart was in my throat the entire time."

"I've never seen one," Harriet said, "but I got that much from Wyss'huk. He described a particularly beautiful mating he'd seen to me—and he did it all in terms of the couple's response to the winds they were flying."

St. Elsie's Field was in sight now, and Harriet slowed her chair to ask, "Sylvaine's Custom House? We can continue this over drinks if you'd like."

"Yes, please. I would."

Harriet keyed the chair for Sylvaine's, then brought i
to a full stop. "Oops," she said, "I almost forgot. How
does Bingo feel about cats? Does he consider them
edible?"

"My uncle had six. Bingo got on with them fine—and
they seemed to like him, though nobody could ever figur
out why."

"Okay," said Harriet. "I'll take your word for it. Bu
if he shows the least interest in eating His Highness, I'l
personally wring his neck."

He nodded equably. The nod reassured Harriet more
than the tale of his uncle's cats had and she set the chai
in motion once more.

She was glad she'd thought to ask when she did, be
cause they'd only gone some hundred yards farther when
His Highness shot from the patch of lithe-grass at the edge
of the road, bounded a few feet beside the rolling chair
sprang to the running board, and from there made a heroi
leap to land squarely in Harriet's lap. "Cat," she said
"if I'd felt that you'd be dangling from my longest set o
pinchers right now—by your tail." She looked down
"Since I'm not bleeding, I assume you didn't do an
damage . . . but I wish to hell you could find some wa
of being affectionate that didn't include fifty-pound attack
with open claws."

His Highness fixed a pair of crossed blue eyes on her
dropped something into her lap, and told her in no un
certain terms that he thought all humans—and Harrie
in particular—had no manners, no taste, and no clas
whatsoever.

In perfect Siamese cat back-street slang, Harriet tol
him he was gutter-bred, ignorant, and a judge of the bette
breeds of dahalfs on LostRoses. Then she scratched hi
ears to thank him for the gift. He butted her shoulder wit
his head and purred furiously, while she held his gift u
by the tail to admire it properly.

"What is it?" Joppich asked.

He was only interested, not appalled, which led her to wonder if maybe Bingo didn't bring him presents too.

"It's native and it's a pest. One of the earliest of the settlers dubbed it 'lizard-and-a-half'—because of the six legs—but only the 'dahalf' stuck."

"Pretty," he said. "And I'm impressed by your friend's hunting abilities—that's almost as long as he is."

His Highness turned his cross-eyed glare on Joppich and told him no one had asked his opinion and, furthermore, that no one ever *would* ask his opinion because he was clearly incapable of forming one without the assistance of a ghost-thinker.

Joppich suppressed a smile and said, in Crotonite, "May the Raiser of Winds be out of breath when She speaks to you and may you walk until your talons wear to stubs."

His Highness stepped—delicately now—across Harriet's lap to thump his head soundly against Joppich's shoulder.

"You pass," said Harriet, amused. "Though I'm not sure you could have managed that quite so well if you'd tried it in Nevelse."

"Probably not," said Joppich, equally amused. "He's got some mouth on him."

"Wyss'huk says he curses like a sapient," Harriet said, and watched with amusement as Joppich filed *that* for further information.

Joppich and the cat continued to regard each other with matched fiery blue glares—His Highness was trying to stare Joppich into submission, Joppich attempting to show the cat who was boss. The result of the contest had to wait for another time, however, for Bingo swooped close enough to distract them both.

His Highness sniffed the air carefully and followed every move of the bird. He had a good cursing relationship with most of the Crotonites, so a flyer of Bingo's size held no terrors for him. Still, the damned thing clearly didn't smell Crotonite, so His Highness kept a wary eye on it.

Harriet said to Joppich, "Bingo must be as confusing to him as he is to a Crotonite."

"Confusing?"

"The ability to fly is everything to a Crotonite," Harriet said. "You know that as well as I do. It's a sign of their natural superiority, to hear them tell it. Then along comes Bingo, who can fly with the best of them—but who's clearly *not* sapient. What does that say for wingspan as a measure of superiority?"

"Oh, ye gods," said Joppich. "I wasn't thinking." He put his head in his hands, narrowly risking the loss of his seat as the chair hit a bump. Grabbing on again, he said, "What'll I do? I can't give Bingo away—I'm the only one he takes to—but if he bothers the Crotonites, how can I find out anything more about them?"

His distress was genuine, so Harriet gave the question genuine thought. When she'd done so, she said, "I don't think it's that much of a worry. Besides, isn't learning their reaction to a nonsapient flyer learning something worth knowing?"

Bingo wasn't all that dumb, Harriet saw. Having earlier worked out just how close to Harriet he was allowed to come, Bingo came to light on the tine of the chair. From there, he crowed a challenge at His Highness.

Harriet gave a worried glance at Joppich, who said, "So far, so good. That's what he always said to Uncle Jamie's cats. . . ."

His Highness laid his ears back and arched forward for a good sniff and look. Then he inflated his lungs and, on full reverb, said, "OHWOOOOOOW!" It was a mystery to Harriet how a creature that small could make a sound that large.

"Heh-heh-heh," said Bingo, snaking his neck forward. Unlike Harriet, His Highness seemed to consider the cackle cajoling: he jumped from Harriet's knee and stepped forward to take a closer look.

To Harriet's surprise, Bingo sat perfectly still while His Highness checked him out. His Highness, who was nothing if not thorough, sniffed the bird from talon tip to wing tip. Bingo bent his head and graciously permitted His Highness to savor his beak, as well.

Inspection finished, His Highness gave Bingo a whap on the beak. Harriet jumped, expecting the worst. Joppich only laughed, as His Highness swaggered back to Harriet. Bingo hooted and flapped into the air once more.

"Same thing my uncle's cat always did," Joppich said. "I think you've made a friend, Your Highness."

His Highness told Joppich that this so-called friend reeked of carrion, couldn't catch his own food to save his life, and was the ugliest sucker he'd seen in years, unless you counted Joppich. Then he snagged Joppich's hand with a claw and demanded that Joppich rub his ears some more.

The chair pulled up in front of Sylvaine's Custom House and beeped arrival. His Highness leaped off, cast a few more insults over his shoulder, and headed back into the brush. Harriet shouted a "See you later" and rolled on into the bar.

This nice a day, Sylvaine's was practically deserted and Sylvaine himself was curled up in his reserved chair, reading. He smiled and waved a greeting, then he held up one finger to let her know he'd be with them the minute he finished this bit. Harriet nodded, and noted with amusement that the hardbook that held Sylvaine so engrossed was one of Joppich's.

She rolled to her favorite table, using the heavy-duty pinchers to pull up a human-suited chair for Joppich along the way. The fine pinchers made an independent grab of their own.

"Thanks for the ride," Joppich said, as he stood to stretch. "I'd better let Bingo know where I am."

"You needn't bother," Harriet said, grinning. "He's still vulching me." The fine-work pinchers had caught Bingo again. She whistled them to set him on the table. "What am I going to do with you, bird?"

Bingo glared.

Harriet had an inspiration. "What can he eat safely?"

"About anything your cat can, but he prefers his food somewhat . . . ripe."

"Let me try him on this, then." Harriet picked up the dahalf by its tail once more. "It may be a little nouveau for him but at least it's dead. What do you think?" This last, she addressed to Bingo. His snakelike head swayed, following the swing of the dahalf. Taking this for interest, Harriet flung him the carcass.

Bingo speared it on his beak in mid-air. Then, using the talons on one foot, he scraped it onto the table and inspected both it and Harriet warily.

"Won't His Highness be upset that you've given away his present?"

Harriet looked at Joppich in surprise. "His Highness doesn't give presents with strings attached. I'm shocked you'd think that of him." She grinned instead. "Seriously . . . he doesn't mind what I do with his gifts. That I accept them is the important thing."

"Oh." Joppich unfolded his hand and looked at the leaf gall he'd been holding all this time. He put it in his pocket.

Harriet suppressed a smile and gave the bird a long look. "You could always hang on to it until it *is* ripe," she suggested.

"Not in here," said Sylvaine, from behind her. "Bad enough everybody comes here to practice insults on each other. I won't have that thing aging its meat on one of my tables." He scowled at Bingo. "You," he said, "eat it or take it outside."

The firmness in Sylvaine's tone must have gotten through the bird's skull. Giving Harriet one last glower, it gobbled down the dahalf. Then it cocked its head at Joppich and flapped off the table and out the door.

"Good tone," Harriet said admiringly to Sylvaine.

He grinned and said, "It works on Crotonites. I wasn't sure it would work on that, but I figured it was worth a try, given the overweening wingspan." He took orders and vanished behind the bar for a long moment.

Leaning back in her chair, Harriet took the time to admire the mural that was slowly spreading the length of the north wall. Looking at it almost made up for the flight time she was missing: Fastas had brought the sky—and the feel of flying—into Sylvaine's Custom House.

The wall behind Joppich was alive with Crotonites and winds for which only the Crotonites had words. "Sylvaine made a deal with Fastas," Harriet said. "Free drinks for a mural." She turned Joppich to it with a point.

Joppich followed her point and his jaw dropped open. "Ye gods!" He leaned forward so abruptly, Harriet had the momentary feeling he was about to fall into Fastas's sky; his sky-colored eyes looked like a reflection from the painting.

"Nice, isn't it?" said Sylvaine, who had returned with the usual for Harriet and a steaming cup of chimmel for Joppich. "Really brightens the place up. I told Fast As if he wanted to make a turn to the right after he hit the corner and keep going, I'd keep bringing his drinks free." He smiled happily and added, "I think I'll let him do the whole place if he's willing."

"Nice?" Joppich seemed to have gotten stuck a few sentences back. He flapped his jaw twice before he found enough voice to say a second time, *"Nice?"*

"Hey, if you don't like it, you don't have to drink here." Frowning and looming, Sylvaine could be about twice as large as anybody on LostRoses.

"Down, Sylvaine," said Harriet. "He's not disparaging Fastas's work—he thinks *you* are."

Joppich let out a breath. *"Nice* doesn't begin to describe it. Try *magnificent!"* He looked at Harriet almost wildly. "It's . . ." Words failed him again, and he shook his head as if despairing of them altogether. He turned and looked again, then he swung his chair around beside Harriet's so that he could sit facing the painted wall.

After he'd let out another long breath, he took a sip of his chimmel—without taking his eyes off the mural. At last he said, in a more normal voice, "I think it's my turn to astonish you, Harriet. I know a museum curator who'd pay—oh, at a guess—about twenty times the worth of that leaf gall you gave me for that wall.''

Sylvaine laughed and said, "Tell him he can come look for the price of a drink." He was silent for a space, silent and appreciating of Fastas's work. Then he wandered back to his chair and reopened his book.

If Sylvaine didn't believe Joppich, Harriet did. "Well, we might as well appreciate it while it's still here."

"I'm serious," Joppich said. "And that's nothing compared to what he'd get from an art dealer. LostRoses is getting a masterpiece—for free drinks."

Ah! Harriet saw his problem. "Tell Fastas if that makes you happier, but I'll bet Fastas doesn't think he's being cheated. He's painting the mural for the sake of painting the mural. When the weather turns bad for flying, come in and watch him at it and you'll see for yourself."

She took a long contented look at the painting again, then added, "And I suspect he's also doing it to impress a certain gold-eyed Crotonite female who's been in the forefront of the kibitzers ever since he started work on the wall. It's really coming along . . ."

Joppich smiled. "The mural or the courting?"

"The mural, for sure. I won't know about the courting until I've had a few days to catch up on gossip." She shrugged and smiled, "Or maybe tonight, if Fastas comes in to do some more painting. I'm rooting for him—Prist is charming. Seems a nice match, given the limited experience I've had with Crotonite matches. She's a painter in her own right, maybe even a better one than Fastas."

His eyes widened again at that, and Harriet grinned. "Besides," she added, "I'd like to see a mating flight for myself. Wyss'huk found a spot just off the Singing Crag that *he* says has the perfect—wait, these two are tough to wrap my tongue around—the perfect *pssstrit* and *tripssst*." If there was a literal translation of either into Nevelse, Harriet hadn't gotten that far yet. "You'll want Wyss'huk to pronounce them for you. When he says them, there's a poetry about the combination that's almost as lively as the winds themselves.''

She paused to take a sip from her glass. ''Once he found that the winds were always good or perfect in that spot—something to do with the shape of the crag, maybe the same thing that makes it sing—he abandoned the Pssstwhitian Embassy building we made him and extruded the official one at the foot of the crag. The Stiss followed suit—though I'm not sure that had as much to do with the perfect mating winds as it did with the rivalry between Pssstwhit and Stiss.''

''How strong do you gauge the rivalry?''

''As I said, strikes me as mostly bluff and fluff. I haven't seen anything hotter than that one-up contest Wyss'huk and Katuk had when they were cursing you out in turn. I've *never* seen a Crotonite strike another Crotonite, though Katuk tells me he has.''

''It does happen. It's rare, but I've seen it.''

Harriet cocked her head, inviting further details.

''Like tomcats,'' he offered. ''They'd worked themselves up into full blow, and one of them said the unforgivable thing. The result was nasty; those talons can do some damage.'' His face darkened. ''I imagine it was months before either of them flew again.''

Harriet frowned. Hard to picture, even though she'd seen any number of Crotonites use their talons to shred dinner. That was polite Crotonite table manners, but she was quite capable of extrapolating from dead meat to live.

Hard to picture because . . . ''Joppich? Once a month or so, we get the obligatory bar fight in here—between humans, I mean. Sylvaine drops the antagonists before it gets nasty, but . . .''

Joppich finished for her: ''But the Crotonites are long gone by then.''

''Yes,'' said Sylvaine. ''Eavesdropper,'' said Harriet, and Sylvaine grinned and told her, ''I only eavesdrop the interesting conversations. Be boring and I'll ignore you completely.''

To Joppich, he said, "It upsets the hell out of the Crotonites when the Erthumoi start bashing each other. I had to shorten my intervention time. I used to let them each get in one punch before I stopped them. Now I try to get it before the first punch. Can't have good customers run out of the place just because some Erthuma doesn't like some other Erthuma's face."

He pulled up a chair, settled his huge frame into it, and said, "There's nobody here but us Erthumoi . . . What's the unforgivable word? I need to know it so I can move fast if I hear it."

"That's not the kind of fight you'd want to intervene in," Joppich began.

"Rules," said Sylvaine. "Nobody gets hurt in a fight in my bar." He gave the problem visible thought, then smiled and said, "And I suspect I can stop 'em dead if I grab 'em by the breathing masks."

"Might stop you dead too," Harriet said. "That stuff's poisonous to you and me."

"Pinch, not pull." Sylvaine closed a hand as if tightening it around the tube to a breathing mask. "Have you ever known me to be careless, Harriet?"

Harriet grinned. "No, I haven't." To Joppich, she said, "If you don't tell us, I'll ask Wyss'huk."

"You wouldn't!" Joppich stared at her in disbelief.

Grin broadened all across Sylvaine's face. "She would," he said. "And Wooshuck would tell her, too, I bet. Those Only Birds are as thick as thieves."

Still staring, Joppich slumped ever so slightly in his chair. Harriet knew resignation when she saw it, but Joppich gave a careful scan of the room before he straightened again. No Crotonites had come in while he'd been speaking. "All right," he said and leaned in close. "The unforgivable word was *hashas'sit*. And they really punch the *'sit*."

Sylvaine took a deep breath, stared at Joppich, and opened his mouth.

Knowing exactly what Sylvaine was about to say, she

gave the barkeep a quick negative jerk of her head—she genuinely regretted she wasn't able to kick him under the table—and said, "That's a new one on me. What's it mean, do you know? Are we talking something on the order of 'rapist' or 'murderer,' or are we talking something that would only make sense to another Crotonite?"

Sylvaine shut his mouth abruptly and leaned forward—this time to listen only. Harriet let out the breath she hadn't known she'd been holding.

"More on the order of nonsense to a non-Crotonite," Joppich said. "From what I've been able to gather, it's a derogatory reference to some religious sect." He held up his hands to fend off questions. "I honestly don't know enough about Crotonite religion to tell you much more than that. That's not a question I get a lot of answers on. And I'm not sure it's safe to ask about it, either, Harriet," he added firmly. "So don't."

Harriet gave him her best imitation of His Highness's *Who me, boss? Would I ever do a thing like that?* It didn't fool Sylvaine for a minute, but Joppich bought it.

Luckily, she didn't have to preen her invisible whiskers for long. A flutter of wings brought Bingo back inside. This time he landed neatly on the table—just beyond pincher-reach—to glare not at Harriet but at Joppich.

"I thought, since you'd eaten the dahalf," Joppich began. Logic cut no ice with the bird, to judge from his expression, and Joppich knew it too, to judge from his. Resigned, he rose to his feet. "Feeding time for the bird," he said. "Nice to have met you, Sylvaine, Harriet." He hesitated. "Any chance I might find you here later?"

Sylvaine swung a hand to take in the room. "Best place in town," he said.

"*Only* place in town," Harriet added, with a grin.

"I'll be here, then," said Joppich. "Come on, Bingo."

Bingo gave Harriet a long look to say he hadn't forgotten her, then took off after Joppich.

The minute the two vanished through the door, Sylvaine leaned forward and opened his mouth. Harriet held up a hand and made him wait until Joppich's footsteps had passed beyond her earshot.

When Harriet lowered her hand, Sylvaine said, "Harriet, *Prist* is a *hashash*—whatever the damned word was. I may not be able to pronounce it but I know what I heard him say and I know what Prist said . . ."

"I know. I know. So's Fastas. So are half the Crotonites from Stiss—maybe *all* of them, for all I know." Thinking hard, Harriet drummed her fingers on the chair's armrest.

Sylvaine let her think for a moment, but only a moment. "Prist said never to tell another Crotonite because Erthumoi weren't supposed to know about such things," he said. "So what was the problem with telling that guy? It's not like *he's* Crotonite."

"That guy is Joppich, the author of the book you're reading. He knows about as much as there is to know about Crotonites, unless you are one . . ."

That still didn't explain her reaction, Harriet realized. She reached for her drink and took a healthy swig. Sylvaine didn't believe in interrupting a person who was drinking, and it gave her time to put her thoughts in order. What *was* wrong with telling him?

"So here's this expert on Crotonites who says that calling somebody a *hashas'sit* is a criminal offense—and here's Prist, who says she is a *hashas'sit* and acts like she's proud of it."

"So the expert's wrong," said Sylvaine. "Oh! You didn't want me to embarrass him in public." He cast a glance at the hardbook lying beside his reserved chair. "I wonder if he's wrong about the rest of it, too."

Harriet shook her head. "He's not. What he knows matches with what I know, and I think we've got a problem."

Tipping back his chair, Sylvaine considered her carefully. "Problem? I don't see it, Harriet. They can't *both* be right—Joppich and Prist. Joppich must have heard the word wrong."

"His Crotonite is too good for that. And they *can* both be right. That's what's setting my teeth on edge."

"Explain it in simple terms," said Sylvaine.

"Okay," said Harriet. "Suppose somebody calls you a barkeep . . . what's your reaction?"

"I am a barkeep." Sylvaine shrugged. "Why should that bother me?"

"It wouldn't," Harriet said. "But suppose somebody calls you a barkeep and you know that, to *him,* the word means 'not fit to live'? *Now* what's your reaction?"

"Oh," said Sylvaine, in a very quiet voice. "Oh, boy . . ." He rose to his feet. "Shall I call Wanwadee Li and tell him he's got to be *El Presidente*?"

"No need to make it official. Let's just tell Wanwadee Li what we know so far; he likes to be prepared. This is only a hairy feeling as yet. I'd better do some poking around before we get everybody else excited over something that might be nothing."

Raising an eyebrow, Sylvaine said, "If the word's unforgivable, Wushshock might not take so kindly to . . . Be careful where you poke your nose."

She held up both hands. "I promise to be extremely careful. Full ritual and all. Who's in charge of nosy and possibly dangerous questions?"

Thoughtful furrows crossed his brow. "Let's see—it'd be Albie for secrets of the universe and Hans Stefan for good gossip . . . but neither one of them quite covers this sort of thing. Hang on"—he strode to the bar, ducked briefly behind it, and came up with a well-thumbed hard-book—"lemme check the catalog."

He flipped through to the back and read snatches of the index aloud, " 'Questions . . . secrets of the universe,' yeah, yeah, we know about Albert Einstein . . ." He muttered for a moment then said, " 'Personal, sexual'—would that be it, do you think?"

"Maybe. Joppich seems to think it's religious, though. How the hell do I know until I ask? And then it'll be too late."

"Aha!" said Sylvaine, triumphant. Grinning, he brought the book and held it out to her, his finger marking the spot.

" 'Questions—nosy, see The Quid Nunc,' " Harriet read. "The Quid Nunc? I've never even heard of that one."

"Most people haven't," Sylvaine said—and then he chuckled. "But she's the one you want. Look her up, and see if I'm not right."

Turning to the page indicated, Harriet saw the reason for Sylvaine's chuckle. "She was a cat! I thought they were all people—and she was a cat!" She read carefully through the text. No doubt about it. "Yes," said Harriet, delighted. "A cat could get away with it. She's perfect, Sylvaine. Thanks."

"Anytime, Harriet. Part of the job, after all. I hope it helps."

He was getting that furrow of worry again, so Harriet said, "It will, I'm sure of it. But in the meantime—"

"In the meantime, I'll keep my mouth shut." The twinkle returned to his dark eyes, and he added with a smile, "Except to drink my beer, of course."

Harriet smiled back. "You might also open it long enough to fill me in on the gossip . . ." That was an invitation she'd never known Sylvaine to resist—and this was no exception. The courtship, it seemed, was coming along as nicely as the mural.

From Sylvaine's map, the Quid Nunc's shrine was somewhere along Niles-Canfield Road but closer to the Canfield's end of it . . . which put it very near the new Pssstwhitian Embassy. Harriet took that as a good omen as well.

The day was a lousy one for flying—for hang gliding, at any rate. She could see a handful of winged Crotonites circling the embassy on a quick morning stretch of the wings.

Sylvaine had assured her the route was well enough kept

that she'd have no need of any of the special adaptations to her chair, but she had fixed on the brolly. No point getting soaked to the skin. In her lap, His Highness snoozed mightily. For no apparent reason, he'd decided to accompany her today—and she took that as an even better omen.

Choosing a gift for the Quid Nunc had been something of a puzzle but, after rereading her attributes, Harriet had brought the string of lostroses that His Highness sometimes deigned to play with. He preferred a length of ribbon, mostly for the pleasure of shredding, but she thought perhaps the Quid Nunc would prefer something a little more lasting.

The chair rolled to a stop-and-beep in front of the Pssstwhitian Embassy. Wyss'huk waved to her from the cliff side, gave one last glance upward at his winged staff, and came to meet her. He looked naked and vulnerable compared to the rest of the Crotonites. On the ground, with their huge batlike wings furled, they always looked to her as if they were cloaked. Wyss'huk had no cloak.

Harriet extruded his perch from the side of the chair. He shook rain from his fur and climbed on. His Highness lifted his head sleepily and gave him the ritual greeting, something about the ugly warp of his beak and the putridity of his breath. Wyss'huk ticked and answered in kind, then delicately scratched the cat's head with his talons. Permitting the liberty, His Highness even purred a moment or two before going back to sleep.

Having discovered that Wyss'huk had to curse less in Nevelse than in his own language and all too aware that she couldn't live up to his standards at this hour of the morning, Harriet decided to opt out of the game temporarily. She gave him a simple, "Rotten morning to you, Wyss'huk," in Nevelse.

"Hi, slugger," said Wyss'huk, also in Nevelse.

" 'Slugger'?" said Harriet, putting the accent on the last syllable.

Wyss'huk ticked like a time bomb. "I am in the process

of convincing the entire staff—brain-burned idiots that they are—that 'slug*er*' is a worse insult than 'slug.' "

Harriet laughed out loud. Disturbed, His Highness opened a blue eye and glared. "Sorry," she said to him soothingly. "Sorry, Wyss'huk, but it *is* funny."

"I know. What's funnier is that no Erthuma can tell them different: it's my word against yours." That set him to ticking all over again, as Harriet set the chair into motion.

After a while, he said, "It's not a rotten morning to a Crotonite, you know." He switched briefly to his own language and gave her such an appealing description of the winds that she wanted to hightail it for home, grab her wings, and dive off the nearest cliff.

Instead she sighed. "So we'll have to make our own fun today." His orange eyes widened sharply—and Harriet knew she'd startled him somehow. "Wyss'huk? If I've said something wrong, please tell me what. I don't *mean* to offend. You know that."

"You surprised me. I had understood you to mean we would see something religious—having to do with your gods. I am not accustomed to hearing the word 'fun' in this context. Have I misunderstood?"

"These aren't exactly gods. Unless you count the Raiser of Winds—who's a bit of a newcomer—we don't really have any resident gods. These are more like spirits. We don't exactly worship them; we invoke them when we need a little specialized assistance. And there's even one whose specialty *is* fun—you leave him a gift if you're having a party and want to make sure everybody has a good time."

Wyss'huk was silent as he worked that over. "You're different," he said at last. "You are not Crotonite. You do not think like a Crotonite; you think *differently*. You approach your spirits *differently*."

He was not really talking to her; he was reminding himself. Harriet recognized the procedure because she had to run through it often enough when she was with him, and for all the same reasons.

Then he said, "What sort of spirit are we visiting today? Should I be solemn or merry? Which is appropriate to this Quid Nunc of yours?"

"This one's a bit unusual even for LostRoses. This one was a cat—so whatever's appropriate for His Highness is equally appropriate for the Quid Nunc."

"Harriet, you're making this up."

She shook her head. "Ask Sylvaine to show you the book next time you're in the Custom House—or get Wanwadee Li to print you one of your own." When he wasn't being *El Presidente* of LostRoses, Wanwadee Li was the world's only publisher. If Harriet knew Wyss'huk, he'd stop by for a copy the next time he was in town.

"Let me understand properly. This was a cat, a real one, that actually lived . . ."

"As real as His Highness," Harriet said. "And she's the right spirit for us, too—she's helpful with nosy questions." Wyss'huk gave a double tick—which Harriet added to her list of good omens—then she went on, "The story is that she was even nosier, if you can believe that, than His Highness. She was *so* nosy that she tagged along with a group of kids exploring a cave they'd found, just to see what they were up to. The kids were very young and very inexperienced, and they got themselves very thoroughly lost. They'd never have made their way safely home if the Quid Nunc hadn't been there to lead them back to sunlight."

More ticking. "Perhaps she should be the spirit that helps you find your way through a maze, then."

Harriet chuckled. "Wyss'huk, can you think of a worse or more convoluted maze than the two of us trying to find each other in all this messy universe?"

His ticking was steady and loud now, so Harriet smiled and turned her attention to the road. "Start looking along the right shoulder now. The shrine should be somewhere near here. Look for an eye carved in a stone stela."

"I know where that is," said Wyss'huk. "About a tenth of a mile from here. First you'll come to a row of very old scroll trees, then a leaf-rustle"—that was a wind that came up in certain wooded conditions; Harriet would recognize it when she felt it—"then one more very old scroll tree, and the stela is about three wingspans beyond that. I've been taking the slug's tour," he added, by way of explanation.

His ground map was almost as good as his sky map, though on the ground his idea of a wingspan was somewhat exaggerated—Harriet almost passed the stela. A quick whistle brought them to a halt in time, and Harriet turned the chair onto the narrow winding path down to the Quid Nunc's shrine.

The shrine was small but well kept. Sylvaine's doing, perhaps. In the center of a small clearing in the wood stood the life-sized statue of a cat. It was made of bronze, she suspected; the patina was that strange and wonderful shade of green she'd once seen on a copper roof.

The Quid Nunc sat on her regal haunches, surveying her domain and her treasures—a ball, a tuft of dried catnip, a length of string—with as haughty and possessive an air as ever Harriet had seen His Highness display. Come to think of it, His Highness was very probably a distant descendant of hers. The only difference between them was the gold hoop the Quid Nunc bore in her left ear.

Harriet gave the snoozing cat a thorough rubbing about the head and ears and said, "Up, cat. Say hello to a relative of yours . . . and be respectful—she's reputed to have a few powers you haven't." To Wyss'huk, she added, "At least, he's never displayed them around me."

"He doesn't like you to know he can manipulate gravity at will, either," said Wyss'huk.

Grinning, Harriet shook her head admiringly. "You've caught on quick to cats."

"I had to, for self-preservation. His Highness classifies me as a bird and therefore potentially as a meal."

Harriet shook her head. "Not anymore. He thinks you curse like a sapient."

Two ticks, like a chuckle, from Wyss'huk. Then he turned solemn and cast an orange eye at the ground. "Any special form here?"

His Highness, having finished a leisurely stretch, sprang from Harriet's lap and sauntered over to sniff the statue of the Quid Nunc.

"I guess not," said Wyss'huk, answering his own question.

His olfactory inspection of the statue finished, His Highness turned his back on the figure disdainfully, licked a few hairs into more perfect order, and began to investigate the Quid Nunc's gifts.

"Your Highness!" Wyss'huk's voice took on a tone of sharp warning. "Those are gifts to a spirit—"

His Highness flicked back an ear, copped the tuft of catnip, and disappeared with it into the brush at the edge of the grove.

"Harriet!" Wyss'huk said, in alarm. "He took—"

"If that were a human, I'd worry, Wyss'huk. But it's a cat—and what happens between cats is no business of a human's or of a Crotonite's. They'll work it out to their satisfaction, not to ours." She whistled herself to the ground beside him, within hand's reach of the statue.

As she'd never appealed to the Quid Nunc before, she opted for good manners and held out her knuckles for sniffing. "Hello, Quid Nunc," she said. "I'm Harriet Kingsolver and the fellow with me is Wyss'huk. I don't know if you've met any of his kind before but the cat that just copped your catnip will vouch for him—and for me, too, I think."

Wyss'huk held out his own stubby knuckles to be sniffed. With a sidelong glance at Harriet, he addressed the statue and told it a few of the things he habitually told His Highness. ". . . And do it *twice*," he added, apparently feeling the need to give a spirit a little something extra.

Harriet grinned. "I brought you a present, cat." From her pocket, she took the string of lostroses and dangled it enticingly in front of the image's forepaws.

There was no reaction or acknowledgment from the image; of course, Harriet had gotten the same response (or lack of response) from His Highness in similar circumstances. She'd hardly expected the statue to pounce, after all. Come to think of it, she didn't know what she expected, if anything.

She wriggled the string of deep red gems past the verdigris paws one last time, then coiled it into a rich glowing heap beside the image. "Okay. I'll leave it for later." To Wyss'huk, she added, "Most cats do it on their time, not yours—but you already know that."

She whistled again and the cargo pinchers gently lifted her back into her seat and settled her comfortably.

Wyss'huk made no move to regain his perch. He was still considering the statue. Harriet couldn't read his expression. At last, he said, "Perhaps I should make her a gift, too?"

"I don't think it's necessary," Harriet said. "The problem is mine; I'm the one asking for the helping paw." Like the paw His Highness stuck down a dahalf's hole, snatching for the meat by feel alone.

"What happens now?" Wyss'huk asked, his eyes still on those of the statue.

"Aside from waiting for His Highness to turn up? That's it—we've done the ritual, now we head home."

At long last, Wyss'huk turned to face her, his orange eyes vivid in the long green shadows of the wood. He said, very carefully, "Did you get the help you need?"

Harriet shrugged. "I don't know yet." She gazed at him thoughtfully. "You're asking do I really believe she will help, aren't you?" She leaned back and cocked her head. "I don't know if that's done me the least damned bit of good," she said, "but I simply can't pass up *any* shot at help on this one. Does that answer your question?"

"Yes." He fixed her with a steady eye and said, "What's your nosy question, Ha'reet? I'll answer it if I can."

Harriet chuckled. "Erthumoi are getting pretty transparent to you, aren't they?"

"Not all Erthumoi," he said, "but you and I have flown together." He scanned the edges of the grove. There was still no sign of His Highness. "Being at His Highness's beck and call, we've plenty of time."

"It's a *tough* nosy question," Harriet said. "I'm told it's been cause for actual bloodshed between Crotonites. . . ."

He drew back a little but his expression was one Harriet had learned to interpret as thoughtful. The stubs on his shoulders, the still-healing remnants of his wings, twitched minutely—as if he did his best thinking on the wing. Finally, he said, "You instructed your chair to defend you against that . . . that mindless flyer. Will you instruct it to defend you against me, please?"

Harriet jerked in outrage. "I don't *want* to defend against you, Wyss'huk!"

"Not forever, Ha'reet. Only while you ask your question. Please. If the question is as nosy as you believe, I might lose my temper with you. . . ."

"I don't want you to lose your temper with me. That's why I wanted the Quid Nunc's help."

"Ha'reet, *pippest*," he said, "I promise you, on the Raiser of Winds, that even if I lose my temper with you over this question I will find it again in time for the two of us to fly together in the next high heart-wind."

And he was not going to listen to another word until she did as he asked. The set of his body gave Harriet the distinct impression that he'd put his fingers in his ears—wherever they were. Sighing resignation, she keyed the necessary instructions into the chair's memory, labeling the macro n for "nosy" and absently writing it to file. If he asked her to do it once, he might again.

"Done," she said. "Ready or not, Wyss'huk, here it comes." She took a deep breath, saw him do the same, and began, "I've been told by someone I credit with intelligence that calling a Crotonite one certain name will lead to bloodshed. The problem is, the word does not sound the least bit like a curse to me."

The little Crotonite took two steps backward—careful not to disturb the Quid Nunc's treasures—and eyed her chair's pinchers warily. Another self-reminder, thought Harriet. How do I get myself into these situations?

He said, "What is the word you need to know about?"

"*Hashas'sit,*" said Harriet . . . and she held her breath.

Wyss'huk crooked his talons and took a single step toward her.

His Highness shot from the underbrush at the edge of the grove and charged directly into the Crotonite's path.

Wyss'huk jumped back to avoid having his toes run over—with cleats—and, having jumped back, stayed where he was, making a visible effort to settle his ruffled nonfeathers.

Harriet let out her breath. "Good timing," she said to His Highness. His Highness, smug, circled the Crotonite's ankles once and then laid a dead fricket at his taloned feet. Harriet gaped at the two of them. "He brought you a gift, Wyss'huk! You see? I told you he thinks you curse like a sapient." She shook her head, as much to clear it as to express her disbelief. "Or have you been holding out on me? Has he done that before?"

"No," said Wyss'huk, staring down in equal astonishment. He spattered and sputtered a few words of the purest, most vile slander at the cat, who responded with a considerably worse assessment of batlike things that were too oversized to be considered edible and then permitted his ears to be scratched.

When he'd permitted his ears to be scratched to his satisfaction, he swaggered over to the chair, settled again in Harriet's lap, and closed his eyes to sleep.

When Harriet looked back at Wyss'huk, the Crotonite was holding the fricket in his two-fingered, two-clawed grip, as if it might just be a palatable snack. Still nosy—

and unwilling to press the previous question—Harriet said, "Can you eat frickets? Without poisoning yourself, I mean."

"I doubt it," he said. "You told me once that His Highness doesn't give his gifts with strings attached . . ."

"Well, I wouldn't toss it away in front of him; he hates to see a good fricket wasted."

"I won't waste it." He turned and laid the fricket before the statue of the cat. In his own language, he said something that Harriet couldn't quite catch, then he added, "I've got some nosy questions of my own, but I'll save those for another time and another gift. This fricket is thanks for helping Harriet with hers."

Then he walked slowly back to stand beside Harriet, just beyond the reach of the pinchers. "I want your promise," he said in Nevelse, "that you won't use that word in front of any other Crotonite."

"I can't promise that, Wyss'huk. I don't know enough to make promises."

His wing stubs twitched furiously, but his orange eyes glared directly at her. "It's not a curse word, though many of my people would take it for one."

She'd assessed the situation correctly, then. "If I promise you I'll never use the word as a curse, will that satisfy you?"

"Only partially. So many of my people take it for a curse that you could hurt—badly—anyone you applied the word to . . ." He made an odd ducking motion with his head; if he'd still had his wings, he'd have been hiding his head beneath them.

When he raised his head again, he said, "This is very hard to explain, but I'll try. The word refers to a Crotonite who has accepted the teachings of a new . . . god? I'm not sure, here, Ha'reet. This may be a spirit, like the Quid Nunc—I believe he was originally a real person. He taught, or teaches, that life began on the ground and only later took to the air."

Harriet knit her brow. "More likely, life began in the waters of your homeworld, the way it did on Old Earth."

"I'm not speaking of evolution," he said, orange eyes flaring. "I'm speaking of religion, which is a much touchier subject." He paused, wing stubs twitching. Harriet could see that his breath came fast and furious, fogging the transparent breathing mask from within. He went on, "A . . . *hashas'sit* believes that life sprang from the ground and believes accordingly that a winged Crotonite is somehow related to slugs—including *you*."

"And most Crotonites would prefer not to hear that," Harriet said.

He ducked his head once more. "Worse," he said, without raising his head. "Most Crotonites would kill the messenger who brought that message."

"Oh," said Harriet. "Oh, my sweet wings!"

Sensing her distress, His Highness opened his eyes and chirruped an inquiry. When Harriet didn't answer, he rose and thumped her soundly in the chest with the flat of his head until she had to rub his ears out of sheer self-defense. When he was satisfied he'd calmed her, he turned a hot blue glare on Wyss'huk and told him where to put what and how quickly. Not even the most limber of Crotonites could have managed that one.

Wyss'huk said, "That's why you're not to say the word to a Crotonite, Ha'reet. If you were believed, the Crotonite would be put to death."

And Prist and Fastas had entrusted their secret to a handful of Erthumoi . . . ! Harriet gulped and said again, "Oh, my sweet wings!" She stared wildly at Wyss'huk. "You—would *you*—" She faltered, unwilling to imagine her favorite flying partner party to a lynching or whatever a winged people did to each other in such hate.

Orange eyes locked on hers. "You know about the *hashas'sitta* in the Stiss Embassy," Wyss'huk said. It was not a question and Harriet made no answer. Lapsing into Crotonite, Wyss'huk began an elaborate description of the caliber of self-destructive fool that staffed the Stiss Embassy. His voice was low, as if he feared being overheard by anyone.

By anyone but Harriet, that was—he stepped closer to make sure she got an earful. So close, in fact, that the pinchers reached out to seize him. Caught and held, Wyss'huk merely went motionless and continued to curse the Crotonite Stiss for the fools they were. His Highness watched with intense interest.

Startled, Harriet whistled to the chair to let go, wishing she could add an emphatic "dammit!" to the order. The pinchers released him as gently as they'd seized him, but Harriet said, "Sorry."

"I would not hurt a single one of them, Ha'reet. By the Raiser of Winds, you must believe me. I've fought the rulings against them to the full stretch of my wings." Wyss'huk's use of the Pssstwhitian expression was ironic but the emotion behind it was genuine. "Why do you think *I* was chosen ambassador to Erthumoi on a little backwater planet—your own description—like LostRoses?"

That was an easy one, now that Harriet knew the context. "You made yourself politically unpopular—so they ditched you." *And cut off your wings for emphasis.* "Punishment duty," she said aloud.

"My punishment is that I may be forced to watch helplessly as the *hashas'sit* Stiss . . ." He shut his beak with an almost audible click. "*I* would tell no one, Ha'reet, but there are members of my staff who may recognize that style of artwork. It is unmistakable, if you have any eye for painting whatsoever." He glanced over his shoulder at the statue of the Quid Nunc. "If you have a spirit that oversees the keeping of secrets, we would do well to pay that one a visit. As carefully as I chose my staff, I cannot be sure I haven't a . . ."

Wing stubs once again a-twitch, he glanced up and said, "Do you know a creature that substitutes its eggs for those of another?"

"Cuckoo," she said.

" 'Kukoo,' " he repeated. "I may have a kukoo in my nest. I won't know until my own children are dead."

"Or the *hashas'sitta* are," Harriet said.

"Yes, I'm afraid so."

Harriet took a deep breath. "Hop on, Wyss'huk. I think we'd better pay a visit to *El Presidente* and work out a contingency plan."

Dejectedly, he resumed his perch. "I appreciate the thought but I don't see how—forgive me—a bunch of slugs could help the poor *hashas'sitta*."

"No offense taken, slug," she said. "Thanks, Quid Nunc," she called to the little statue as she keyed the chair for home. To Wyss'huk, she said, "We'll just have to wing it . . . and that's worked for us before."

The storm that raged outside Sylvaine's Custom House the following day might have been a bad omen for "winging it," but Harriet chose to see it as the perfect opportunity to speak with one of the *hashas'sitta*. Rotten flying weather would bring most of the Stissian staff in to watch Fastas's mural work its way across the wall. While she waited for them to arrive, she shared a cup with Joppich— and gave him a hang glider's eye-view of the winds that swept the painting.

"Yes," said Joppich. "I'll have to learn to fly to appreciate . . . the Crotonites. Thanks, I owe you."

The other Erthuma experts were well out of earshot, so Harriet said, "Then tell me about your colleagues. Anybody here particularly good in a crisis?"

"I got here five days ago, special delivery. I don't know them all yet." He gave a quick glance around the room, then lowered his voice anyway. "I've run into Gomperson and Ellis before, though. If you're having a crisis, leave them out of it—they're government flacks." His dark brow knit. "Helene Justin knows her stuff—and she seems the sort to keep her head in a crisis."

That matched Sylvaine's assessment to a T. Harriet nodded. "Thanks," she said. "We're even."

Joppich gave her a quiet thoughtful look. "*Are* we having a crisis?"

She appreciated that *we*. "Not yet," she told him, "but any minute now, maybe." She watched him file that, too.

Then she said, "Excuse me, will you? I see Prist and I need a word with her." The word would have to be in private, given the Erthuma experts and the handful of Pssstwhitians who'd trickled in. Leaving a still-thoughtful Joppich behind, Harriet whistled her chair over to the gold-eyed Crotonite and said, "Hi, Prist, you motheaten excuse for a winter cloak . . . I need a word with you."

"Crawl back under your stone, slug," said Prist amiably. "Lest the sun crisp your skin to a fragrant black."

That sounded enough like a yes that Harriet turned her chair and started for Sylvaine's back room. "This way," she said, and Prist followed, carrying her pipette mug of glavsa with her. A nod from Harriet brought Sylvaine along as well; he ushered them both into the back room and sealed it for privacy.

El Presidente, wearing what Harriet thought of as his war-paint, was waiting for them. The frown lines of his office were drawn with elaborate care, this time in vivid crimson. However shocking and bloodthirsty he might look to someone unfamiliar with LostRoses customs, Harriet found his masklike face reassuring. She'd explained the extent of the possible problem to him and he'd taken her at her word. Wanwadee Li meant business.

Prist stopped short as she caught sight of him and unfurled her wings ever so slightly. They made a rustling sound, like taffeta. "Wanwadee Li?" she said, in passable Nevelse. "You look most ugly than usual. I didn't think that was possible for a slug." To Harriet, in Crotonite, she added, "Have I said that right?"

"Close," Harriet said. " 'Uglier,' not 'most ugly.' He looks that way because he's acting in his official capacity today, as *El Presidente* of LostRoses."

She cocked her head to one side. "Perhaps you want

to talk to Katuk,'' she said to Wanwadee. ''Katuk is official, too.''

Wanwadee Li shook his head. ''We need some information, Prist, and we think it's safer to talk to you. You are *hashash* . . .'' He held out his hands in appeal. ''Harriet, I'll butcher it.''

''You said you were *hashas'sit*, Prist.'' Harriet said the word so softly that only she could hear it. ''I'm given to understand that the Crotonites would kill you if they knew that.''

''Many would. Some would not.'' She ducked her head briefly under wing. When she raised it again, she raised it high, looked Wanwadee Li straight in the eye, and said, ''And now that you have found out what the word means to a Crotonite, you wish us to leave LostRoses.''

Half rising in shock, Wanwadee Li said, ''No! No, Prist! That's not it at all!''

''No, Prist,'' said Harriet—in Crotonite and with all the proper improper flourishes so there could be no misunderstanding. ''We're here to work out a contingency plan in case *your* people find out; we don't want you or Fastas hurt.''

''What happens if Katuk—or anybody else in the embassy, for that matter—finds out?'' Sylvaine put in. ''Where would you go? What would happen to you? That's what we need to work out—and that's why we need your advice.''

''They know,'' said Prist.

''They know what you are,'' Wanwadee Li said, for clarity's sake.

''What we all are,'' said Prist.

That surprised the hell out of Harriet. ''Even Katuk?''

''Katuk arranged it. He was giving us a haven—or so he thought.''

''Then we'll have to arrange just that: a haven,'' said Wanwadee Li. ''Would you call Katuk and invite him to join us? And then I would appreciate it very much if you would record a small piece of tape for Sylvaine. I want you to explain who and what the *hassas* are, so *I* can explain it to the rest of the LostRosians if need be.''

"I will do my best," she said. "May I show some of my paintings? They often explain better than my words—especially my words in Nevelse.''

"Whatever makes you happy," said Sylvaine. "Come on, let's get to it.''

" 'Whatever makes me happy,' '' Prist repeated slowly. Then to Harriet, she said, "I like Nevelse. I don't think I could say that in Pssstwhitian.''

By the time Wyss'huk had arrived, Sylvaine's was doing a rousing business. Lilac was behind the bar serving drinks as fast as she could pour them. Harriet saw a couple of faces she'd never seen in town, some of the true outlyers come in to take a gander at Fastas's mural. They liked it, that much was obvious. Old Hairy and Jebediah had both asked Harriet to translate their praises to the Crotonite.

Harriet collared Joppich—with the fine-work pinchers—and said, "Help translate. I'm running out of *nice* things to say in Crotonite.''

When Joppich grinned and rose to her assistance, Bingo hopped to the floor and stalked her on foot. The damned thing had gauged the range of her pinchers to a nicety now and stayed a quarter of an inch beyond; from there, his hungry glare was all too palpable on the back of Harriet's neck.

The storm had tapered off, but Katuk arrived dripping water. Old Hairy tossed the Crotonite a towel from the rack beside the door—and Harriet tossed him a quick explanation of the offer. When Katuk had wiped the worst of the mess from his fur, he handed the towel back and thanked Old Hairy—politely.

Beside Harriet, Joppich gaped at the exchange. Harriet suppressed a smile and said, "Old Hairy doesn't know he's not supposed to like Crotonites.''

"*Katuk* was polite.''

"He was speaking Nevelse. It's easier to be polite in Nevelse." Harriet turned to greet Katuk with a few polite Crotonite insults, then she added, "Thanks for coming, Katuk."

"I haven't come to make plans with you. I've come to tell the rest of my staff we're being recalled." The little alien made a keening noise in the back of his throat. "You can do nothing. Our replacements are already on the way, and the same ship will take—" He faltered.

"They know," said Harriet. "How long before the ship gets here?"

Katuk spat a phrase. Harriet, whose time-telling in Crotonite was too shaky to take the chance, turned sharply to Joppich. "That's about twelve days," he supplied.

"That's a long time, Katuk," Harriet said. "Let's make the most of it." She raised her voice over the chatter and sizzle of conversation. "Sylvaine!" she shouted. "Get out here—you're wanted in your official capacity."

Beside her, Joppich had been watching too closely. "What's going on?"

"*Now* we're having a crisis," Harriet told him. To Sylvaine, who'd appeared with the fearsome Wanwadee Li at his side, she called, "There's a ship coming in from Stiss. Remind them they'll have to clear customs before they do anything else." To Katuk, she added, "If we need extra time, Sylvaine can make them take apart everything they've brought to check for contraband."

Sylvaine smiled only with his mouth. "And as many times as need be," he said.

Silence spread slowly but inexorably throughout the bar. Perhaps it was Katuk's keening that had done it, perhaps Wanwadee Li's warpaint. Whatever the cause, conversation trickled off and all eyes began to turn in the direction of *El Presidente*.

"So much for contingency plans," he said. The scarlet lines across his brow were merged by his frown to resemble an open wound. To Katuk, he said, "Have they come to take you away?"

"Yes," said Katuk.

"Then we'd better think in terms of a fait accompli."

Fastas, still holding his brushes, crossed the room to stand beside Katuk. Harriet thought perhaps he was looking for Prist, but it was Sylvaine he fixed his orange eyes on. "I wish I could paint the entire bar, as you suggested—but now . . . if you can give me the time to finish the wall I've begun, I'd be most grateful." He cast a quick glance at Katuk. "I know what they'll do to the paintings in the embassy, but—they wouldn't dare to destroy a painting on Erthuma property, would they?"

Well, that's done it, thought Harriet. Now *everybody* knows there's a crisis. Pandemonium reigned—for all of three minutes. Then it was cut short by the reverberating blast of Sylvaine's shotgun.

Lilac had fired the first round into the ceiling. She handed the gun to Sylvaine, who fixed it on the crowd. "Shut up," he said politely. Erthuma and Crotonite alike shut up and gave Sylvaine their full attention. Sylvaine gave Wanwadee Li his full attention. "Go, Wanwadee," he said.

It was like watching the buck be passed. Harriet gave an exasperated sigh as Wanwadee Li turned to Wyss'huk and said, "Wushok, can you put the Stiss up in your embassy? We could claim they've all left. They could just disappear." His eyes scanned the bar. "*I* haven't seen any Stiss around here, have you?"

Two dozen Erthumoi shook their heads and muttered variations on "No. Stiss? Never heard of them . . ." Even one of Wyss'huk's staff said, "There were some here once, but I don't know where they got to."

Harriet held her breath. Perhaps that *would* work, at least until they could plan something else. Then in the waiting silence, Harriet heard ticking.

She was not the only one who heard the sound. Handing his shotgun back to Lilac, Sylvaine rounded the bar for a better look at the crowd.

The ticking redoubled. The sound came from Chelrek,

another of Wyss'huk's staff—and, to Harriet, it sounded malevolent, as if she were listening to a radiation detector warning that this was too hot to handle.

"Slug," said Chelrek. "Brain-burned slug who wants to cherish the slime at the bottom of the sea. Wyss'huk may call you a person, slug, but I know better. You wish to protect this slime?" Two crooked talons indicated Fastas. "This slime is *hashas*—"

She got no further. Sylvaine had the tube to her breathing mask between his clenched hands. "Don't say it, Chelrek. Saying that on LostRoses will leave you quite out of breath."

"Saying that *as a curse* will leave you quite out of breath," Harriet corrected. "But I think you've had your question answered, Wanwadee. Wyss'huk can't take them in. He can't watch all his staff members all the time."

Beside her, Katuk said, "They'd kill him for harboring us, Harriet. I couldn't permit that. None of us could."

Harriet turned a steady eye on Wanwadee Li and said, "They couldn't kill *us* for harboring them . . ."

He nodded, slowly and firmly. "Referendum," he said. "Sylvaine, you put the question to the voters."

Still holding Chelrek's breathing tube, Sylvaine nodded. Slowly, he relaxed his hands. To Wyss'huk, he said, "Chelrek is no longer welcome in my bar. Get her out of here. I don't even want to know if she's the one who told the Stiss about Fastas and Prist—it's safer for her that way."

To Harriet's surprise, the Crotonite Sylvaine released did not resume her ticking. "I did not tell the Stiss," she said. "I tell the Stiss *nothing*. The Stiss are. . . ." She switched abruptly to Crotonite. Obviously, Nevelse hadn't the proper words to describe Chelrek's view of the Stiss— listening to her invective with half an ear, Harriet was not surprised. Chelrek was using obscenities that Harriet recognized as crude even by Crotonite standards.

Wyss'huk cut through the torrent with a single word, also in Crotonite. "Out," he said. Chelrek glared at him but shut her beak. Wyss'huk went on, "Sylvaine has forbidden you entry. You have breached local mores and you are now a liability to the Pssstwhitian Embassy. You are confined to quarters until you can be shipped home."

That meant no flying, as well, Harriet bet. Wyss'huk was mad as a wet hen.

Chelrek spread her wings to their full extent. All around her, Erthuma heads ducked, arms came up to protect eyes from the flap. "When I return home," she said grandly, "I shall fly." Then she furled her wings again and stamped toward the door.

She'd gotten Wyss'huk where it hurt most. Harriet could see his breath come fast.

From behind Harriet's chair, there was a flap of wings. Apparently, Chelrek had offended Bingo as well. Croaking a few choice insults of his own, Bingo swept across the room and dived at the Crotonite, harrying Chelrek to the door and hastily through.

"Bingo!" said Joppich angrily. "You get back here. *Now!*"

Having come smack against a closed door, Bingo was quite happy to comply, but Harriet would have sworn he was chortling to himself as he did.

Wyss'huk was ticking softly. He fixed an orange eye on Bingo and then on Harriet. "Isn't being able to fly a remarkable and superior attribute?"

Harriet had to grin. "Bingo's not impressed."

"To my surprise," Wyss'huk said, "neither am I. I think you've corrupted me, slugger."

The rattle of spoon on glass silenced them both. "Quiet for a vote," Sylvaine shouted from behind the bar. "Quiet for a vote!" He pointed to the screen at the far end of the room and dimmed the lights to brighten the image.

It was the tape Prist had made for him, explaining the *hashas' sitta*. Harriet listened with half an ear, her mind distracted by the problems they faced, her eye distracted by the shiny button-black eye of Bingo who sat once again on the tine of her chair.

The distraction was almost welcome. Harriet had to think about something else, if only for a moment, and Bingo was determined she should think about him. She had, actually—but in all the excitement she'd forgotten what she'd brought for him.

Harriet canceled the chair's "grab Bingo" program and reached into a side pouch for the fricket His Highness had brought her the previous day. Ought to be good enough by now, she thought.

Not wishing to disturb anyone else, she unwrapped the fricket quietly and without a word held it out to Bingo. She'd corrupted Wyss'huk, maybe she could corrupt Bingo, too. Why not?

Bingo eyed Harriet, not the fricket. He could probably smell the fricket just fine—Harriet certainly could—and a creature that ate carrion ought to be adept at locating same.

Yes, he could smell it. Casting a wary eye at the pinchers, Bingo stepped cautiously forward. When he passed into grabbing range and one step closer, he gave Harriet a startled look. She leaned forward, offering the fricket between thumb and forefinger.

I hope I don't lose a thumb on this, Harriet thought. Couldn't regenerate that, either.

Bingo's neck stretched and his beak closed delicately around the fricket. "Heh-heh-heh," he said softly. "You're welcome," said Harriet, just as softly.

Prize in beak, Bingo retreated to the tine of the chair, where he shredded it into tiny pieces—must be good, Harriet thought, if he wanted to make it last longer—and savored each before throwing back his head to swallow.

Prist's tape had finished. The question was put to the population of LostRoses. The question was: Shall we do everything in our power to keep the *hashas' sitta* from being taken off LostRoses simply because they are what they are?

Sylvaine passed Harriet the absentee ballot box, and she thrust in her hand and thumbed "Yes."

"Ought to get one of those built into your chair," he

said, as he passed the box to Old Hairy. Old Hairy's hand vanished inside. It was impossible to tell how he'd voted—the box had been designed that way—but Old Hairy nodded at Harriet. "Voted *yes*," he said. "I want to see the rest of Fast As's painting. Maybe he'd paint my place too. I've got so much money stashed from selling LostRoses, I betcha I could afford something that good." Old Hairy passed the box on its way.

Bingo had finished his fricket. Eyeing the pinchers, he started forward again. Harriet let him pass within grabbing range and held out her hand to show it empty. "Sorry," she said. "That's all I've got. I'll save you the next one, though, since you like them so much. It's not as if *I* eat them."

Bingo thrust his beak close to her hand. Checking out the smell, she thought. Then he eyed her one more time. "Friends?" she said.

He croaked a syllable. Then, very deliberately, he turned his back on her and walked to the tine of the chair. He gave a second croak, glanced over his shoulder at her, and settled down—facing outward.

"Friends," said Joppich, confirming Harriet's assessment. "With all this going on, you've got the time to woo Bingo?"

Harriet shrugged. "Just because somebody seems to hate you is no reason to hate him back. I kept thinking of a quatrain from an old book of Wanwadee's . . . you'd have to ask him for the whole quote, but the import stuck in my head." She gestured at the bird, now poised like a hood ornament. "He drew a circle that closed me out." Harriet tilted her head to one side and, finding the couplet, she quoted, " 'But love and I had the wit to win. We drew a circle that closed him in.' "

For a long moment, his sky-colored eyes held hers, then the eyes focused briefly on the middle distance, and Harriet knew he was writing the couplet in that mental notebook of his. She said, "I may be misquoting—check with

Wanwadee if you want the actual words—but I know I got the meaning right.''

Then it came to her—rising like a life-pulse to lift her into the sky. A slow smile spread across her face. ''I *know* I got the meaning right,'' she said again.

''We've got the tally,'' Sylvaine announced, and Harriet turned her attention to the screen. Of the roughly five thousand citizens of LostRoses, all those eligible to vote had. The referendum had passed unanimously. A cheer went up from the Erthumoi assembled in the bar.

''Wanwadee! Sylvaine! I think I've got the answer . . . I think it'll work,'' Harriet shouted over the hubbub.

Sylvaine tinked a spoon on his glass. ''Quiet for a vote!'' he shouted again. ''Quiet for a vote!''

''But Sylvaine—''

This time it was Wanwadee Li's face, oddly hard to recognize beneath the mask of his frown of office, that appeared on the screen. ''As Harriet Kingsolver knows the situation and the Crotonites better than any of us, and as she speaks their language, and as the situation has come to a head and may require immediate action, I nominate Harriet Kingsolver for God and I suggest her term of office be three weeks, to begin with a yes vote.''

Harriet couldn't believe her ears. Even when the referendum appeared on the screen to make the nomination formal, she could only gape.

''No,'' she said, when Sylvaine handed her the ballot box.

''Shut up and vote, Harriet. You know you're the only one who can do it.''

''I also know what happened to the last guy who got voted God. They lynched him for abuse of power the day his term of office ended.''

''Don't get lynched,'' said Sylvaine. He laid the ballot box in her lap and folded her hands about it.

Harriet thrust a shaking hand into the box and voted.

Teeth clenched, she watched the box make its rounds. After a long, long time of waiting, she watched the tally light the screen. This time the result was not unanimous; there was a single vote no.

Old Hairy leaped to this feet and roared, "All right—who's the slug who voted against Harriet?" He glowered at each Erthuma in the room in turn.

Harriet took a deep breath, got it together, and roared, "*I'm* the slug who voted against Harriet! Want to make something of it?"

"No, ma'am!" Old Hairy sat down and shut up; he was grinning. He kept grinning even as Sylvaine climbed onto the running board of her chair to fit the paper foil halo to her head.

Sylvaine stepped down to admire his handiwork. "Done," he said. He tinked his glass. "Harriet Kingsolver is God! Harriet Kingsolver is God! Everybody shut up and listen to God!"

Wyss'huk was peering up at Harriet and her halo with clear astonishment. She could see nosy questions by the thousands in his brilliant orange eyes. Bet the Quid Nunc gets a lot of offerings this week, she thought. "It's not religious," she told him. "It's political. It means that everybody on LostRoses has to do whatever I say as long as I'm wearing the halo. Think of it as vast and unlimited emergency powers . . ."

Think of it as dangerous, she added to herself. Don't abuse it and, above all, *don't* get lynched afterward.

Wyss'huk had named another wind for her, one she'd never felt because it was specific to worlds better suited for Crotonites. "Rise-or-be-broken" was the literal translation of the word. Now she knew how it felt to be caught up in one. You've got no choice, she told herself. Rise!

"First," she said, "I need to know if the ship from Stiss is likely to be armed and, if so, how heavily. Secondly, I need to know how much of what you've been importing to maintain your embassy staff we can supply directly from LostRoses, Katuk, and how much can *only* be supplied by Crotonite sources. Then I need to know if the embassy building Wyss'huk abandoned is still airtight."

Lilac laid aside her mug and stepped around the bar.
"I'll check the embassy. If it's not airtight . . . ?"

"If it's not airtight, fix it so it is. I'm confiscating it
for the duration of the emergency."

"If they've got an adviser to spare," Lilac said, "I
could build them something really *pretty*."

Harriet shook her head. "No frills today. Just something
they can live in safely until we have the leisure to build
them safe *and* pretty."

"Gotcha, God," said Lilac. "Let me take Muhammed
and we'll get it done twice as fast." At Harriet's nod, the
two of them were off like a shot.

Katuk watched them go, then he turned to Harriet and
said, "If I may use Sylvaine's equipment, I can tell you
about the ship's armaments."

This time Harriet's nod brought a quick change of light
at the end of the room: someone had taken all the data
available in LostRoses's computer and thrown the ship's
profile and stats to the screen. Katuk said, "There will be
a"—the word was a garble to Harriet—"at the nose and
probably a"—another garble—"at the tail."

"Wyss'huk," she said, "help me out here. I don't
know the words for guns."

"Enough firepower to wipe out everybody on Lost-
Roses," Wyss'huk said. "But the ship can't maneuver
within the atmosphere. Once it sets down, we're safe,
except from hand-held weapons."

God scowled and asked nobody in particular, "How
fast can we get Erthuma backup?"

The nobody-in-particular who answered was Joppich.
"The ship that brought me should still be in range. It took
us a month's time in real-space to get here from the local
hyperpoint."

"Are *they* armed? Can we get them to turn around?"

"The ship was a Cappio-5D," someone in the crowd—
Effie, it was—volunteered. "Two Steinholz guns and an
Eye of God, begging your pardon, Harriet. That ought to
handle anything Stiss can throw."

"Don't sound so cheerful about it," Harriet said. "I'm not trying to start a shooting war. I'm just trying to keep the *hashas'sitta* alive."

"Yes, ma'am," came Effie's subdued reply.

"You're frowning, Joppich," Harriet said. "What's the problem?"

"They won't turn around to keep Stiss from removing its own people from LostRoses."

"I know," said Harriet. "But they'll turn around to keep Stiss from removing *citizens* from LostRoses."

All around her, shock spread across faces. It took a long moment before they understood what she was suggesting, but slowly the shock was pushed aside by broad smiles spreading in its place.

"It might just work," said Sylvaine, his smile the broadest of all.

"Wanwadee," said Harriet. "Call the Erthuma ship back."

"*Yes!*" Wanwadee, his own grin distorted by the warpaint, headed for the back room, to make his call where he wouldn't disturb God.

"*No!*" someone shouted, just as forcefully.

Harriet glared and the room went silent. The speaker wasn't a LostRosian but, in the end, that didn't matter. "You're telling God no?" she inquired quietly.

Gheorghe and Jebediah, the two LostRosians on either side of the negative young man, picked him up bodily and carried him forward. They dropped him on the left tine of Harriet's chair none too gently. At her side, Joppich said, "Gomperson."

Harriet remembered—one of the government flacks. "Well, Gomperson?" she said. "What's your problem?"

"You can't make a bunch of Crotonites citizens of LostRoses."

Harriet turned to Sylvaine. "May I have your copy of the constitution, please?" Sylvaine grinned at the "please" and rummaged behind the bar. "Which reminds me—somebody make up a copy of the constitution for each of the *hashas'sitta*."

Majnoun said to Katuk, "How many of you are there?" Still unsure of numbers in Nevelse, Katuk told Wyss'huk, who said, "Fifteen, not counting Katuk."

Harriet nodded to Majnoun. "We'll worry about a translation later. Just make up enough of the Nevelse version to go around."

"This has nothing to *do* with any constitution," Gomperson shouted.

"It certainly does," said Sylvaine, handing Harriet a scrolled copy of the LostRoses constitution. "There's nothing in our constitution that says citizenship is limited to Erthumoi."

"You can't do it!"

From where Harriet sat, Gomperson seemed to be having some sort of fit. "I don't have time for this," she said. "Get him out of here." Gheorghe and Jebediah obligingly picked up Gomperson again and started for the door with him.

"You can't! You can't throw away all my work," Gomperson shouted at Harriet, as he struggled frantically against the two. "Think of the advantage I've given the Erthumoi . . . !"

"Wait a minute, Gheorghe," she said. "Bring him back."

They brought him back and set him down once more. Smugly, Gomperson dusted himself off, glared once at Gheorghe and Jebediah, and said, "I thought you'd listen to reason."

"Reason with me," said Harriet, in tones so sweet even Sylvaine looked shocked. "Just how did you give Erthumoi this advantage?"

"You don't know much about the Crotonites, do you?" he said.

Gheorghe cocked a fist and aimed, but Harriet held up a restraining hand and Gheorghe's stopped a scant quarter inch short of Gomperson's face. Gomperson hadn't even noticed—nor did he notice that while Gheorghe might have lowered his hand he was keeping the fist clenched and ready at his side.

To Gomperson, Harriet said, "I don't know *enough* about the Crotonites, true. Tell me."

Gomperson grinned. On him, it was unpleasant. "The Crotonites from Stiss are *hashas' sitta. All* Crotonites hate them. By embarrassing Stiss in front of Pssstwhit, Erthumoi gain an advantage in their dealings with the Stiss—"

A muttered undercurrent ran through the crowd. Harriet raised her hand slightly higher and silence prevailed. She leaned closer. "You were the one," she said. "*You* told the Stiss that Katuk and his staff are *hashas' sitta.*"

Gomperson straightened. "I was," he said.

Stunned by the look of pride that accompanied this admission, Harriet put her head in her hands. Without looking up, she said, "Take him out and—" Her fingers brushed the paper halo and she shivered. She'd been about to add *and shoot him*—and they would have. Very carefully, she finished, "And lock him up somewhere. I don't want to have to look at him again. Old Hairy, go tell Wanwadee to tell that ship they're to pick up Gomperson while they're here. He's being deported for offending the constitution. Not to mention God. Not to mention the human race. Now get him out before I do something awful to him!"

They got him out—kicking and screaming, but they got him out. Harriet turned wide eyes on Joppich. "You said he was a flack . . . you *didn't* say he was a sociopath."

"I didn't think he'd go that far, I swear." Joppich looked as stunned as Harriet felt. Shock still ran in ripples up his forehead.

From the tine of her chair, Bingo made a hacking sound that reminded Harriet of His Highness about to upchuck a hairball. Disgusting as the sound was, it expressed Harriet's feelings better than any words she knew—in Nevelse or Crotonite.

To condemn Fastas and Prist and the rest to death for

the sake of political advantage . . . What kind of a mind did that take? Harriet shuddered and shook her head. "Joppich? Am I going to have trouble with the other one?"

"I don't know." The sky-colored eyes were wide.

"Round up the 'experts' and put 'em under house arrest," Harriet said. Old Hairy reached obligingly for Joppich and Harriet said, hastily, "No, leave me that one."

Despite "expert" protests, it was quickly done. Still hacking insults at them, Bingo followed them out. Back to business, Harriet thought. "Katuk, what's the verdict on your imports?"

It was Tomas of the Only Birds who answered, "They can keep breathing—that's no problem. We've got everything in the way of natural resources they need to synthesize their atmosphere. But food's another story. It's *all* imported. I don't see a damned thing here we could grow."

"So we have to figure we keep importing food for them. Katuk's turn now—will Stiss sell us food or do you think they'll be mad enough to embargo?" Harriet turned to Wyss'huk and added, "And, if Stiss institutes an embargo, what are the chances we can buy food from Pssstwhit?"

"We can find sources that will sell the Stiss food, even through an embargo, Ha'reet," said Wyss'huk.

Beside her, Joppich whispered, "There's a thriving black market. If they can't contact it, I can." At full voice, he said, "What's your estimated cost per shipment? Or range of costs—from Stiss, from Pssstwhit, from . . . other."

Tomas, Katuk, and Wyss'huk bent over the computer—Tomas's fingers flew. When he was done, he wrinkled at the brow and read the figures aloud. Wyss'huk said, "It won't work, Ha'reet."

Even the highest of the three numbers was less than the price she'd get for the lostrose gall she'd handed Joppich so little time ago. Harriet growled and said, "God doesn't understand the problem."

Katuk ducked his head. Harriet suddenly recognized the gesture to mean embarrassment. "I apologize for the rude way I put that," she told him, "but I need to know the answer."

"We have no money, and no source of income. We're all diplomats—"

"I think he means," said Tomas with a grin, "they never learned an honest trade."

The door opened and closed behind her, and Bingo flapped back to his perch.

"We'll give you the crash course; you can peddle lostroses like the rest of us," Harriet said.

"And when the fad for them goes bust, they starve to death," Wanwadee Li said. "They're here forever if they do this, Harriet."

Harriet shook her head. "Only until they colonize a world of their own. Look around the system, we've got five perfectly good planets going to waste here—maybe one of them's right for Crotonites. If you don't see one you like, look further. But it'd be nice to have neighbors."

"You're still not thinking money," said Sylvaine. "Gods are always lousy at economics. A ship, even leased, would cost them a massive amount of credits. I doubt we could peddle enough lostroses to cover it without *pushing* the bottom out of our market."

"Okay," said Harriet. "Shut up a minute. This God's got to think about money." The Erthuma faces in the crowd were all so expectant—and the Crotonite so disappointed—that Harriet couldn't look at them and think at the same time. She turned her gaze to the sweeping serenity of Fastas's mural and . . . she had it!

"Fastas," she said, slowly, carefully. "Prist gave me one of her paintings. Now, I understand your painting has something to do with your . . . worship? With your reverence for your God?"

"The painting is more like . . . like giving a party for him," Fastas said.

"Celebratory," said Wyss'huk. He spattered a word at Fastas, who spattered back. "Celebratory," Wyss'huk said, again, this time with full assurance.

"Then," said Harriet, "would you mind if others joined the celebration by looking at your work, by displaying your work in their museums or their homes? Wyss'huk, translate for me—make sure he understands."

Wyss'huk did, and then translated Fastas's words back, rapid-fire. "He says, of course not. He says they would be delighted and honored to share the celebration of *hash-as'sit* with anyone who wished to do so."

"Here comes the tough one, Wyss'huk. We've got to get this one right. Ask him if he would mind if someone *paid* him for a painting."

Beside her, Joppich gave a gasp of understanding. He leaned forward, waiting as anxiously as Harriet while the question was officially translated. Fastas turned to Katuk and the two of them held a rapid-fire exchange that sizzled and spat. It was so fast, and the vocabulary was so unfamiliar, that Harriet could only wait—and patience was hard to come by.

A smile started to work its way across Joppich's features. *He* could follow—Harriet turned her attention to him. Even before Fastas switched back to Nevelse, Harriet knew what the answer would be.

"We would take money for our paintings," Fastas said. "This is a very strange question, Ha'reet. We would sell our paintings—we would give them to people who"—he lapsed into Crotonite but this time Harriet understood—"would use them to rise on."

"Sell," Harriet repeated. "Would you *sell* them?"

"Of course," Fastas said, and because he couldn't say it in Crotonite, he added in Nevelse, "Why not?"

Harriet let go a breath she didn't know she'd been holding and turned to Joppich. He was grinning so hard the grin had worked all the way up his forehead to vanish only under the thick black hair. His eyes were perfect sky for soaring. "Photos—I need some photos of their paintings," he said.

"I've got a whole collection," Isobel volunteered from a corner table. "Good photos, then," Harriet assured Joppich, who said, eyes bright, "It'll work, Harriet. Where's a comunit? It'll work."

"Dealers," Harriet said. "Not just museum curators."

"I'll call the curator first," Joppich said. "I'll explain that, unless somebody shows up with money—and lots of it—all the artists will be put to death. I know him, Harriet; you can bet he'll pass the word."

"Well?" Harriet did her best to loom at the entire room. "What are you waiting for? Let's start swearing in our newest citizens. The sooner we can let the ship from Stiss land, the safer we'll be."

"Who's first?" asked Wanwadee Li. "You, Fast As?"

The Crotonite unfurled and furled his wings; they made a restless sound, like the rustle of taffeta. He ducked his head briefly beneath one wing, then he fixed his eyes on Harriet.

Oh, my sweet wings, thought Harriet. There's still a problem. "What is it, Fastas?"

"We have no money," Katuk said. "Until we sell some lostroses or some paintings, we have no money. We can't live on your—charity? Is that the word? That *would* be against our principles."

Into the silence that ensued, Bingo again made the disgusted glack-glack-glack sound of a cat with a hairball. His sinuous neck rippled and he disgorged a long string of lumps onto the tabletop. With a croak of pleasure, he picked it up by one end and flew straight to Harriet, to lay his dripping prize in her lap. "Heh-heh-heh," he said.

As disgusting as it was, Harriet recognized it—and it was undamaged by its stay in the bird's craw. *Thank you, Quid Nunc,* Harriet said silently, breathing a sigh of relief. *I'll bring you ribbons every color of the rainbow.* Aloud, she said, "And, thank you, Bingo."

To Katuk, she said, "One of our resident spirits wishes to make you a welcoming gift. Would you be able to accept that?"

Again there was much hasty discussion. "Yes, of course," said Katuk, at last. "We acknowledge the existence of other gods and we're pleased to accept."

"Then there's no problem about money. You have it to hand." She held up the string of lostroses, running her hand down it to wipe off the worst of the guck. "The Quid Nunc has sent you this to cover your expenses until your own money starts coming in."

"Will it?" asked Fastas. "Will it, really?"

Old Hairy peered at the string of lostroses and grinned at Harriet. "Oh, yeah. Top quality. Look at those little beauties glow!" Then he turned to Fastas and said, "I been meaning to ask: when you're done with Sylvaine's mural, would you come out and paint my place? I'd like it lots—sky on the inside. Here"—he thrust a pouch at the little alien—"I got a down payment . . ."

From the clink of the pouch, Harriet knew it held credits, not lostroses. Maybe the Crotonites needed actual money, not just the potential a string of unsold lostroses represented. Old Hairy wasn't taking any chances; he genuinely wanted his cabin "sky on the inside."

Five minutes later, there was a heap of credits on the table in front of Fastas and Katuk, and Fastas probably had more commissions than he had wingspan.

"Now?" said Wanwadee Li.

"Now," said Harriet.

"Fast As," he said. "Hold up your right hand and repeat after me: 'I, Fast As . . .' "

"I, Fastas," the Crotonite repeated after Wanwadee Li, "pledge allegiance to the Constitution of LostRoses, second planet of the Ashmore system. I pledge to help my neighbor at my inconvenience. Other than that, I pledge to let my neighbor sin his own sins and never force him to do something for his own good, 'cause it's none of my damned business how he goes to hell. All this I swear by those things I hold dearest . . ."

Wanwadee Li stopped there. Fastas waited for the rest but Wanwadee shook his head. "The rest is up to you, Fast As," he said. "I can't tell you what you hold dearest. You tell us."

Taloned claw still raised, Fastas said, "All this I swear by *hashas' sit*, by Prist, by the sweet winds off Singing Crag . . . and by the friendship I've found on LostRoses."

"Congratulations, Fast As," said Wanwadee Li. "You're now a citizen of LostRoses." He handed him a scroll.

Who ever had made up the copies of the constitution had done a loving job: each one came wrapped in a red ribbon, tied with a bow. Harriet felt tears burn the corners of her eyes. To Fastas, Wanwadee Li added, "Which means you too have to obey God over there for the next three weeks . . ." God sniffled happily and grinned at them both.

If he'd been physically capable of it, Fastas would have grinned back. "Yes," he said, with a sweep of his wings for emphasis. "What shall I do to help, God Ha'reet?"

"Go round up the rest of the Stiss *hashas' sitta*," Harriet said. "Let's get them sworn in as fast as we can."

"I fly to obey!" he shouted, and ran for the door. From his perch on Harriet's leg, Bingo croaked encouragement.

Wyss'huk considered Harriet, his orange eyes very bright. "I think," he said at last, "that the Quid Nunc is a very useful spirit to know."

"Want to know what I think, Wyss'huk?" Harriet leaned over the arm of her chair and said quietly, "I think Joppich visited the Pssstwhitian Embassy today."

"Yes, he did," said Wyss'huk, clearly not understanding the implication.

"And I think Bingo got bored and went exploring . . . and found the Quid Nunc's tribute. He ate the fricket and tried the string of lostroses—when it didn't agree with him, he returned it to the person it smelled most like."

"Heh-heh-heh," said the bird.

Wyss'huk looked so disappointed, Harriet added, "How seriously do you expect God to take a simple spirit?"

"But—"

She grinned. "But the Quid Nunc will get her ribbons. I promised and I plan to deliver."

"I'll come too," he said, and his fur settled in relief.

"Good," said Harriet. "Now, shut up, will you? I want to hear what the rest of the Stiss hold dearest."

Half an hour later, as the last two Stiss were being sworn in, Joppich returned. He waited and watched until Prist had finished her oath of citizenship—she swore by Fastas, Harriet noted with delight—then he said, "In two months, you'll have more art dealers here than you know what to do with. I see you've won him over."

He meant Bingo, but Harriet couldn't help grinning. In quick, quiet words, she caught him up on what he'd missed. When she got to the part about Bingo's gift, Joppich eyed the bird. "Part magpie, too, then," he said. "Thieving bird. Good for you, Bingo."

He reached out to caress the bird's feathers. "Oh!" he said, suddenly. From his pocket, he took the leaf gall she'd given him. "Prist," he called, "may I commission a painting too?"

He could and he did. "Sorry, Harriet," he added. "I didn't know what to do with it. It was burning a hole in my pocket but I couldn't just throw it away."

"You did the right thing, then. I hate to see a good fricket wasted," Harriet said, and was all the more pleased to see that he got the joke.

Katuk said, "We're done; they're safe. We can let the ship from Stiss land now."

Frowning, Harriet said, "You haven't been sworn in yet, Katuk."

"I'm going back to Stiss."

"No," said half a dozen people and Crotonites in chorus. Harriet shook her head violently.

"I must. I have enough political influence still that they

can't kill me. The worst they could do is cut off my wings, and . . ." His stumps twitched.

"And they've already done that."

"Yes," he said. "I want to go back, Ha'reet. I want to tell some people I know what's been done here. Perhaps they too might find their way to this world—"

"We'd be happy to have 'em," Wanwadee Li said, catching on immediately.

"Ha'reet," said Wyss'huk, his fur ruffled in warning. 'Stiss will want a scapegoat . . ."

There was a word for that in Crotonite, all right. Harriet said to Katuk, "Is Wyss'huk right? What happens to your influence when the high muckamucks find out you've 'embarrassed' them in front of a bunch of Pssstwhitians and Erthumoi?" Harriet wasn't sure which the muckamucks would consider worse.

Katuk wasn't sure what a 'high muckamuck' was, but once Wyss'huk had explained the expression, Katuk said only, "I want to take the chance."

Well, Harriet had sworn herself to let people go to hell in their own way . . . but she didn't have to like it.

"Wait," said Wyss'huk. "Give me a moment, Ha'reet. I may have a solution."

Harriet nodded, hoping against hope, even though she couldn't see a damned thing Wyss'huk could do. Wyss'-huk motioned one of his aides—Chellet, Harriet recognized belatedly—into Sylvaine's back room. After a moment, the two returned. Chellet rustled her wings and said to Wanwadee Li, "Would you accept a Pssstwhitian as a citizen of LostRoses, too?"

"Of course," he said.

"Then I wish to take the oath of citizenship. I, too, am *ashas'sit.*"

Harriet crowed her delight—and Bingo added his own croak. "Thank you, Wyss'huk."

"Harriet, *pippest,* I was afraid for her. Someone would have found her out sooner or later."

As Chellet took the oath, Harriet kept grinning at

Wyss'huk. With Pssstwhit as officially embarrassed b·
scandal as Stiss, they'd *both* have a good reason to hus·
the incident up—and high muckamucks of Stiss woul·
have no reason to punish Katuk.

Chellet had finished. The Stiss Crotonites welcomed he·
with open wings, and Harriet narrowly missed getting a·
eye put out by one of those fluttering wing tips in all th·
excitement.

"Now I know how you recognized the characteristi·
style of art," she said to Wyss'huk. "How good *is* she?"

"You'll want one of her sculptures for your collectior
too," he said. "I have several."

"Wyss'huk, *pippest*," Harriet whispered. "You are on·
brilliant little bat-out-of-hell."

He shrugged. "A mere matter of diplomacy, Ha'reet,"
he whispered back. "Some of us have 'learned a trade.'"

Harriet laughed. Then, raising her voice, she said t·
Sylvaine, "You won't have to overdo the customs searc·
after all. Unless, of course, you're feeling vindictive . . ."

He shook his head. "I'll be too busy to be vindictiv·
Harriet. I've got to extrude an addition to this place—·
much bigger one. There's not enough room in here t·
spread a Crotonite."

All over but the shouting, Harriet thought, as she hea·
the roar of the Stiss ship landing. She needed some shou·
ing to put the finishing touch to her arrangements, b·
she hoped to limit it to that. "Wyss'huk—who's better ·
cursing, you or Katuk? I think I'll need a translator o·
this."

"Katuk is," said Wyss'huk, much to Harriet's surpris·
With a tick or two, he added, "By a slim margin."

"I'd have said different," said Katuk. "And it's ju·
as well, because Wyss'huk will have to do the job. The·
won't believe me anymore. Don't worry, Ha'reet. I kno·
the muckamuck they've sent: Wyss'huk can out-curse *an·*
out-fly him."

"Stiss's answer to Gomperson, hunh? Good."

The Crotonite gomperson flung open the door to Sylvaine's Custom House with all the arrogance of a . . . well, of a winged Crotonite. There on the threshold he poised to make his grand entrance.

But before the Crotonite could step into the Custom House, His Highness shot through the open door and whipped around to face the Stiss and inform him he had the manners of a pig, the face of a dog, and the breath of a three-day-old dahalf . . . and that, in all probability, no one would ever take him for a meal, much less for a mate.

Having settled that to his satisfaction, His Highness swaggered across the room to leap to the armrest of Harriet's chair. From there, he whapped Bingo once on the beak for the hell of it—and to shove him over to make room—and tucked himself up on Harriet's knee.

He was wet, he was muddy, he was inordinately pleased with himself. With all the superciliousness of a few thousand years of Siamese cat ancestry, he sneered down at the gomperson.

His grand entrance spoiled beyond recognition, the gomperson burst into sputtering vituperatives—all of them aimed at Katuk. Katuk had been right: this one wasn't in the same class as any of the Crotonites she'd matched curses with. Harriet let him ramble on long enough to gauge his lack of talent, then she nodded at Wanwadee Li, who obligingly bellowed, "Shut up!"

In the stunned silence that followed, Harriet—bird and cat rampant on either knee—fixed her eyes on the gomperson and said, as ominously as she could, "Who dares to speak without my permission?" She jerked her head at Katuk and said, "Well? What does this call itself?"

A tick almost escaped Katuk. "It calls itself Pitset, Great Ha'reet."

"Pitset." Harriet made an extra effort and got it out in perfect Crotonite. "Appropriate to its status." When Katuk obliged her with an inquiring look, she explained graciously, " 'Pitset' is the Eften word for pond scum."

That was good enough to bring her to Pitset's enraged

attention, and Harriet said, "Tell the pond scum to state its business quickly and briefly, without flourish. Its voice offends me."

"And just who and what does this slug think it is?" the gomperson asked Katuk in Crotonite.

"Ha'reet is God of LostRoses," said Katuk. "I suggest you be respectful and do as She commands."

They'd done the exchange with flourishes, but Katuk had easily out-flourished Pitset. Pitset swirled his wings angrily about his body and said, "I've brought LostRoses a new ambassador and staff. I am here to remove the previous ambassador and staff."

Harriet gave a nonchalant wave of her hand. "You may take Katuk with you. As for staff, he has none. Now go away. You're not worth insulting." She said it in Crotonite.

Pitset exploded in rage, spreading his wings to their fullest reach. On Harriet's knee, Bingo spread his wings in mocking imitation. Wyss'huk ticked delightedly. So did several of the other Crotonites. None of which did Pitset's temper any good.

"I've come to take the other Stiss slugs away!" He flapped his wings as he sputtered.

Harriet made a show of scanning the room. When she had completed her inspection, she said, "Aside from Katuk, there are no Stiss here."

Pitset drew a weapon—from where, Harriet never knew, but she knew she'd overplayed her hand. He trained the weapon on her. To Katuk, he said, "This god is like yours: easily disposed of."

Without looking down, Harriet felt the keyboard. Her finger found the *n* for "nosy" and touched it in.

Katuk said, "Pitset, ask your new ambassador's advice before you do such a rash thing."

Behind her, Sylvaine must have gone for his shotgun, because Pitset said, "Don't move. Any of you. I am taking the former Stiss staff with me, where they will be made as truly former as such slime deserves." He'd said it all in Crotonite, but the gesture he made with his weapon was unmistakable in any language. He switched to broken Nevelse and said, "Lift your hands."

Harriet raised her hands . . . and whistled. The chair's heavy pinchers flicked out to snap closed on Pitset's hand. Harriet heard the sound of bones breaking and winced—but she kept whistling, and the pinchers wrenched the weapon from Pitset's two-fingered grasp to lay it obligingly in her outstretched palm.

A collective sigh of relief went up from behind her. "Disintegrator," said Wyss'huk. "*That* was risky, Ha'-reet—the kind of risky Majnoun would yell at you for."

"Good thing I didn't know it at the time," she told him. She looked the little weapon over, very carefully. Made for the Crotonite grip. Her hand could not hold it comfortably; what was more, she couldn't fit her fingers correctly to pull what was so obviously the trigger.

Pitset screamed and—in a flutter of wings—leaped at Harriet, unbroken talons first. Bingo shrieked defiance, His Highness spat and bristled, but before Harriet had the chance to think of shredded lunch meat, the chair's pinchers had caught the Crotonite in mid-leap.

There they held him, flapping and cursing. Unlike Wyss'huk or even Bingo, Pitset hadn't enough sense to settle down. "Hold still," she told him, irritably. "Hold still or you'll damage your wings."

He wouldn't. Harriet thought a minute, then slipped her hand into the waldo glove for the fine-work pinchers. She picked up the Crotonite's weapon in her "fingers"—yes, the two pinchers were an adequate substitute for the two Crotonite fingers. She could fire the gun if need be.

She pointed it at him, then she whistled for the heavy-duty pinchers to set him down. "Now," she said, "are you ready to behave yourself like a civilized Stiss?" She aimed his gun suggestively between his eyes.

He stopped flapping and screeching and held very still.

"Good," said Harriet. She whistled for the pinchers to release him. The gun remained aimed at his head. "Now, why don't you call in the *new* ambassador to LostRoses, and we'll see if we can't work something out diplomatically.''

He did as God asked. Nothing like a disintegrator to back up a commandment, thought Harriet . . . His Highness told Harriet she was getting too big for her britches which had never fit right anyway as she hadn't the sense of style of a slime mold. ''All right, all right,'' Harriet told him. ''You've put me in my place. Consider God properly deflated.''

With His Highness around, Harriet thought, she might just make it safely through the rest of her term as God . . .

As it turned out, though, her first sight of Ambassador Terchep deflated her with a vengeance: the Stiss had clipped the wings of yet another of their own people.

Unsure whether to weep or rage her frustration, Harriet could scarcely trust herself to speak. She took a few deep breaths and, at last, she said, ''Wyss'huk, would you be vile enough to explain to the new ambassador from Stiss that a member of his party has just attempted to kidnap a number of citizens from LostRoses?''

Wyss'huk was vile enough, all right. By the time he was done explaining, the *hashas' sitta* (and Harriet) knew that *all* the citizens of LostRoses would be left in peace by both sets of Crotonites, that Katuk was in the clear (as much as possible), and that Pitset was in deep shit.

Ambassadors Terchep and Wyss'huk had come to the happy sputtering conclusion that the less said about *hashas' sitta* among the Stiss *or* the Pssstwhitians, the better.

All over but for one last detail. ''Ambassador Terchep,'' Harriet said. ''Stiss owes LostRoses major compensation for what the pond scum over there tried to do to us.'' And let's see just how much we can get away with, she added silently.

''Yes,'' said Terchep, and he ducked his head beneath his wing. ''I'm sure we can agree on a fitting punishment for the pond scum.''

''The pond scum's punishment is up to you. I'm talking

about what Stiss owes LostRoses . . . I am confiscating
current Stiss Embassy and all its contents.'' There, that
would save the murals in the embassy. ''You, Ambassador
Terchep, may use the abandoned Pssstwhitian Embassy
until you can extrude a new one more to your liking.''

Just to make it official, she asked Wyss'huk to translate
it all. When he'd finished, he turned to her and made a
slight motion with his taloned hands. Rise! the motion
said.

Harriet grinned—and asked for more. ''Also in compensation, we want three years' worth of supplies for the
LostRosian Crotonites.'' And Wyss'huk translated that as
well . . . though somehow the amount of supplies asked
for went *up* in translation.

''Heh-heh-heh,'' said Bingo, appreciatively.

''Yes,'' said Terchep. ''Given the extent of your griev-
ance, my government will agree to that.'' He added a few
choice words in Pitset's direction, then he said, ''If the
abandoned embassy is airtight, I shall move my people in
and then your eye will no longer be offended by the sight
of such pond scum.''

''Thank you,'' said Harriet. To Wanwadee Li, she
added sotto voce, ''I wonder what we can get for
Gomperson?''

''Worth giving it some thought,'' he said, and from his
expression she knew he'd do just that.

A few hours later, they all went down to the ship to
see Katuk and Pitset off. Harriet kept the gun she'd con-
fiscated trained on Pitset until he vanished into the ship—
taken away by two of his own crew. To be put in irons,
she hoped. What little of Ambassador Terchep's description of his fate she'd been able to follow had been undeniably unpleasant, though not nearly as unpleasant as the
fate they'd planned for the *hashas' sitta*.

Good-byes were harder than Harriet had expected.
''We'll miss you, Katuk,'' she said, at last. ''You leave
a hole in our sky.''

The little Crotonite looked up and read the skies over

LostRoses for her one last time. It was beautiful flying weather for hang glider or winged creature. He mapped perfect flights from Fallaway Point . . . and then he gave her a glimpse of the winds along the gentle slope Majnoun favored for ground school. They too were perfect today. "Fill the hole with Ambassador Terchep," he said. "Give him my wings and teach him to fly."

"We'll do our best to get him back in the air," said Harriet. "Even as God, that's the best I can promise. You never know how stubborn a Crotonite can be until you try to teach one to fly."

Katuk ticked quietly all the way to the ship, and Harriet listened to the gentle sound until the hatch closed on it. "Good luck, Katuk," she said softly.

When the ship had lifted off, Harriet gazed down from her chair at the crowd around her. Her shoulders felt like she'd been carrying her chair instead of vice-versa. Her head felt leaden—she reached up and her fingers touched the rim of the halo.

"Majnoun," she said, and waited until he'd made his way to the forefront of the crowd. "Katuk says it's a great day for ground school. Are you in the mood to give lessons?"

"Always," said Majnoun. "Who's the student, as if I didn't know." He grinned at the new ambassador from Stiss.

"Two of them this time." Harriet pointed out Joppich, then she grinned down at Wyss'huk and added, "Let's see who's quicker to learn to fly, Erthuma or Crotonite, shall we?"

"My money's on Joppich," Wyss'huk said. "He has a head full of sky already."

Harriet shook her head. "Mine's on Terchep—*nobody* flies like a Crotonite, once he gets the hang of it."

From her knee, Bingo gave raucous voice. With a flap and a flutter, he launched into the sky to execute a series of aerobatics that would have turned even a Crotonite slime mold green with envy. "Heh-heh-heh!"

Wyss'huk ticked, a slow and reassuring sound like the purr of His Highness.

"All right," she grumbled at the bird. "Call God a liar . . ." She shouted suddenly after Bingo, "I was talking about Erthumoi and Crotonites, dammit! I wasn't talking about you!"

Raising a hand to shade her eyes as she watched Bingo swoop, Harriet once again touched the halo. "The hell with it," she said. She swept the halo from her head and sent it sailing back to Sylvaine.

"Hold that for me, will you?" she said. "God's going flying. That's the best way I know to keep Her out of trouble."

Sylvaine grinned and looped the halo over his forearm, and God rolled off to go flying with a dozen Erthumoi, as many Crotonites, winged and wingless alike, and one mutt of a cormorant who could outfly them all.

His Highness watched them go in silence. He had more important things to see to . . . and all the words he had on the subject he was saving for a certain lowlife un-Siamese tom that lived on the far side of St. Elsie's Field.

WATER OF LIFE

GEORGE ALEC EFFINGER

THERE IS SOMETHING ABOUT BEING IN THE MIDDLE of a large-scale disaster that seems to make time run more slowly. One of the first things Ph'anjan learned—after assuring herself that she had, indeed, survived the disaster—is that this effect was an illusion. She barely had enough time to get herself clear, and no time at all to grab up those items that would make continued existence the least bit comfortable.

Ph'anjan was an Ilonian, a subspecies of Cephallonian, the only aquatic starfaring race. She wasn't ranked very highly, though; she'd been seventh officer in the *Ses'kol*'s entire crew complement of twenty-two. The most important difference between her and the other officers and crew members was that she was still alive, while her twenty-one companions had died after the *Ses'kol* had come violently apart during the landing maneuvers.

Now she swam in the warm water of the ocean of this strange world, with only a Crotonite-made robot to speak with. The robot had been built to Cephallonian specifications, with only the intelligence the Crotonites had given it to perform certain tasks. Also, the Crotonites had never liked the Ilonians, and this bias tended to show up now and then in the robot's speech and behavior.

Now, though, Ph'anjan's first worries were food and shelter. This was an alien world, of course, and some of the higher officers had known its name and quite a bit about its natural history. Ph'anjan had learned only that there was a huge, dark gray carnivore called a mor'ul that roamed this sea, and if she intended to survive at all she'd better not forget it.

Shelter was simple enough. Part of the ruined hulk of the *Ses'kol* lay on the ocean floor, surrounded by a small quantity of items that might prove useful in the future. She ordered the Crotonite robot to gather these things up and stow them in the section of the starship she now called home.

Ph'anjan loosed a stream of bubbles tinted blue with thoughtfulness as she considered her other immediate problem: food. The galley of the *Ses'kol* had vanished with the remainder of the ship; that meant that if Ph'anjan were not going to starve to death, she'd need to find food locally. There was no guarantee that the body chemistry of this world's sea creatures would sustain a half-ton Cephallonian. The first taste might be deadly poison.

"Attention, please, robot," said Ph'anjan. Her voice was half an octave lower than normal, at least for a little while, because she realized that she'd been promoted. Through catastrophe it had come, of course, but she was presently and without a doubt First among them. She tried to impress the seriousness of that change on the robot.

"I am at attention," replied the Crotonite robot.

"Because of the destruction of the *Ses'kol* and all its officers and crew except myself, I am now First among us. Do you understand?"

"How much better for the universe at large if the annihilation had been just a trifle more complete," said the robot in its annoying, side-of-the-mouth, Crotonite voice. "One less fish—"

Ph'anjan made a sort of fist of one of her manipulative members. "There are planets that have fish," she said fiercely, "and there are planets that do not. I and my race are *not* fish. It occurs to me that you and I have had this conversation before."

"Yes, First among us," said the robot. "But please remember that *you* are the one with the great intellect and learning, while I'm only a Grade-Two Testing and Analysis Robot.''

"You continue to miss the point," said Ph'anjan. "Or else, you ignore it intentionally. We'll leave that alarming possibility for another occasion. Let us first look at your primary vital error.''

"In all of the known universe," said the robot, "Cephallonians have the greatest love of debate and rational discourse. If I may point out one small item, I think it may benefit us both.''

"Now you present me with 'a small item.' My courses of action are several, with two chief among them: either I listen to your jot of mechanical-minded wisdom, or I don't. Then we have the formation of what we Ilonians sometimes refer to as a logic tree. That is, supposing that I listen to you, do I act upon your information, or do I overrule it with my immensely superior knowledge? Or supposing that I do not listen to you, do I live to regret it, or do I perish immediately, a victim of my own self-centered interests? You can see that such a logic tree can quickly become very complex and difficult to interpret.''

The Crotonite robot found another tool fitted out for the Ilonians' vestigial hands—and its own—and looked at it thoughtfully. "You are supposing free will on your part,'' it said. "But you do not always have free will. For instance, I could use my own—''

"Robots do not have free will," said Ph'anjan. "That's what differentiates them from living, sentient creatures.''

The robot stood very still, without changing its appearance in the least. It paused a few seconds before responding. "Perhaps in the happy future, we'll have the freedom and leisure to discuss that point," it said. "But getting back to my original inspiration—''

"Robots are incapable of inspiration," said Ph'anjan, loosing a stream of deep red bubbles that expressed impatience.

"—my original inspiration," continued the robot, well used to the Cephallonian method of conversation, and not caring for it an atom's weight more than did the robot's bat-winged manufacturers.

"For the sake of the argument you love so much," continued Grade-Two Testing and Analysis Robot, "let's pretend something. Let's pretend that we've switched places, just for a moment. I am now the masterful Cephallonian, although only an under-officer in the Communications Section such as you were, and you are the lowly Grade-Two Testing and Analysis Robot. After some horrible mishap, we find ourselves alone and virtually without resources. What do you do?"

The deep red bubbles of impatience flowed forth again. "I'd do exactly what I have been doing. I'd begin organizing and putting things in order. I'd rely on my master's special mental talents, a unique racial quality among all the six interstellar life-forms, to optimize the odds of survival."

"You declare positively that you *are* utilizing those 'special mental talents,' even now?"

"You, a mere Crotonite-built robot, have delighted in reminding me again and again that we Cephallonians in general, and my sub-race from Ilon in particular, a world I may never see again in my lifetime, spend an absurd amount of time in debating. I will grant, for the sake of argument, even as you granted something for argument, that someday a machine might be developed with a more logical 'mind,' if you'll permit me to use the word 'mind' in connection with some inorganic, nonliving, artificial personality-construct such as yourself. This hypothetical mechanical mind might be superior to any of the Six Races; we need not bicker and wrestle over who make up those six races; that is only a cheap debater's trick and not worth our dwindling time. Yet you don't realize that such speculations are what enable us to put the chaos of the universe into a form that begins to make sense to our organic faculties. I think the proper direction for our contest of wills to proceed—"

The Crotonite analysis robot raised a mechanical arm

and cut off Ph'anjan in mid-sentence, a feat of near-impossibility. "I've let you go on at length," it said in its raspy, Crotonite voice, "because you've proved my point for me. Now, if we'd truly changed places, I wouldn't have spent the last several indispensable minutes arguing about abstract truths that don't concern our present situation in the least. If we'd switched identities, I would've begun a furious yet thorough analysis of the water content, the typical biochemistry of the local life-forms from the microscopic to the macroforms, those larger than us. And I would've begun to use my under-officer in the Communications Section to get us saved, or at least to make a report of our crash. There would always be the hope that someone—a Cephallonian, preferably, but any of the other Six Races would certainly do in a worst-case scenario—might be near enough to save our tired, hungry, fearful, and not entirely competent hides. That goes for the single metal-skinned hide, I might add," whacking itself on its front control panel.

Ph'anjan was brought up short. "Is *that* what I've been doing? Wasting and burning up our severely limited consumables in idle though nonetheless thought-provoking speech? Yes, you've earned yourself a point, and I'm not too proud to award it to you, robot. Priorities are priorities, and we should already know much more about this 'adopted' world we find ourself on. Well, then, let's get to work. As I see it, my first chore is building a communicator. You, surprisingly, have a good grasp on what your immediate duties are. Before we separate and devote ourselves to our—"

"First among us," said the robot, turning and streaming down toward the small remaining wreckage of the *Ses'kol*, "I feel another entertaining and possibly deadly debate will soon begin. If I have your permission, I've already gathered my equipment and begun the most essential of the tests. We'll know more about the environment shortly."

The Crotonite robot disappeared in the gloom of the depths. Ph'anjan loosed a stream of deep green bubbles, which signified excitement, followed by the deep blue bubbles of embarrassment, which she wanted no one to see or record.

There were logical replies to the robot's arguments, of course; but Ph'anjan was intelligent enough to know that each such reply would lead only to further and ever more abstruse discussions. The true, actual, real problem was not Cephallonian attitudes, but survival.

Ph'anjan followed the robot down to begin making a long, detailed list of all the tools, objects, instruments, implements, utensils, still-functioning mechanisms, devices, engines, and appliances she could rely on, down in the chunk of the *Ses'kol*'s wreckage. Everything was lit by the green emergency lights, making the place seem even more nightmarish.

When she searched carefully, she felt as joyful as at any time since the catastrophe had occurred. The reason was that this piece of the wreckage had been *her* piece of the wreckage. At least, as an under-officer she had been granted freedom to spend time in this area of what had been part of the Communications Section, and she had actually performed several small and insignificant chores here. More importantly, she knew what some of the whispering readouts meant, and she knew how to get some of the unlabeled hardware and software to do what she wanted.

Her hope and joy were interrupted by the grade-two Crotonite robot. "I've spent some time analyzing the immediate area," it said. "You fish would die before you found that time, but I decided to use my small amount of discretionary liberty to do for you what I knew you would never do for yourself."

"I am *not* a fish," shouted Ph'anjan. "I am an Ilonian first, a subspecies of the magnificent star-traveling Cephallonians, and although we live in water, we have overcome the technological problems that limit an aquatic race, and if you don't begin to show the proper respect, I may decide that I can do just as well without your services!"

"Threaten me!" said the robot in a cold voice. "I am the product of a race far greater than the Cephallonians—and here I mean the Crotonites. I was schooled by them in no uncertain terms that all creatures without wings were 'landgrubbers,' or 'mudsuckers.' Even I, deep in my mechanical body, have emergency, temporarily functional wings. And of all the Six Races, the Cephallonians were the most to be despised, if not hated, because they didn't even live on land."

Ph'anjan trembled in the warm sea, unable to come up with an appropriate response. There was only a trickle of gray bubbles that indicated intense offense. Ph'anjan didn't care in the least if the robot comprehended, and it had dwelt among the Cephallonians long enough to learn the significance of each color and shade of bubble.

"You have your tasks," said Ph'anjan in a level voice. Inside, she shook like a humiliated youngster, but certainly no Crotonite second-grade robot was going to see that.

"And you have yours," said the robot. "I might point out to you that you are getting hungry, and that you are beginning to starve to death. I have other information, but I do not wish to offer it freely to a fish. Not at this time."

Ph'anjan labored to control her rage. She swam about, and the familiarity of the single piece of wreckage cheered her a little, but only a little. What had the robot meant by "*other* information it wouldn't impart to a *fish*?" It was probably only part of the robot's Crotonite-based programming; the Cephallonians and, if Ph'anjan were not mistaken, the Naxians, the Erthumoi, the Samians, and the Locrians found the bat-winged creatures repellent and of a smug, self-worshipping turn of mind, which would be reflected in their products.

Grade-Two Testing and Analysis Robot was just such a device; perhaps, if Ph'anjan survived, she'd engage a few Erthumoi in an intellectual discussion of the Erthuma concept they called "advertising." The phrase "Need help? Buy Erthuma!" was known throughout the Galaxy. Erthuma machines and equipment were well respected for their dependability and quality.

Now, however, was not the time to engage some Erthumoi in a philosophical debate concerning the differences between their robots and the Crotonites'. There were no Erthumoi around, for one thing. Also, it was the wrong time because Grade-Two Robot had reminded Ph'anjan that she had much more life-threatening emergencies to attend to. She certainly didn't need to get into a lone-Ilonian philosophical debate at this particular moment. Without giving further thought to the matter, she loosed bubbles of irritation, aqua in color.

The bubbles changed to the bright orange of pure joy when Ph'anjan's attention returned to the piece of wreckage, and she realized how much of the demolished Communications Section had been salvaged, and what a superlative job Grade-Two Robot had done in fitting tools and materials back into their original positions.

"Now," she thought, "the first order of business is reestablishing contact with Ilon. Failing that, admitting that the chances are extremely slim as the *Ses'kol* had traveled at hyperjump interstellar velocities before arriving at this hospitable yet uncolonized world, we can hope to achieve contact with any of the various other Cephallonian planets. That is much more likely. The only difficulty is that I don't have all the essential apparatus and fittings to build a modulated-neutrino hyperspace communicator. So the robot's cryptic words about 'other information' might have meant that I had little time to find that equipment, here in the seas of . . . of Ph'arcan." She named the world after the Number One among them who had perished in the landing disaster.

Ph'anjan took stock of what she did, after all, possess, and made a list of what she would need. Even as a seventh under-officer, she'd learned enough here in her work station to build a modulated-neutrino communicator, if she could find the proper materials. She hoped that Grade-

Two Robot was already collecting such resources, and that the communicator might be constructed quickly.

Just as she completed that thought, her assistant robot entered the shelter and laboratory. "There's good news, and there's bad news."

Ph'anjan gave the Cephallonian equivalent of a frown, a string of light green bubbles expressing her severest irritation. "Why do you speak in that time-wasting way? And why can't you just give me the essential facts immediately?"

Grade-Two Testing and Analysis Robot waited a moment. It had no facial expressions to change, or bubbles to emit. Its Crotonite programming also gave it no means for expressing the irony it felt. "I apologize, First among us. It's a manner of speech we've learned from the Erthumoi. One of the few things, I might add, that we've found useful to adopt from the Erthumoi."

"Get on with it!" cried Ph'anjan, letting loose yet again the deep red bubbles of utter impatience.

"The good news first," said Grade-Two Robot. "None— or few—of the local marine creatures will poison you with their physical makeup alone. Of course, some have unusual protective mechanisms of which you'll have to beware, but I'm sure you take that as an assumption and appreciate it already."

"Your news causes me great happiness," said Ph'anjan, "in the limited sort of way it can, considering for the moment that we're trapped on a planet whose very name and location I don't know. Yet we have shelter, and you've just told me that I didn't have to worry about the local sea creatures as sources of food. Yet thinking back over your recent words, you implied there was bad news, as well, and I'm certain that I—or we—will need to know the bad as well as the good. What is it? Have you spotted a mor'ul, the great swimming carnivore of this world? Or is it something even more threatening, such as small, ocean-bottom volcanoes preparing to erupt not far from here? Or, even worse, the effects of—"

"I ask your pardon, First among us, for interrupting

your reasoning process, such as it is," said Grade-Two Robot. "When I told you that this planet's sea creatures wouldn't poison you if you ate them, I told you only part of the story. They won't nourish you, either. You just don't have the necessary enzymes in your gut to digest them fully and properly. And further, the fishes, invertebrates, and plants are based on a completely different set of amino acids. The Cephallonian cells expect to receive from the digestive process certain chemicals in order to build up even the simplest microstructures. It's in this kind of problem that a second-grade robot has it all over a living fish. My Crotonite creators made sure that I'd never have to face a similar inconvenience."

"Don't behave so self-importantly," said the Cephallonian, deep in thought and loosing blue bubbles to prove it. "I'm very sure that you're powered by something—batteries, more than likely. Even if you were built with a small fusion reactor, sooner or later you'd require servicing. One thing we Cephallonians have determined is that there is no such thing as sustained existence without an occasional input of *something*. You'll have your moment of truth eventually. Everything, living or mechanical, does. And don't call me a fish ever again. I'm a Cephallonian, and you know it."

"As for my moment of truth," said the Grade-Two Testing and Analysis Robot, "that's why Imiqulor put so many Crotonites in the universe."

"Imiqulor?" asked Ph'anjan, expelling a small string of light violet bubbles, indicating initial confusion.

"You'll come to worship Imiqulor, but no doubt too late," said the robot. "As for your long-term survival, during which various organelles and even the unique Ilonian bones and muscles will wear out and need to be replaced, the very idea is beyond the realm of possibility here. Your cells anticipate the regular delivery of proline, glycine, tyrosine, and leucine. These are the essential amino acids, the building blocks of Cephallonian life. They are another proof that fish are inferior to winged

Crotonite life, which demand a more logical set of essential acids.''

''One group of amino acids is no more 'logical' than another,'' said Ph'anjan.

''Wait until you learn the inner mysteries surrounding Imiqulor. I know that you, as a seventh officer with no specific duties, had only a fundamental knowledge of your own body's construction. But even so, I feel a certain satisfaction in informing you, Number One—''

''Don't call me that,'' muttered Ph'anjan, loosing the colorless bubbles of increasing horror. ''Number One was Ph'arcan, and as far as the *Ses'kol* is concerned, Number One will always be Ph'arcan. Number One died during the landing accident.''

''Then, First among us, let me put it this way: you can gorge yourself until you are so full you won't be able to swallow another bite, but the local life-forms have been created around different amino acids—cystine, sarcosine, proline, and lysine. As I said, you can make a glutton of yourself, but you'll never find sufficient tyrosine and leucine. Proline is here in abundance, but it is the *d* form, not the *l* form that you require; there are sources of glycine, it is true. But from the moment of the crash, you have been slowly starving to death, and all the eating of the many-colored fishes around you won't help.''

''By the Water of Life!'' exclaimed Ph'anjan.

''As a prime example,'' said the Grade-Two Robot, ''like the Erthumoi, the Cephallonians form the molecule adenosine triphosphate to provide energy for every major or minor task in each cell and throughout the bodily tissues generally. Here on Ph'arcan, ATP is unknown; the sea creatures about us use instead a string of azide ions, useless to you.''

Ph'anjan didn't need the situation explained to her in such detail. The Cephallonians were magnificent biologists, and Ph'anjan fully understood what the robot had been saying. She knew that her deliverance had just taken on an urgency it hadn't had before. Rather than merely being marooned on a moderately comfortable ocean world, she had been cast loose into a watery desert without nourishment. Now her rescue meant her survival. It would mean that the *Ses'kol* had not destroyed itself in vain, as well.

There were two philosophical approaches to Ph'anjan's dilemma. The first was that she could swim over the piece of wreckage and wish there were more; she could eat her fill of the odd sea creatures, knowing as she did so that she wasn't taking in enough useful nutrients; she could think up endless and useless tasks for the Grade-Two Testing and Analysis Robot, because if she didn't, it would spend most of its time mocking her.

The other approach involved doing something productive. At first Ph'anjan didn't feel like doing anything meaningful. She had long, silent debates with herself, in which she demonstrated the pointlessness of any kind of action. The only thing that had meaning was getting off this trap of a world; anything less was a waste of time and energy.

Then it occurred to Ph'anjan that she could do something, after all. How, her argument went, does an aquatic race reach the stars? Living in water, without fire, the race is unable to smelt metals or join them in the kind of gigantic joined and welded constructions that were favored by the other five races.

The Cephallonians rarely went into space, and never for the reasons that motivated the Erthumoi, for instance, or the Crotonites. The Cephallonians did not accumulate things to own or trade—their lives were spent swimming about their worlds, forever immersed in an environment that provided everything they needed. When they left the surface of a planet, it was usually in a smaller spacecraft than one of the other races would have built, and it was for motives that only other Cephallonians could comprehend.

Without fire, the Cephallonians had had to become expert biochemists, and what the built, they built by organic procedures. The concept of nanotechnology was known to the Cephallonians before the Erthumoi were walking upright on whatever their homeworld was called.

All Cephallonians, including the Ilonians, had this basic knowledge. And, finally, the choice came to Ph'anjan: use the knowledge to find a way home, or accept the Crotonite robot's verdict of starving to death.

Ph'anjan didn't want to give the Grade-Two Robot the satisfaction of watching her die. She returned to the half-pod of wreckage, still glowing with its green emergency lights, and made an inventory list of the materials, tools, and special equipment that were accessible. She had more than she'd realized; her hopes went up.

Even as a young Ilonian, she'd known how to make a template that would make use of enzymes, minerals, and carbon compounds in the water that was everywhere around her. Such a template would begin the nanotechnological assembly of a toy or a simple mechanical or electronic device.

The Communications Section was well stocked with templates. Most were for objects or instruments that were of no use to Ph'anjan. There was, however, a variety of templates that would produce modulated neutrino communicators of varying sophistication. In order to obtain the necessary building materials, of course, some of the fish and other sea creatures would have to be sacrificed—a beautiful lavender and yellow bottom-dweller for a specific acetate here, a rock-mounted bivalve for a particular ester there. Once begun, the template took over and found its components wherever it could in the environment. The only restriction written into each template was that no use was ever to be made of a Cephallonian, in any capacity.

Ph'anjan began making lists of enzymes, proteins, minerals, and other chemical components that she could find in certain organisms . . . sea life of this planet she'd named Ph'arcan. Bit by bit, element by element, compound by compound, she discovered what she needed. And all the while, the Crotonite-made robot hovered in the warm water and spoke to her.

"You've never shown me that you had the knowledge to use all of this," it said.

"You wouldn't know what it would take to use it," said Ph'anjan calmly. "You're just a mobile testing apparatus, a convenience we bought from the bats."

"They aren't 'bats,' " said Grade-Two Robot. "They're Crotonites."

"Ah," said Ph'anjan, emitting yellow bubbles of amusement.

As the days passed, and the information accumulated in the data decks, two things happened. The first was that the template for the modulated-neutrino communicator that Ph'anjan had chosen had begun its work. Its limited intelligence had decided that it had enough of the basic materials on hand to start the nanotechnological process of "growing" a communicator.

"So that's how you Ilonians do it," said Grade-Two Robot in its flat, empty voice. "Until now, I assumed you went out and bought everything you needed from the other five races, as you bought me."

"No race is rich enough to do that," said Ph'anjan.

"What do I know?" said the Crotonite machine. "I'm just a Grade-Two Testing and Analysis Robot."

The second event that happened in those exciting days was that Ph'anjan made a friend. It was a large white and blue creature, shaped not very differently from Ph'anjan, although perhaps a couple of hundred kilograms smaller.

"A mudsucker!" cried the robot. "If this were a normal world, that creature's race wouldn't have the intelligence to achieve space travel. It would be only another of the negligible beasts that crawl across the face of the world— except here, it's in the ocean! You've made friends with a seagoing mudsucker!"

"Don't mind him," said Ph'anjan. "He's not even alive, and he thinks that gives him special critical powers."

"He did not insult me," said Ph'anjan's friend, whose name was Slen and who had lurked near the Communications Section for a while, learning Ph'anjan's language. "I didn't even know what he was talking about."

"See?" said the robot.

"See?" said Ph'anjan. "Slen is vastly more intelligent than you, because he did not take offense when you did your best to offer it."

From that day on, Ph'anjan and Slen were fast friends, allies from different worlds. Slen took the Ilonian on a tour of the nearby area, warned it of the places where the mor'ul liked to hunt or rest, and mentioned several other dangerous species. Grade-Two Robot was all but forgotten; but, because of its mechanical nature, it didn't really care. When it realized that neither Ph'anjan nor Slen was paying it any attention, it stood in a corner of the Communications Section, in case it was ever needed again.

Ph'anjan used her time to recircuit the lighting system of the Communications Section, turning off the green emergency lights, replacing them with the normal, soothing blue. "An improvement, I think," said Slen.

Ph'anjan was about to reply when an audible alarm interrupted her. She was upset at first, but then she realize that the alarm was coming from the nano monitors, and it was telling her that the modulated-neutrino communicator was finished. Ph'anjan was so excited that for the moment she forgot her friend, turned off the alarm, and removed the communicator from the nano tank. It didn't look any different to her than a piecework device made by the Erthumoi or Crotonites. She had full confidence in its ability to do its job.

"How does it work?" asked Slen.

"Well," said Ph'anjan, "it's a little complicated." Explaining the notion of modulated neutrinos to a being that didn't even have the concept of "atom" in its background could take quite a long while. "I just have to tune it correctly, and I'll be able to talk to others of my kind."

"Tune it?" asked Slen. "Like this?" And then he began to sing, in a powerful voice that thrilled Ph'anjan. She had never suspected that Slen or the others of his species could communicate this way. A few seconds later, another voice, higher pitched, answered him.

"What did it say?" asked Ph'anjan.

"She," said Slen. "She said, 'Thanks, but I'm not interested.' "

Ph'anjan loosed yellow bubbles of merriment. "I've said the same thing, on more than one occasion."

Slen snorted. "I've found myself wishing . . ."

"Yes, I know," said Ph'anjan. "So have I."

It was time to speak of something else. Ph'anjan held the communicator in her stubby, somewhat clumsy hands. She felt tremors of excitement in her vestigial limbs. "This used to be my specialty," she said. "When they permitted me the privilege, that is."

Slen said nothing. He hovered nearby and watched and waited for a miracle.

Ph'jan murmured into the communicator, waited, waited some more, and then decided they were too far from Ilon for the low-powered communicator to be of any use. However, there were still other and nearer Cephallonian worlds. She murmured again into the communicator, and waited—and this time there was an answering voice!

Slen was so startled that he fell over and downward toward the sea bottom before he recovered. Ph'anjan pretended that she was calm and professional, but if Slen had been able to understand, her deep green bubbles of excitement would have given her away.

The news was not good. After some time for consultation on the Cephallonian world, Ph'anjan was informed by a second voice, this one much more serious and sad, that they didn't have the resources to travel to the planet Ph'anjan had named Ph'arcan, merely to rescue a single Ilonian. There had to be some solution, but neither Ph'anjan nor the Cephallonians could think of one. At last, gravely, the Cephallonians ended the transmission. Ph'anjan was, for the time being, truly stranded.

It was the Cephallonian way—and the Ilonian—to debate the various aspects of every subject, sometimes beyond the point when any of the other Six Races would have accepted one side or the other or a reasonable compromise. Sometimes the Cephallonians considered first one side of a question, and then another, until disaster struck. This may well explain the destruction of the *Ses'kol,* and the point had occurred more than once to Ph'anjan. She had discussed the subject with herself and with Grade-Two Robot several times. It was this propensity for philosophizing that most characterized the Cephallonian mind to the other five races, and often made it difficult for the others to bear the presence of the starfaring aquatic creatures.

"The nearest Cephallonians have declined to rescue me," observed Ph'anjan thoughtfully, emitting blue bubbles. "Does this necessarily mean that still more distant Cephallonian planets would by force of reason reach the same conclusion? Or is it possible that the qualities of generosity and compassion were distributed unequally among the planetary sub-groups of Cephallonians? What I suppose I'm trying to put into words is, should I continue to use the communicator until I've exhausted its range, in the hope that Cephallonians on some other world be more moved to pity, and launch a mission that would return me to the civilized portion of the Galaxy? Or has my experience indicated that my operating definition of 'civilized' is in need of revision? Could the answer be that I should use different templates to construct ever more powerful communicators, while I languish here and cling to what remains of my life? For all I know, an unimaginably faraway Cephallonian planet—perhaps Ilon itself—has a ship on some assignment in nearby space, and would be happy to make a quick stop to liberate me from my ravenous end. Slen, what are your thoughts on these matters?"

That was the moment when Ph'anjan, in an analytical mood, realized that as handsome, good, and kind as Slen was, he was no Cephallonian. "Would you like to swim over to the easterly chasm today?" he asked. "We haven't been there in days, you've been so intent on your little machine.''

"It's a modulated-neutrino communicator!" cried Ph'anjan in an unseemly, un-Ilonian tone. She was so distressed, her voice split into triple harmonics. Immediately she began to debate with herself on the rightness or the wrongness of her attitude toward Slen. Certainly, she couldn't expect him to understand her situation in its entirety, including all the subtle ramifications both moral and ethical; and yet, to be blunt, she was dying. He ought to be able to grasp *that*.

They did make an excursion to the easterly chasm that day, and it was fortunate that they did. Ph'anjan discovered an object buried almost completely by the gritty layer of sand that covered the rocky bottom. She used her manipulative fins to free it. Slen couldn't have accomplished that much; he didn't have even Ph'anjan's undeveloped hands.

The object was a roughly carved figure. "It's not anything that lives on *this* world," declared Slen.

"It's difficult to state with any degree of accuracy," said Ph'anjan, always in the mood for an intellectual argument. "Who knows what frame of mind the artist might have been in when he created this thing?"

"Artist?" said Slen.

Ph'anjan let loose some deep red bubbles of impatience. Lately, more frequently, her bubbles had been the deep red shade. "'Artist' may be too strong a term, I'll admit," she said. "Craftsman, perhaps. In any event, I was referring to the individual who carved this object."

Slen flipped his tail, his equivalent of a shrug. "It's definitely not a representation of a member of your race or mine."

"Perhaps not," murmured Ph'anjan. "Yet I wouldn't go as far as to rule out a Cephallonian altogether. The main point we must bear in mind is that there are five other starfaring races. This may be an unskilled likeness of one of them, or an example of how they see you or me."

"You've mentioned these other races before. Where are they, and what are they like?"

Ph'anjan released a stream of yellow bubbles, and her thousand-pound body shook with Ilonian laughter. "The one place those races are *not* is here, so you don't have to worry about them," she said.

"You still haven't told me much about them."

"I don't think you'd be pleased," she said seriously. "For one thing, none of the other five races is aquatic. Even I find that more than a little disturbing."

Slen looked as if he were trying very hard to understand. "Not . . . aquatic?" he said. "Then where do they live?"

Ph'anjan's bubbles were light green, showing her indignation, an emotion she rarely felt. "Each of the other five star-traveling creatures has adapted in some way to life on dry land, although the sorts of planets they find comfortable are all very different from each other."

Slen stared at her for a long moment. "What is . . . dry land?" he asked at last.

Ph'anjan just shook her large head. Explaining the Six Races and dry land would be at least as difficult as talking about neutrinos, and she didn't have the energy to attempt any of it. "We'll get into all that sometime," she said. "For now, I just want to get back to the Communications Section of the *Ses'kol* and see if I can learn anything more about this bizarre sculpture. You're sure that no civilization on this world could have produced it?"

"I'm certain of it," said Slen. "I've never seen such a thing in my life. What purpose does it serve?"

"It may just be decorative," said Ph'anjan.

"Decorative?" asked Slen. There was another long silence between them. "I'm not stupid, you know. Sometimes you treat me as if I had an inferior intellect or something. Just because we've never build starships that explode over strange planets. I'm not even sure I believe there *are* other planets. None of us has ever seen one. *You're* the only odd element in this situation. Maybe I should reassess my relationship with you.''

''Slen,'' she said, emitting the gray bubbles of offense, ''I've never said that you were stupid. Go ahead and do whatever reassessing you think is necessary.''

They swam back to the Communications Section in silence, each feeling deeply insulted. Ph'anjan carried the strange object, but her thoughts were on other matters.

When they arrived at the wreckage of the *Ses'kol*, Grade-Two Testing and Analysis Robot approached Ph'anjan, ignoring Slen completely. ''I've had an idea, First among us,'' it said.

It had been many days since Ph'anjan had had to listen to Grade-Two Robot's condescending, arrogant voice, or put up with its repellent, Crotonite thought patterns. In fact, she had concentrated so heavily on her own vital problems, and on Slen, that she'd almost completely forgotten about Grade-Two Robot. Until it spoke up and reminded her.

''I didn't know that machinery of such meager intelligence could develop its own ideas,'' said Ph'anjan, loosing a stream of light green bubbles of indignation. She swam past the robot as if it didn't even exist.

''Crotonites are generous,'' said Grade-Two Robot, ''in their way. They can't help it if the ground-crawling races don't always understand. So I'll pretend you didn't say what you just said, and give you the full benefit of my idea.''

''I might point out,'' said Ph'anjan, ''that I've never crawled any ground in my entire life. Then that would elicit from you an even greater insult directed specifically at Cephallonians, and then I'd have to find a way of disabling you completely. It would all be a huge waste of time, and I don't have time.''

The machine made the sound that Ph'anjan had decided mimicked Crotonite laughter. ''My creators design all their robots so they may not be turned off or on by their clients," it said. "This is a basic difference between the Crotonites and, say, the Erthumoi, who also build robots. I've never seen one of the Erthuma variety, so I can't attack them directly. I'd just be willing to wager that the majority of them can't fly, and leave it at that."

"What is flying?" asked Slen. Neither Ph'anjan nor Grade-Two Robot responded.

"What is your idea, then?" asked the Ilonian.

"As we've discovered," said Grade-Two Robot, in a tone of voice one would use in lecturing an eager but somewhat blockheaded pupil, "the food sources on this planet—"

"Ph'arcan," said Ph'anjan. "That's the name of this planet."

"Yes, of course," said the robot.

"That's not what *we* call it," said Slen. "You've never even asked me what *we* call it."

Ph'anjan turned to Slen, releasing deep red bubbles. "Well, what in the name of God and Goddess *do* you call it?"

"We don't really call it anything," said Slen triumphantly. "If there were other worlds, perhaps we'd have to differentiate them all. But, as I pointed out earlier, none of us has ever seen evidence of another planet. Here is just . . . here."

Ph'anjan and Grade-Two Robot exchanged glances. "You were saying?" she said.

"Yes," said the robot. "I will grant that the Cephallonians are the greatest biochemists among the Six Races."

"Thank you," said Ph'anjan.

Grade-Two Robot merely paused. "And you've proven it by using nanotechnology to 'grow' a communicator, using a huge assortment of enzymes and other catalysts. Why, then, can't you use those enzymes to change the unsuitable amino acids in the local food sources to the amino acids you need to remain alive? Why didn't either of us think of this earlier?"

More deep red bubbles. "*One* of us did," said Ph'anjan. "The problem is that there are more enzymes than you can imagine, and here in the Communications Section of the *Ses'kol* I have only a small part of the ship's normal supply. If I'd been better equipped, I could have grown a much more efficient, powerful communicator. But each template for those better communicators always seemed to require something I didn't have. Just as I don't have the proper enzymes to alter cystine, sarcosine, lysine, and *d*-proline into glycine, tyrosine, leucine, and *l*-proline, among other nutrients."

Grade-Two Robot took a few seconds to process that information. It didn't really care if the Ilonian lived or died. It had merely tried to solve an intellectual problem. "What is that you're holding?" it asked.

Ph'anjan showed the strange carving to the robot. For some reason, she felt defensive about the object, ready to answer any critical comments Grade-Two Robot might offer.

It surprised her by saying nothing about the unrefined nature of the figure. "Oh," it said, "one of those."

"What is it?" asked Ph'anjan, streaming deep red bubbles. Ph'anjan was not a patient Cephallonian; perhaps that was in the nature of those from Ilon.

"Well, First among us," said Grade-Two Robot, "originally the Crotonites thought they were left behind by the extragalactics; but my creators have decided that's not the case. Yet there does appear to be some kind of link between those carvings and the extragalactics."

"Your creators have definitely decided then," said Ph'anjan, emitting mocking light orange bubbles, "that the builders of those vastly ancient cities, now ruins, came from another Galaxy? They couldn't have developed in our own?"

"At least as far as I've been informed," said the robot. "I find none of this interesting any longer." It went back to stand in its place.

"I have some questions," said Slen.

"I should hope you do," said Ph'anjan. "I'd be worried

if you didn't demand more information. Yet now is not the time."

Slen gave an angry flip of his tail. "It's never the time to answer my questions!"

Ph'anjan turned to face him directly. "Can't you understand? Unless I think of something, I will die in less than two more weeks. I have a great deal to do before then. If I find a way to survive, then I will gladly answer all your questions; but at the moment, they have a low priority."

Slen gave another angry tail flip, but said nothing.

Ph'anjan began debating with herself, aloud, in a quiet voice. She had many moral questions to consider, and she was running out of time, just as she'd told Slen. She wished that he, or even the Crotonite robot, was her equal when it came to philosophizing. Unfortunately, there wasn't anyone on this world that fit that description. Then, suddenly, she let go a string of deep green bubbles, showing her excitement. She still had the modular-neutrino communicator: she could consult with other Cephallonians!

Ignoring Slen for now—after all, although he was sentient and somewhat intelligent, it was clear to her that his race would never join the Six—she initiated a transmission to the same Cephallonian world that had declined to rescue her. This time she spoke with some female government official. She learned that her case had become famous, and was now the subject of much debate. The Cephallonians still weren't prepared to send a ship to fetch her, but the rightness or the wrongness of that decision was argued almost constantly.

"There is something we can do," said the female official, whose name was Ph'orza. "We can transmit to you the necessary templates to build a small interstellar craft. Our estimates indicate that if you begin immediately, you can have the ship finished, and make the journey here before you perish of starvation."

"I'm tremendously grateful for your help," said Ph'anjan. "The trouble is that I'm working with only a fraction of the *Ses'kol*'s supply of catalysts. Any templates would have to be carefully chosen not to include enzymes or catalysts I don't have.''

There was silence from Ph'orza. ''I had no idea your situation included limitations such as that,'' she said at last. ''It may be impossible—''

''Tell her about the carving,'' said Grade-Two Testing and Analysis Robot. ''Tell her it wasn't done by the extragalactics, but it's definitely a link to them.''

Ph'anjan turned and regarded the robot for a few seconds, then passed on the information. The only change she made was that she used the term ''Ancient Ones'' for what the Crotonite robot called extragalactics. There was still considerable speculation concerning the origin of the strange cities and structures that had been left behind by the vanished elder race. It was obvious that the Cephallonians preferred to think of that race as arising in the Milky Way Galaxy, and the Crotonites insisted that they hadn't.

''That's very interesting,'' said Ph'orza. ''Still—''

''Tell her that you have an important piece of information that you'll only reveal in person.''

''What information?'' asked Ph'anjan.

The robot paused. ''That although a great number of these carvings have been discovered—''

''It's the first one I know about,'' objected Ph'anjan.

The robot paused again. ''I can't be held responsible for the ignorance of the Ilonians, First among us,'' it said at last. ''Tell Ph'orza when you see her that although a great number of these carvings have been discovered by members of all Six Races, none has ever been found on a world that wasn't suitable to at least one.''

Ph'anjan emitted the blue bubbles of thoughtfulness. ''Do you mean, then—''

The robot's voice deepened. ''We don't have time to argue significance now. You're trying to get this Ph'orza fish to save your life.''

''We're not fish,'' said Ph'anjan calmly. She returned to her negotiations with Ph'orza. At last, the distant Cephallonian agreed to take down a long list of the catalysts Ph'anjan had to work with.

"I can't promise anything," said Ph'orza. "I'm not an engineer. There is so much interest in your plight, however, that perhaps someone on one of the Cephallonian worlds will design a small spacecraft specially for you. I will say this: if you have a Crotonite-made robot, we will not permit you to bring it here. We are trying to keep our culture pure of Crotonite influences."

"I don't want to go there, anyway," Ph'anjan told Grade-Two Robot. "I want to go back to Ilon."

"Ask Ph'orza for Ilon's coordinates," suggested the robot. "As part of the bargain."

"Then how will she see the carving?"

"Worry about that later. She doesn't have to see the carving. I'll bet they know quite a bit more about them than the Ilonians do. All Ph'orza needs to hear is the information I gave you."

With all due compliments and courtesies, Ph'anjan and Ph'orza concluded their transmission. Eleven hours later, recorders in the Communications Section began storing the templates that came from some Cephallonian world without a name that Ph'anjan recognized. And Cephallonians on other worlds had listened to Ph'anjan's transmissions; together, using simple mathematical techniques, they located her. They told her how to find Ilon from her present position. Everything seemed fine. It definitely looked like a happy ending in the near future.

It looked that way until Ph'anjan studied the templates before she began construction. There were more than two thousand templates, but only one concerned her. That one called for a complex manganese-based compound she could not build, but which occurred rarely in the life-forms of Ph'arcan. In fact, the manganese-based compound could be found in only one species, to Ph'anjan's knowledge: Slen's.

He saw the light gray bubbles that signified worry. "Trouble?" he asked. "It looks to me as if your nano tanks are working away just fine. You'll have your space-craft, and in enough time to get you back to Ilon alive."

Ph'anjan nodded her large head. "Yes," she said slowly. "And I have important information that needs to get back to Ilon with me."

"You mean that strange carving," said Slen. "I heard the robot say that it represented a link between the Six Races and what you call the Ancient Ones. Does that mean the Ancient Ones were our—I mean, your ancestors? Or that your Six Races are some sort of experiment? Why haven't more starfaring races developed? I have so many questions."

"I know," said Ph'anjan wearily. "I know. So do I." And she told him about the one template that demanded the manganese-based compound.

His reaction almost frightened her. He laughed. "I'd been hoping to go back to Ilon with you, but I was too afraid to ask," he said.

"You don't understand," she said, loosing the aqua-colored bubbles of great sorrow. "To get that compound, to build the section represented by that template, you'd have to die."

Slen laughed again. "I knew that. I'm not stupid, you know."

"Listen," she said. "Before you got into the nano tank, I could map your cells. All the species on this planet store their genetic information in a self-replicating molecule. It's not the same molecule that Cephallonians have, or the Erthumoi, or the Naxians; yet I could map that molecule and recreate it when I reached Ilon. You would be the parent of a line of your species that would swim the seas of Ilon forever."

"Ph'anjan," he said quietly, "I would be proud. Show me what to do."

Later, when all the templates had been used and all the finished parts had been assembled, Ph'anjan left the ocean world of Ph'arcan. It did not take her long to return to Ilon, even though she had to use conventional fusion engines to get her far enough from Ph'arcan to make the hyperjump across the Galaxy. Then she used the fusion engines again to approach Ilon. By that time, she was faint and weak, but her fellow Ilonians knew she was coming, and she would be well taken care of.

Grade-Two Robot performed most of the pilot's chores as the unnamed craft fell into orbit around Ilon. Ph'anjan was going into and coming out of increasing periods of delirium, and the watery atmosphere was filled with the light violet bubbles of confusion.

At one point, she wondered if Slen's race would prosper on Ilon. Her answer, either reasoned or dreamed, was that there was always a niche in the ecology for slightly dumb but good-looking creatures. Then, the next time she regained consciousness, she was surrounded by waters with a particular tang that she hadn't even known she'd missed.

—With thanks to Hal Clement
    for the chemistry lesson

EYEBALL VECTORS

HAL CLEMENT

THE BACKGROUND WAS DARK TO BOTH ERTHUMOI and Cephallonians fifty meters down. Habranha's sun, an M-type dwarf, had little of the blue and green light that might have penetrated that far, and here at The Cataract was usually hidden by clouds anyway. Frequent specks and threads of luminous plankton appeared in front of the travelers and fell quickly behind, but Janice had only one interest in these. Even the rare explosive ones were usually too small to be dangerous, but they did provide a little warning of Thrasher's maneuvers.

The Cephallonian was avoiding the larger plants with his usual grace, now swerving sharply one way or the other, now diving or rising as suddenly. He could trust most animals to dodge him. The carrier in which Janice rode, on the right side of his suit, was full of water to make it match the bulk and drag of the oxygen tanks on his left, so she was not being thrown around; but for the first time in years she was feeling motion sickness. If she couldn't have seen what was coming, it would have been much worse. Happily the vertical currents in particular were outlined most of the time by the glowing dots, lines, and patches of Habranha's more electric life forms.

She was not sure what nausea could do when one's body cavities and breathing passages were full of diving fluid, and she didn't want to find out. Eating took care enough, and vomiting might be really dangerous. The reflexes that normally let only gas into the human windpipe had had to be blocked to let her use the pressure-guarding liquid. No one had known how far down the Pupil Study Group's work might lead it into the little world's ocean, but someone had to be ready for a deep dive. It was merely funny that the someone had to be an Erthuma rather than a Cephallonian. The cetaceoids had personal limits of a few kilometers, and their technology had never produced anything like the pressure fluid.

Janice tried to keep her mind off the possibilities by conversation. This took much attention, since it had to be by code; human vocal cords don't work in liquid.

"Can you spot them yet, Thrash?" she keyed.

"Not certainly," replied the Cephallonian. He could speak normally, since there was water inside his suit as well as outside, and the translator could handle sounds in both water and air. "There's something which seems big enough ahead of us and, I think, at the surface, but I can't make it out clearly. Too many verticals and density variants around to distort the sound, and too much suspended, floating, and swimming junk besides. It does seem to have edge behavior like the raft, though; surface waves are damped as they approach it, if I'm interpreting correctly. That could be the deck."

Janice didn't want to hear about vertical currents. They were the main cause of her discomfort. An ocean should be quiet near the substellar point of a tide-locked planet, where only simple evaporation ought to be taking place, but Habranha had its own ideas about practically everything. Very little on this world was simple.

She and her husband had learned this the hard way earlier, in the Sclera section near the edge of the dark hemisphere. The ice there was water, relatively pure except for trapped silicate dust. Ammonia stayed mostly in liquid solution at that low temperature; near the dark rim, an Erthuma could breathe the air without too much discomfort—for a while, as it also contained traces of hydrogen cyanide. The planet, however, was largely ice, like Titan or Triton in the Solarian system; and since it was

close enough to its small sun for the ice to melt on one
hemisphere, there was a very deep ocean made principally
of water but holding much dissolved ammonia and suspended solids such as silicate grains, various phases of
water ice, and an enormous variety of biological material.
Warm water could not be depended upon to rise, or cold
to sink; ammonia and other content could rule otherwise.
An iceberg might be carried up or down in a density current and change phase as it reached a pressure boundary,
either abruptly or at some unpredictable later time when
it finally yielded to internal stresses, shattering to fragments or to dust and releasing or absorbing enough heat
to invalidate the most detailed calculations. The weird behavior in the ocean was reflected in the overlying atmosphere; native Habranhan meteorologists were far more
skillful than the visiting aliens who were sometimes arrogant enough to try to teach them their own art. They still,
however, had poorer prediction scores than did those
aliens on their own worlds. Hence the arrogance.

Far from the ice hemisphere, past The Iris, the ring-
shaped floating continent of merged icebergs, and on to
the center of The Pupil, the ice-free sunward ocean, it
seemed as though things should be simpler. They weren't.
Janice Cedar, her husband Hugh, and the two Cephallonians who formed with them the Pupil Study Group knew
now they were all in trouble, though they had not yet
accepted that they were doomed.

"How far?" she asked. Some seconds passed before
Thrasher's voice came from the translator. "I can't be
sure. If it's really the raft, then I'd say about twenty kilometers. I can't get any of my own echoes, though. All
I'm spotting seems to be wave sounds from the source,
so distance is guesswork. That's why I think it's at the
surface, and can hope it's what we want. Why don't you
try calling? Your low-frequency stuff gets through better,
and an answer would give us travel time. Hugh'll be listening, I expect."

If he weren't, the woman thought, it wouldn't matter;

The Box will be. And I hope it isn't really twenty kilometers; the tracker says it should be seventeen point seven one, and even this turbulence shouldn't have thrown it that badly off. She switched to her outside transducer and tapped out a here-we-are. The Box's response, at Thrasher's distance guess, should take about fifty-five seconds but one would have to allow a bit more for human reaction and decision time if Hugh were involved.

After a minute and a half, the cetaceoid voiced the more pessimistic interpretation. "Not the right target, I guess. I hope you're not getting worried."

"Should I be?"

"Well, frankly, if that's not the raft, I have no idea which way we should be going. I suppose we can trust your tracker? It *said* we should head this way when we came back up—or at least you told me it did when I got my senses back. You seemed pretty sure of it. That was as rough a dive as I've ever made, though, and even this leg of the swim has been pretty snaky."

"It isn't a planetary range instrument, but it should be good within a few centimeters in what we've logged so far. The raft should be just under eighteen kilos, in the direction we're heading right now—or were half a second ago." Thrasher had swerved again to avoid a larger than usual patch of luminous weed. It took him several seconds more to come up with an answer. He might have been concerned with the weed, a type that was normally highly charged, or with something entirely different.

"Then why no response to your call?"

"Hugh and The Box could both be busy, and Splasher probably wouldn't have heard it even if she's there. She could be away for any of a hundred reasons."

"But you're not worried?"

Janice repeated her evasive counter. "Should I be?"

"Well, I'm getting a little tired. Fighting turbulence is work. It's lucky the downs are denser so our buoyancy helps, and the ups less dense with the same result."

"That's not luck. It's laws of physics."

"I know. But isn't it lucky the laws are on our side?" The woman might have answered this if she had had the use of her voice, since several responses occurred to her at once. However, spelling out philosophy via code key seemed hardly worth the trouble. The Cephallonian paused only briefly for an answer, and gossiped on. "Can't you imagine what these verticals would be like in decent gravity?"

Janice could, but didn't want to. Decent gravity for either of them was roughly five times that at Habranha's surface, and convection currents are driven by gravity as well as density difference. Also, she *was* getting just a little worried. If Thrasher were actually tired, they could really be in trouble, something more immediate than the basic problem of the whole group. Swimming even two or three kilometers alone would take her hours, and the thought of towing her huge companion would have been funny if it weren't so grim. She was of fairly standard Erthuma-female proportions, a hundred and fifty-four centimeters standing height by forty-five kilograms of mass. Thrasher, while much better streamlined hydrodynamically, had over ten times her mass, and even adjusted to neutral or slightly positive buoyancy would have represented a hopeless task for towing.

Deserting him never occurred to her.

Her own buoyancy was set slightly positive, of course. Her companion's should be even more so now that a lot of his oxygen must have been used. Habranha's partial pressure of the gas was high by Erthuma standards, allowing Hugh and Janice to make do with filters when out of water, but not by Cephallonian ones, though the swimmers could survive at low activity without extra supplies.

She and Thrasher would float, and could therefore breathe, if their strength gave out. Maybe Splasher would find them eventually, but maybe she wouldn't, and away from the raft there was the problem of food. Worrying, of course, was never much use, but planning might be in order.

Her suit would supply her for a while, but it wasn't a real full-recycling exploration unit. Thrasher had only the stored food and oxygen he had brought along, and with his size and metabolism those would go quickly. Neither could eat the local life, not even the sort that used DNA and ATP, and neither was carrying the fermenting units which could turn Habranhan biomass of that kind into edible "cheese." There were four of these back on the raft, two for human and two for Cephallonian use, but none was small enough for even Thrasher to tow conveniently.

So they had to get back to the raft reasonably soon, and their only guide was her tracker. The target Thrasher was hearing had better be the raft, and its failure to respond and the distance discrepancy had better not mean trouble there. Of course, her companion had felt unsure of his distance estimate, she reminded herself; but why the silence?

She keyed out another signal and, a kilometer or so farther on, still another. Thrasher said nothing at either lack of response, but was swimming more slowly. This was a comfort in one way, as her stomach quieted down, but not in the other. How long could the old whale last?

There is *no* point in worrying, Janice told herself firmly. We can float for days. Maybe we'd better surface now, and just wait. Of course, the surface will be rougher still, and the motions a lot less predictable, but let's not think of that; we're facing a practical problem. Splasher is bound to come looking, but of course she won't have tracking data, and when we started the test dive The Box had a clear image for only a couple of kilometers' radius. We left the raft straight downward, with no idea of what lateral currents we might meet. She'd have to make a full circle search starting from the raft, and she couldn't assume we'd have been able to surface. She'd have a hemisphere, not a circle, to explore.

Not so good. We'd better keep going. The closer we are when Thrasher gives out, the smaller the search volume will be, at least.

That is, of course, if we *are* getting closer.

"It keeps sounding more and more like the raft," her friend remarked at this point.

"Can you make it?" she keyed.

"Eventually. I wonder why they haven't answered you?"

The Erthuma still had no explanation to offer, but took the query as a hint to try again. She was getting just a little uneasy about this; each lack of answer made it that much harder not to worry. She had just touched the keypad when Hugh's voice came through the transducer.

"Hi, there. How deep did you get? Any problems?"

Again his loving wife found the code frustrating. There were *so* many ways she'd have loved to reply to that one—

She settled for "Any trouble there? You didn't answer the here-we-are." She couldn't even underline the *there*. Her husband could have read a lot from her voice, but she didn't have a voice. Now the darling idiot was assuming that the dive had been uneventful, since she hadn't answered his question.

"Sorry. We've been busy. The Box has been making more sense out of its echo data, and has a practically real-time chart of the currents for nearly thirty kilometers horizontally and over three down. They're really something, aren't they? We spotted you ten minutes ago, once The Box was able to allow for all the refraction and scattering of sound, and it could tell you were on the way back, but we weren't in time to see you at depth. How far down did you get? Any useful material? *Can* we ever get out of here?"

"Of course you weren't listening, since you could see us."

"That's right." Hugh suddenly seemed to sense a touch

of emotion even in the code buzzes. "You *are* all right, aren't you?"

"Thrasher's wearing out. Deep currents even worse. He got more determined to go on the worse they got. I had to use The Order."

"You didn't tell me that!" the Cephallonian cut in.

"I was afraid to after you woke up. I thought you'd have guessed. How's your memory?"

"Well . . ." The translator paused. "I see. Yes, I should have figured that out. Was I really bad?"

A simple yes seemed easier than "You were starting to talk to the currents as though they were personal enemies, we were half a kilo deeper than we had planned for the test limit, and you were swearing by something that wouldn't translate that you weren't going to be thwarted and frustrated by something that wouldn't translate either," so yes was all Janice keyed.

"Splasher says she bets he's starving," Hugh cut in.

Thrasher also limited himself to a simple yes, more because the response delay was still nearly forty seconds than because he couldn't have expressed himself more forcibly.

"She's on the way with food, or will be by the time this gets to you. The Box will guide her; she can't hear you yet herself. Better hold off reporting until she's close enough not to need help. Relax if you feel like it."

"We'll surface," Thrasher returned. "It'll be easier to eat with the suit open."

"I didn't think." The man's voice, clearly contrite, partly overlapped the swimmer's. "I let her go off with no human food. Do you need any, Jan? Surely you're not out."

"All right here. Don't worry." She was rather hungry, now that she thought of it and they had stopped charging through verticals, but there was a good supply of the tape-like recycled stuff in her processor. She worked the control that began delivering the strip to her mouth, and bit off a few lengths. It was fibrous and hard to chew by design, and by the time she had dealt with it satisfactorily Splasher and her companion were able to talk directly to each other. Practically unburdened except by her environment suit and its oxygen tanks, the female Cephallonian had an impressive turn of speed.

"I can't get echoes from you yet, but I can hear your voice. Keep talking, sweetfish."

"Sure. We're going up so I can open up and eat properly. I hope you brought more than concentrate. I'm starved . . ." Thrasher kept talking as ordered, but it became mere babble to Janice.

"Sorry, I wanted to travel fast. There'll be a real feast back at the raft, if you can still stand cheese. You'd have trouble enjoying it now, anyway; it's been stormy as ever with at least a dozen spouts since you dived, and it's just as rough now, so don't be too casual about opening your hood away from the raft. I think I can get your echo now."

"Likely. I'm spotting yours, and mine should be stronger with the equipment and Janice. We're only ten meters down now—you're right, the waves are still—" The translator gave its burping sign for no-symbol-equivalent, which did not surprise Janice; any Cephallonian language has more words for wave conditions than clothing stylists have for colors. As far as she was concerned, the appropriate word was "terrible"; even at ten meters she was starting to feel the surface roughness. Maybe she shouldn't have eaten, after all. She knew what the top was like; she had lived enough of it in the last few days. In theory, wind had a long reach—hundreds of kilometers from The Iris, which bore the Habranhan cities and farms, to cloudy Cataract in the strong evaporation zone under the sun. Waves should reasonably have been long and regular. Coriolis effects had to be negligible; not only were they practically at the little world's equator, but its rotation period was over three weeks.

Even here, however, chaos reigned. A patch of ocean would grow just slightly warmer than its surroundings, either from sunlight or from biological effects. Ammonia would become correspondingly less soluble and escape into the atmosphere, which would drop accordingly in density and start a strong updraft. The water would of course grow denser and settle. Wind and surface flows would race toward the spot with essentially no inertial deflection until the final moments and even then in an unpredictable direction. There might be a waterspout, a whirlpool, or both; neighboring spouts or eddies might attract or repel each other; whatever happened, no wind or waves got very far undisturbed in this region. Regularity in either was unknown. Farther away from the evaporation center, of course, there *was* an effective long reach. Long, high waves *did* build up across The Pupil, focusing on The Cataract, and found their way into the chaotic mass of rocking, swirling local storm centers where even the winged Habras didn't try to fly. Once there, though, they merely complicated the local chop.

Janice began to doubt that the surface was for her. Not just now. Not just in a suit, or even riding the massive Thrasher. The raft was bad enough.

She tried valiantly to concentrate on the Cephallonians' conversation, but with less and less success as they neared the heaving surface.

She shouldn't have thought of that participle.

"Thrasher," she buzzed, "I'll have to go back down. I can't take the motion—I'll explain why later, or you can ask Hugh. I'll be swimming toward the raft; you two can catch me when you've eaten." Without waiting for an answer she opened the carrier in which she had been riding, emerged, and headed downward. It was rather hard work, but not impossible. The temptation to reduce buoyancy was easy to resist when one knew that the darkness extended five hundred kilometers that way before anything except perhaps a wandering iceberg on the verge of explosive shattering would stop a sinking body. She had no intention of sleeping, and expected no accidents that might knock her out, but common sense insisted on positive lift.

Waves or no waves, she would be easier to find and possible to reach on the surface.

She keyed a brief message to Hugh, telling her plans.

"Why?" came his reasonable question. "Thrasher can bring you here in a few minutes."

"Surface rough. Stomach."

"Oh. All right. The Box will keep track of you, and I'll have the two pick you up when Thrasher's eaten. I hope—" He fell silent.

"What?" There was still a long wait for his answer.

"The raft isn't exactly steady, either. Maybe when you get here you'd better get rid of the diving juice and let me take over the deep work. I don't get queasy."

"We'll see." Janice had no intention of giving up what promised to be the interesting part of the trip, but arguing by code was far too much nuisance.

Having Hugh come with her into the depths, as he had before during the Sclera investigation, would of course be different. In fact, it seemed a very good idea, and there was enough reserve diving fluid to allow it. Maybe the need for a surface monitor could be ducked somehow. If not, however, Janice Wind Cedar would not be filling *that* job. It would be her beloved husband Hugh who stayed on deck watching instruments, regardless of how protective he might feel.

She was still firmly of this opinion, tired as she was getting, when the Cephallonians caught up with her. She resumed her place in Thrasher's carrier without comment, and in half an hour they were at the raft.

This was simply a resting tank for the swimmers and support deck for equipment. A large framework outlined a volume of water shallow enough so that they could keep their blow-slits near the surface and breathe occasionally with minimum effort. Some sort of streamlining was achieved by covering the sides with polymer sheeting. From below the surface, the main body of the structure looked a little like a canoe submerged to the gunwales and with the open stern cut off flat. Decks of stiffer polymer formed the tank's bottom and a rim some five meters wide all around at the waterline. A low shelter stood on this for the convenience of the Erthumoi. Between this cabin and the nearest edge of the tank was a roughly cubical structure some three-quarters of a meter on each edge; why this was called The Box was obvious. Near this was a compressor and filter system to charge oxygen tanks, and inside the resting place near it, mostly under water, a rack of high-pressure gas cylinders. Half a dozen smaller structures, sheltered like The Box from rain and spray, were scattered around the edge of the tank, accessible to both Erthumoi and Cephallonians, to house the research equipment and fermenters.

Floats of polymer foam were attached at scores of seemingly random points all over the structure—under the deck, at its edges, and around and under the tank. No one of these was highly buoyant, since the designers did not want wind to have much of a grip on the craft, but there were enough of them to satisfy the firmest believer in the value of redundance. A dozen hydro-jets were mounted on as many of the floats, allowing the whole unit to be maneuvered rather clumsily. No one had studied the currents closely enough to foresee the need for more. The winged Habranhans had reported that the aerial storms in The Cataract were violent, but no one seemed to know much about the sea.

Someone *had* made a casual estimate of centripetal currents based on calculated evaporation rates, and powered the raft to move at twice their speed. This was why the Pupil Study Group was in trouble. Evaporation had been calculated simply from cloud observations made from space. No one had computed the amount of ocean that sank from ammonia loss and thus created more inbound current. In fact, the surface flow toward the planet's sunward pole reached a speed much greater than the raft's thrusters could override. None of the four living explorers had paid enough attention to the trackers to notice this on the inward trip, and no one had told The Box to watch out for such matters. Winds feeding into the same zone reached speeds five or six times as great as the ocean currents, resulting in spectacular waves; but the raft had very little structure above the surface and no one had really worried about air motion until they reached the really chaotic region almost under the sun.

One does not use or even carry radio transmitters on Habranha, since they interfere with native speech. There was no neutrino set on the raft, so they could reach nothing off the surface. It was wildly unlikely that they could be spotted optically from orbit against a stormy ocean background even if The Cataract's cloud cover should happen to open briefly, and even more unlikely that a flying native would pass anywhere near. Habranhan researchers concentrated on the Sclera region, the low-sun rim of their small world, where grew the icebergs making up for the ever-melting warm edge of The Iris. The stormy hot pole was not only a dangerous flying area, but promised little useful knowledge. The net result was four explorers entirely on their own.

Hugh was summarizing. His wife would have been better at it, but code was too slow.

"As far as food goes, the fermenters will keep us alive indefinitely, or until we let something into them that poisons their pseudolife. Statistically, somewhere between a hundred hours and old age. We Erthumoi have partial recycling units in our suits which would take a thousand hours or so to run down if we lived on nothing else. You swimmers don't have any recycling, and need the fusers to concentrate oxygen for you, so there's a limit to the power we can commit to getting out of here."

"We can't get the raft out. We know that already," Splasher pointed out, "and without the raft we can't carry the fermenters. If we try to build something smaller, it's an all-or-nothing project."

Janice made a negative gesture, and the others paused to listen to her code.

"*One* can go for help."

Hugh pursed his lips thoughtfully.

"I suppose so. Thrasher or Splasher couldn't swim all the way with supplies they can carry, though, and you or I would have to use some sort of jerried boat, either surface or sub. I suppose if we mounted several jets on something small enough it might make it. Would it be better to ride the surface and keep the oxygen problem down, or stay below and use diving juice? And if it doesn't work, what happens? One person at some unknown spot on or in the ocean, out of touch with both the raft here and the rest of the world, lost or out of power or both?"

"The Job." The woman's code remark was terse but adequate. She paused a moment, then added, "Submerged. Navigation."

"You mean it'll be easier to hold heading below storm level? I suppose that's right, though from what you and Thrasher say about the test dive it's pretty turbulent down below, too."

"Low speed."

Hugh was silent for some time. He knew his wife was slanting the arguments in favor of letting her make the trip. He'd have done the same if he'd been quick-witted enough, he realized; he couldn't blame her. He still didn't like the idea, though. He was not particularly protective as husbands went, but knew her tendency to overdemonstrate her already obvious competence, and even after four years of marriage couldn't help worrying just a little when they were apart. He curbed his thoughts firmly after a minute or so, since all three of the others were clearly waiting for him to speak.

"All right. We'll have to do some designing and building, though, and we don't have much of a machine shop with us."

"Basics," keyed Janice.

"I know. The inclined plane. We have a knife apiece, and there are a lot of nuts and bolts in the thruster mounts. We'll have to scrounge material from what's around us, though, and make sure it's chemically stable."

"You dry land and flying types have a violent idea of what makes the basic tool," Thrasher remarked. "Every one of you seems to regard the cutting edge as primary."

"Well, what would you offer, and did you bring it along?" asked Hugh.

"The rope, of course. Yes, we have several kilometers of high-tensile cord, though it's so thin we may have to pad it to keep it from cutting through other material. That's the real fundamental. Support for the helpless, towing burdens, nets and nooses for capturing food—the fiber started civilization, with glue and the lens next."

Hugh was about to respond when Janice and Splasher interrupted together in almost identical phrases, though translator and coder didn't sound much alike. "Design now. Philosophy later." The males looked at each other, read what each was sure must be sympathy in the other's expression, and got back to the real subject.

"How many thrusters should we risk? Will two be enough?"

"I'd advise more," replied the Cephallonian. "There's a time question, and while Janice apparently can't travel very fast through turbulence, power is still relevant. It may be well to have drive force in reserve even if she doesn't want to use all of it."

"All right. You two look over the local seaweed supply. I hope you know what's explosive by sight; with pieces the size we'll need, finding out the hard way is risky."

"We know what furnishes safe cordage—which might be wise to use instead of our own reserves, when we can. Thicker samples of the same growths should make adequate frame members. We won't need too much if the rider is to be an Erthuma. Let's go collecting, Splasher."

The seaweed that the swimmers selected was extremely tough and springy, but the knives of the human workers were able to deal with it. As much as possible was done aboard the raft, since a knife dropped over the abyss would be hard to retrieve. The Cephallonians *might* recover it before reaching their depth limit, but there were already enough problems. More of the high-tech cord was used than the swimmers had wanted, since the natural material they had hoped to employ was inconveniently thick when strong enough. In any case, the skeleton submarine produced in twenty hours or so of labor seemed sturdy enough. It was an open framework like those of the natives, partly to save time and material, partly to help the pilot's visibility. Four of the thruster-fuser units were lashed securely to it slightly ahead of what the group hoped would turn out to be its center of drag pressure. The hull diameter held opposite members of the thruster pairs nearly two meters apart; there had been some argument about making the craft so large, but the thought of having to lie prone for the whole trip was not merely unpleasant. Janice knew she would sometimes need to move around and her husband agreed that this was not just a whim.

Lines of Cephallonian cord were gathered at a "panel" in front of the pilot station and led to the thrusters, where they were wrapped around the control potentiometers a dozen times to provide friction and let the pilot handle all four from one point.

She would have to rely mostly on her own recycling equipment for food, and hope to reach the ring continent before it zeroed. Taking one of the fermenters along would have required an even larger craft, more thrusters, and divided attention for the pilot—selecting the right vegetation to feed the device was time-consuming.

Hugh found no adequate excuse for changing the female pronoun of the pilot up to launch time, and unhappily watched his wife disappear into the depths. "If something goes wrong," he called after her, "just shut off the power and call for us. We put enough floats into that thing so the thrusters won't sink it!"

"In the right places, I hope," muttered Splasher.

Janice did call, very quickly. She was back in ten minutes, towed by the swimmers, and for once did not allow herself to be gagged by the code equipment.

"It's lucky we spaced the drivers equally around this thing," she keyed, "and if we do get back, let's not report this whole episode in detail. I could only steer by changing thrust. The jets were far enough apart to have fair torque, but it was too awkward to manage for more than a few minutes. We'd better install some kind of rudders, lateral and vertical."

Her husband raised his eyebrows. "A thought. It didn't occur to me, either, I admit."

"I took for granted you planned to steer that way," said Splasher. "I thought of suggesting we mount them so they could be swiveled, but decided the control system would be too hard to rig and doubted that we could attach them firmly enough under such conditions. I agree about rudders."

Making control surfaces was a fairly quick job: frames were easy, sheeting was cannibalized from the raft, and while the Cephallonians did not regard adhesive as quite so fundamental as rope, they did have plenty in their basic kits. More time was required to rig an additional system of control lines that Hugh could hope would neither tangle nor kink; and he was more uneasy than before when he saw the skeleton hull slide off once more into the weedy darkness, though his wife had spent some minutes in test maneuvers this time before actually starting.

The moment she was out of sight he made his way to The Box. The artificial intelligence was still producing an almost real-time hologram of the surrounding ocean, a picture growing slowly in size and shrinking in scale as more and more sense was made of the chaotic ocean currents. The model depth, Hugh saw, was now nearly five kilometers at the center, the radius over forty. The image of Janice's craft showed clearly enough, and her husband cringed. Unlike The Box and the Cephallonians she had no sonar, and could not detect vertical currents until she was close enough to see the bits of luminous plankton whose motion would sometimes reveal them. After a few moments of watching, Hugh realized that she had accepted this; she wasn't trying to dodge but merely maintain depth, correcting the brief up or down accelerations as they came. Her attention must have been mostly on her inertial tracker, the man judged; he hoped she was sparing a little for really large explosive plants.

He resisted the urge to call warnings as she nosed toward the bigger verticals. The Box could have produced sounds audible to her transducer easily enough, but she was already far enough away for signal delay to make warnings useless. She'd just have to take the jolts.

Which meant she'd better not eat for—how long? He hadn't thought of that in detail. If Janice had, she hadn't mentioned it. And she *had* eaten before departure—stuffed herself as full as she could to give her recycler as long a run as possible! And she was out there, soaked with diving fluid, with a stomach sensitive to motion, no real way to dodge those awful up-and-down currents, and no reflexes to keep vomit out of her trachea if she lost control!

"Jan! Come back! You can't make it through those currents! We should have thought!"

Dragging seconds passed before the code came back— long enough to make him wonder whether she had failed to hear or was actually ignoring him, and tempt him to call out again.

"I did think. It's all right. I'm driving."

He didn't get her point. "But Jan! How—?" he fell silent, not knowing what to say, but realizing his wife was not going to be argued out of *her* mission. Even before the partial sentence could have reached her, another message arrived. "Please don't worry, dear. I know what I'm doing."

Hugh always wondered, but never asked, whether the attention she had given to the second message had anything to do with what followed. He couldn't see how, even after they finally figured out the cause, but there might have been something—

Usually her code calls were extremely terse; this time she had used extra words, and therefore extra time. The coder must have distracted her, at least a little. He never asked, because he knew she'd never tell.

The Box could spot currents, but there must have been something else. The submarine's image nosed into an unusually complex set of vertical patterns, and suddenly Hugh realized that it was no longer countering them but following, going down with the descending ones, rising with the ascending. For some reason Janice seemed no longer trying to maintain depth. Had she lost her tracker? Unlikely; it was part of her suit, and she was holding direction well enough.

Explosive plant? The Box would have seen, heard, and presumably reported. An electrical encounter? Probable enough, but what could that have done? The submarine frame was of wood, which on Habranha did not necessarily or even probably mean a nonconductor, but her armor should be protection from any charge source they had seen or heard of so far.

The Box had been making no speed readings on the image. Hugh had asked it to supply an enlarged view of the region around the craft but given no instructions about scale, so he could not tell how fast the machine was going, and there were of course limits to the resolving power of sonar that even The Box could not overcome. There was no way for it to show him the smaller plankton, and even large seaweed masses and animals were merely featureless dots in the hologram.

But dots motionless with respect to each other were probably seaweed, and they were drifting past Janice's vessel surprisingly quickly . . .

"Box! Doppler the sub!"

Since The Box had merely been correcting for doppler without displaying it, the visible response was immediate.

"She shouldn't be going that fast! All four thrusters must be wide open! Jan! Jan! What's wrong? Are you all right?"

There was no immediate answer, but Hugh was not

completely out of his mind. He could still allow for message delay.

Code finally sounded from The Box's relay unit.

"Thrust control. Shaking loose. May abandon. Watch."

With clenched fists and bitten lips, Hugh watched. He called the Cephallonians, and The Box without instructions set up a larger display in their tank so that they could see as well, but no more was said for the moment. Instructions were useless; Janice would know what she was doing, what she had to do, and when it had to be done seconds before any of the others could tell. It would be nice to know what had gone wrong with the drivers, but asking her now would be somewhere between futile and dangerous.

They watched while the eight-meter-long framework drove into an upwelling current of nearly four meters a second at roughly three times that speed. The display showed a small object separate from the submarine and sink for twelve or fifteen meters, halt with a jerk with respect to the craft and remain matched to its vertical speed. Hugh sighed in relief, but ground out some words between his teeth.

"For sense's sake, dear idiot, *positive* buoyancy!"

Thrasher was almost as upset, but spoke more sensibly. "I don't think that's Jan, Hugh. More likely one of the thrusters, judging by weight, held by part of the original lashing somewhere ahead of the center of buoyancy. Look at the sub!"

The framework was nosing downward, and starting to move in the same direction.

"Cut it loose, Jan!" cried one of the Cephallonians. "You'll never get the bow up with that thing hanging from it!"

Even Hugh realized that his wife's weight could never have produced that much effect, tricky as the sub's balance had proved to be and regardless of any buoyancy she might have adjusted in her suit, and decided the swimmers were probably right. This did little to make him feel better, however.

The Cephallonians were loading oxygen tanks; they hardly ever removed their suits—the ammonia of Habranna's ocean irritated their skins. Even here at the warm pole, where the stuff was least soluble and occurred mostly in the air, forcing their Erthumoi companions to wear breathing masks even out of the water, the swimmers needed protection. Near the Solid Ocean, as the natives called the darkside glacier, where Erthumoi could breathe unprotected for minutes with little discomfort if they were careful about hyperventilation on the extra oxygen, Cephallonians found the water much worse. Now, therefore, they were ready for the rescue in moments. There was no need for talk; they knew The Box would guide them and provide information updates, and they didn't need requests or instructions from Hugh. They plunged into the waves from the open stern of their tank, and the Erthuma watched their departing images in The Box's main display.

If that dangling object were a loose thruster and not Janice herself, why didn't she cut it loose? With the sub now traveling downward, why didn't she cut *herself* loose if that were her own image or get out if it weren't? Clearly the craft was out of control. Granted it represented a lot of work and, for the group, some irreplaceable equipment, but Janice wasn't *stupid*. As long as she were conscious— if she were—

Hugh Cedar clenched his fists and watched the special display even more closely, wondering whether the swimmers would reach the foundering sub before it got below The Box's range of clear perception. He cursed luridly every few seconds as the artificial mind changed its electronic opinion and modified shape or position of some part of the picture to fit new data. He could have argued with it, since the Cephallonians were too far away to be bothered by his treating a machine as a fellow being, but no number of words would have been any improvement in detail on the image, and would certainly have been far slower.

Why was she staying with the sub? Had something knocked her out? Had motion sickness overcome her, and parts of that huge last meal blocked her air passage? Was she still inside the vessel, or was that, in spite of logic, her armor hanging meters below it? He kept reminding himself firmly that she *should* float; even if the suit leaked diving fluid, any freed volume would be replaced from emergency oxygen tanks and the overall density reduced. The dangling blob *must* be a loose thruster, as Thrasher had insisted.

But why wasn't she doing something about it? And when were those jellyfish going to get to her? He spoke to The Box for the first time in minutes.

"How far do they have to go, and what's the closing rate?"

"Six point seven one kilometers equivalent distance. I am guiding them on a path which allows for all current deflections. They should reach the sub in just over eight minutes, which I assume is what you really wanted to know. The meeting should occur well above the depth limit of the Cephallonians, so you need not worry."

"I hadn't thought of worrying about that. Thanks. Just how sure are you whether that hanging thing is a thruster as Thrasher said, or Jan herself?"

"It is much too dense to be human armor, even occupied. That interpretation had not occurred to me. If I had known you were concerned—"

"Then she's still inside the sub?"

"I would certainly have observed her separation."

"Then what's the silly darling doing? Why is she heading down? I know she can take any pressure this world can give, loaded up with diving fluid, but a few more kilometers and she'll be out of reach of any possible help!"

"Are you being rhetorical, or do you want me to ask her?"

Hugh hesitated only an instant. "Rhetorical, I guess. She could be busy enough for interruption to be dangerous. She must know we're watching and worrying, and will report when she can—if she can . . .'' His voice trailed off.

"You are quite sure?"

"No, not quite, dammit." Hugh pursed his lips grimly. "But with Thrasher and Splasher on the way, that's how I'm going to have to play it. Give me all the resolution you can in your images, and all the sense you can make out of any conversation you hear."

"Of course."

"And if I jump off the raft and start swimming toward them, tell me I'm an idiot."

"Why? You will know it already. I will merely direct you back here, as soon as you are far enough away to need it."

"Then I'll go the other way."

"I know."

That silenced Hugh, whose attention had never really wandered from the display. The swimmers were closing in on their target, now, and visible in the special display. The Box had deleted the vertical current symbols to clear the view for the Erthuma, but there was still a good deal of ambiguity that it kept resolving now one way and now another as the weight of incoming evidence, in the form of sound waves of varying frequency and phase, kept shifting.

The electronic intelligence seemed sure that the dangling object was a driver rather than a human form; it had said so. Hugh's mind recognized the weight of the evidence, but even though he was adult and a scientist his mind wasn't in full control. Not until he saw the two swimmers close in on the sub without paying attention to what was hanging from it did he relax slightly. At that range the Cephallonians could easily tell either by sight or sonar what the suspended object was, and if they were concentrating on the craft—

Abruptly the man felt as though his own breathing system were full of diving fluid. Both swimmers suddenly swerved downward toward the suspended object, and their blurred images merged with it and each other. For long, long seconds no change could be seen; then both The Box and through it the Erthuma could tell that the Cephallonians were rising and the submarine once more nosing upward toward a horizontal attitude.

"They've asked for guidance back here," the artificial intelligence reported in its usual calm tone.

"What happened?"

"Janice doesn't know. Something caused all four thrusters to build up to full power almost simultaneously, and the bottom one tore free from most of its lashings. Its weight and the unbalanced push of the top one before she could shut it down caused the sub to nose downward. The hanging thruster had broken its control cable before she could shut it off too, so it was still operating, also pointing down."

"Why didn't she cut it loose?"

"I will ask. I would guess she didn't want to lose the unit, and felt she could pull it back within reach by the lines still holding it. She was in no obvious danger; she is equipped to survive at the full depth of this ocean."

"Except that the power units were not responding to control."

"She did manage to shut the three off. No doubt though, that is why the Cephallonians think she should return. There was argument, though I could not hear all of it."

"At least Jan's all right."

"It seems so. I expect her main trouble will be annoyance, if she has not been able to decide why the thrust units went out of control."

"You have no idea?"

"None. They worked perfectly driving the raft, and I can see no reason why a change in mount should make a difference. Intake and discharge areas were clear on the submarine, if anything clearer than on the raft. The thrusters and fusers are complete units. Nothing like intake filters, ion dischargers, or electrolyzers are separate, so nothing could have been omitted inadvertently during transfer.''

"Since none of us is a mechanic, that's just as well. I guess you're right, then. If Jan hasn't figured it out by then, she'll be highly incensed when she gets here. D'you mind if I arrange for her to take it out on you?''

"I don't mind, but doubt that you'll fool her that easily.''

"So do I,'' Hugh answered gloomily.

But if Janice were angry, she hid it well. She had no explanation for the misbehavior of the drivers, though she felt normal scientific curiosity about the matter. She would also have liked on purely practical grounds to be able to use them in saving the lives of the group. However, she was a rational person, and having accepted that they were not trustworthy she had already dismissed them from consideration. She was still as concerned as the rest over what should be done next, and her remarks focused on this.

They were all feeling increasingly that while time was not exactly standing over them with a poised axe, it was in the front row of seats with a guess-where-I-put-my-money smile on its face.

"I hate to say it,'' Janice keyed as she reboarded the raft, "but I'm afraid the juice had better go back in the tank. No more diving, little more project. We need to get our present information home, not to mention ourselves. Then we can carry on with better-planned equipment.''

Her husband certainly did not object, and they set to work. Getting the last of the chemical out of her system took time and care, and several hours of therapy were needed to restore Janice's damped-out reflexes. Both of them were now experienced at this, however, and the Cephallonians could continue some project work in the meantime.

Janice marked the completion of the therapy by a couple of hours of acute seasickness; the nausea she had been firmly holding back for over two weeks ran wild, probably with some aid from her imagination. Then, with firsthand assurance that her antichoking reflexes were working as they should, both Erthumoi were able to turn their minds back to the survival problem.

"Box, why couldn't Thrasher or Splasher swim back to the continent if we made a small raft for one of their fermenters? Couldn't they maintain an average speed higher than the incoming current?" Janice asked, rejoicing in her voice. This had been suggested before, but not with the tow detail.

"Not even with the most efficiently streamlined raft we could make," replied The Box unequivocally. "Food would not be the limit. They would run out of oxygen much more quickly. The air here is less breathable for them than for Erthumoi, power is needed to separate oxygen for their suits, and you have said that we can't rely on the power units."

"We *have* been relying on them for that," Hugh pointed out.

"Only here on the raft. We don't know why they didn't work *away* from the raft," his wife insisted. "The Cephs couldn't possibly carry tanks enough for the trip even if we had enough or could make them. They'd need separating equipment and pumps—power. We can't take that chance. *They* were able to pull *me* out of trouble when it happened only a few kilos away, but who rescues one of them a quarter of the way to The Iris?"

"We expect to take chances." Thrasher considered his professional conscience as good as that of Janice.

"Reasonable chances only. If the rescue effort fails, we all die, the rescuer in some possibly interesting fashion and the rest starving while we wait and wonder. We already know the fusers are unreliable in travel, even if we don't know why. If someone does figure that out, it's a new game; but until that happens we count them out." Janice was firm, and Thrasher, who had not been really enthusiastic about towing a raft of equipment and food, said no more. His wife, however, cut in rather pointedly.

"Where is all this leading? Someone has to take a chance, and no one has suggested any way of getting out, except swimming, which doesn't use power units. I assume you're not suggesting that you Erthumoi swim for it—or row. You'd make no headway against even the current, much less the wind, even if we could make you a boat."

"We could manage a boat all right," Janice said thoughtfully, "After all, we did improvise the sub, and there's a lot of fabric still on the raft. But you're probably right about the wind."

"In principle," Hugh said thoughtfully, "I suppose one could use wind power to drive us against the current. We could have some sort of wind turbine which drove another rotor under the surface. The water has more inertia—how about it, Box?"

"Quite possible in principle. Very doubtful as a practical project with the material and tools and, I must regretfully point out, the skills available here."

Janice raised her eyebrows. "Come on, darling. In my education they stressed the difference between comprehension and craftsmanship."

"Hmph. In mine they called 'em mentality and manipulation, and said any time we saw a gap between 'em we should try to close it."

"The translators are having trouble," Thrasher cut in.

"Sorry," answered Janice, "we went a bit astray. The question is still how to get someone or something to carry news of our troubles to where it has a reasonable chance of being found. You folks need food and oxygen in huge amounts, we Erthumoi can't travel far or fast under our own power, and The Box—hmmm. What can't it do?"

"It can't handle emergencies," the artificial intelligence pointed out, using third person to keep the Cephallonians a little happier. "It's the gap Janice mentioned. It can *do* practically nothing. You could have built connections which would have let it run your submarine, for example, but it could only have called for help if anything went wrong. No real imagination, only preplanned effectors. If you are proposing that it guide a boat back to Iris, the advice is *no*. The guidance is easy to find, and there would be no food or oxygen problem, but you would have to use a fuser to power the boat; and we are back to our ignorance of just what went wrong.''

''Then we're stuck, it seems to me,'' said Hugh. ''We can't use power. It takes power to buck current below the surface. It takes power to buck wind and current at the surface. It takes power to buck wind above the surface—for that matter it takes power to fly at all. And we can't use—''

''Does it?'' Janice perked up suddenly.

''Does it what?'' both Cephallonians asked simultaneously. Hugh knew his wife well enough to resolve the ambiguity.

''Yes. It takes power to fly,'' he said firmly.

''No. There are plenty of vertical currents in the air as well as the water. A sailplane can use them—''

''If the pilot can find them. And are you suggesting we can build a sailplane? I know they're simple basically, and we've both flown them, but we've never *made* one—remember your remark about craftsmanship a minute ago. And how would you propose to launch it if we did make it?''

''Kite style, with the Cephallonians pulling. There's plenty of wind, reason knows.'' Janice was wearing a smile that Hugh recognized even through her face protection, but he wasn't quite ready to give up yet.

''And you think you can fly one *here*? Where winged natives themselves don't dare come? Where it isn't just a matter of looking for another thermal to head for after you reach the top of the first? You know as well as I that Habranha should have been called Chaos—it just *looks* like an eyeball. There are *no* simple currents here, air or water!

''Box, will you *please* straighten out this crazy woman? Could the Cephallonians pull a sailplane fast enough to get it off the water—wait, dear, I'm not done—*if it were designed to glide faster than the winds it would have to buck?* In this gravity, what sort of shape would it have—what sort of wing loading?''

"Wait, Box!" insisted Janice. "How high would we have to fly to avoid the really strong wind *into* the evaporation zone? Would we need oxygen? And for how long? Remember the winds aloft carry clouds back toward Darkside.''

"True," replied the artificial intelligence. "The scale height on Habranha, particularly in the Cataract area, is large, though there are no exact figures. In view of the high surface oxygen partial pressure, you can probably breathe unaided at heights well above seven kilometers, and at such altitudes the main circulation is toward Darkside. You need not make a high-speed craft; low wing loading, such as you would use on a planet of Erthuma-comfortable gravity, will be adequate—indeed, highly advisable, since there is no reliable information on how far you would have to travel between updrafts. Launch in the way you suggest should be quite possible.''

"It's still silly!" Hugh was almost snarling. "We've flown in calm atmospheres, with nice, steady thermals a few kilometers apart, marked with cumulus clouds at the top. You know it's not like that here! You—''

"What else can you think of?''

The only answer Hugh could have given to this grossly unfair question would have been to point out its unfairness. He didn't bother; Janice knew that as well as he did. He was silent.

The woman refrained from triumphant remarks, which would have been even more unfair, and even blanked her facial expression now. She did love her Hugh. She also knew that he might be right; not even The Box could have considered everything. She was, however, a determined person, and greatly preferred doing *something* even when not sure that it was right. After all, as any scientist knew, there was never any way to be *completely* certain. Not objectively, and faith was inappropriate to the present problem.

The submarine's frame served as basis for the glider. To the long hull, now a fuselage, were added wings of twelve-meter span and one-meter chord at the root, far more area than was really needed in Habranha's gravity. They were designed carefully with the aid of The Box and assembled even more meticulously. It was embarrassing to Erthuma and Cephallonian alike to find that they needed to make their own measuring devices before doing any cutting; construction of this sort had not been planned for the study. Work was not really delayed by the resulting philosophical debate about fundamental equipment, but the debate served as background.

The hull had to be covered carefully with sheeting from the raft, and only the upper surfaces of the wings could be treated similarly before supplies ran short. Hugh would have liked well-shaped airfoils, but a fuselage that would float and not collect weed on its frame members while being launched, as the submarine had done even on its brief trip, seemed still more necessary. Also, there was no easy way to find the center of gravity unless the object were floating, though this could of course be shifted somewhat in flight by having the crew shift. The cockpit was open, longer than necessary merely to contain the Erthumoi; the crude seats were easily movable to permit this.

Seats, plural. Hugh was for once firm. His wife was not going alone this time. She made little argument and the Cephallonians none. It made no difference to the swimmers, and she was glad enough to have him along.

The other possibility, that he might make the flight without her, never crossed her mind, and if he thought of it he had the sense to keep quiet.

The Cephallonians were ready to make another rescue trip themselves, but courteously said nothing about it. They would have more difficulty this time, of course, since The Box had no sense of what went on above the ocean surface and could present no image of the atmo-

sphere. If the glider had trouble, no one below would
know until it reached the ocean, and then only if the accident occurred within the radius of the current sea image.
It was quite possible, everyone including The Box realized, that even within that range a splash might be misin-
terpreted and go unnoticed; once in the water, the crew
would have to use their transducers and signal as loudly
as possible for help.

Splasher remarked to her husband, translator off, that
she didn't think the Erthumoi would get half a kilometer
vertically or horizontally; if the Habras themselves didn't
fly in this region it seemed pretty silly for walkers to try
it. Thrasher gave the equivalent of a nod.

Hugh had not repeated his essentially identical opinion
since the initial argument, but it remained unchanged. He
made sure that their environment suits were still adjusted
for positive buoyancy, and was somewhat relieved when
he saw his wife unobtrusively making the same check.
This might, of course, have been mere routine, not pessi-
mism or even realism, but at least it was being done.

They checked their suit filters with even greater care,
and loaded a few oxygen tanks for possible need—only a
few, since they did not expect the glider to be able to take
much weight, and the swimmers might have a hard time
with the launch no matter how light the machine was kept.

The real uncertainty was in wing symmetry. Even a
slight warp, too minute to spot by eye alone, would mean
a built-in tendency to bank and turn, and eyes were all
they had—no precision assembly jigs or anything else
"precision." With someone at the controls, of course,
such a warp could be countered, but that would mean a
constantly alert pilot. Hugh had planned and started to
build the wings so that they could be rotated around a
lateral axis in flight, the axis represented by a single main
spar, before his wife convinced him that any significant
motion of that sort would mean gross overcontrolling. As
an experienced recreation sailplane pilot himself he had
known this perfectly well but had been highly pessimistic

about their ability to build a really symmetrical pair of wings. He still was, and was not looking forward to the launch with any great confidence. Naturally, he wanted to be at the controls himself during the process. For similar reasons, so did Janice.

To minimize any temporary warping the wings were rigged with cord provided by the Cephallonians, though as little of this was used as possible. Even if weed could be picked up only during launch, any would be too much; there was no way such a load could possibly turn out to be balanced, either as weight or drag.

There was little doubt by the time it was assembled that the glider would fly kitewise, as long as its launching lines were held from below and someone was controlling its roll; there was always enough wind for that. The question was what would happen when those lines were cast off. It would then be necessary for the Erthumoi to find, or better to have found already, a wind with at least some upward component within gliding distance. There were plenty of spouts where ammonia was leaving the ocean violently, and these should have velocity enough to offset their lower density and lift; but whether the glider would hold together inside their violent structures was decidedly doubtful. On more Erthuma-normal worlds sailplane pilots stayed out of thermals that were growing thunderheads at the top; on this part of Habranha one could not see high enough to tell when this was the case. Free ammonia met water vapor, or much more rarely even hydrogen cyanide, in concentrations high enough to form clouds sometimes quite close to the ocean surface, though the adiabatic lapse rate was small. Thunder was nearly constant in The Cataract, the flicker of lightning sometimes detectable even in the constant daylight, but their sources could seldom be located. It was obvious only that they were high. The thunderheads were out of sight.

Janice was in the cockpit, and the Cephallonians a hundred meters away holding what all hoped would serve as launching lines. Hugh was casting off the numerous cords they had found necessary to keep the glider from blowing away as it neared completion. He trusted his wife to hold it firmly down until he could get on board, but made a point of leaving until last the tiedowns at the forward end—after all, neither of them knew just how effective the control surfaces would be in air, though they had worked well enough when the craft was a submarine. The specific question was whether they could hold the tail high enough to keep the wings from lifting at any time on a pitching deck. Several times during the unmooring the man leaped gliderward as the raft tilted the nose up, wind caught under the wings, and for a moment the fuselage rose and strained upward against the remaining ropes. It promised well for the flight, but made the casting off a nervous procedure.

"Box, have them take up the slack in the launch lines," Hugh called as he approached the last two moorings. This order obeyed, he reached for the nearer of the two; then an idea struck him, and he went back to the cockpit, knotted another cord to an exposed longeron by his own seat, and with the other end of this clipped to his suit went forward again. The moorings clear, he ran and hand-over-handed back to his cockpit, wondering simultaneously whether his wife could hold the craft down for five seconds and why they hadn't thought to improvise some means of releasing all the moorings at once from on board. He reached his goal without being lifted off the deck, slid over the side as quickly as his suit allowed without risking the fuselage fabric, settled onto his lurching seat, and tied the multiply-braided cord intended for a safety belt across his legs. Looking up from that precaution, he saw that they were already eight or ten meters above the raft—straight above; the swimmers hadn't yet started to pull.

Whether they were flying, as opposed to blowing around, was debatable. Janice was certainly using her controls. These consisted of a horizontal foot bar on a vertical axis with lines from its ends directing the rudder, and two vertical rods: one for ailerons manipulated by her left hand, and one for vertical control at her right. Each set of lines had another bar within Hugh's reach as he sat behind his wife, though he had to lean forward rather awkwardly for the aileron one. This was from his seat's present position; it might turn out, they knew, that his would have to be moved so far back or hers so far forward to balance the glider properly that only one could reach controls at all.

The craft was far from steady so far, dipping, soaring, and yawing. The wind was doing all the lifting; the swimmers were holding position a hundred meters from the raft, and the Erthumoi were oscillating above it. Janice was still overcontrolling but learning quickly, and their crewed kite began to settle into a steadier pattern—not perfectly motionless, of course, in Habranha's chaotic air currents, but something far more comfortable than it had been at the start. Hugh wondered briefly how his wife's motion-sensitive stomach had been able to take the first few minutes, and then recalled what a difference it made when the owner of the stomach was doing the piloting. She had been right to insist.

She had almost completely stopped the roll and yaw wandering now, and was managing, on the average, a gentle climb. The tow lines were taking on a remarkably steep slant, and Hugh almost automatically began estimating the lift and drag vectors involved. The weight was small enough, but it wasn't zero even on Habranha. Was there an updraft anywhere near that could support them?

A spout showed half a kilometer to the left, reaching up into the haze beyond human vision; another was behind them, presumably being carried away by the wind now holding up the glider. If they cast loose from the Cephallonians, what would be their glide angle? Could he compute it from the present slant of the rope? Not without knowing the wind speed, of course.

Their trackers would let them calculate the last only *after* they were free. Then they could get glide angle from the recent rope slant, assuming wind was reasonably constant, which was asking a lot. Then they would know if they could get close enough to the spout to use its vertical air currents. If they couldn't—if the glide were too steep—well, they could land on the sea and the Cephallonians could tow them back for another try.

Or they could wait as they were until a spout came so close that there would be no doubt about their reaching it.

Or maybe they shouldn't use a spout. A whirlpool should have a less violent lifter above it. Less likely to tear wings off. The endlessly varying howl of The Cataract's wind didn't completely drown out the occasional mutter of thunder that reminded Hugh of what real thermals could do to aircraft—even professionally built ones. Neither he nor his wife had any illusions about the ruggedness of the gimcrack device they were riding.

Hugh saw a whirlpool a few hundred meters to their right, and pointed. Janice nodded silently. The launch cables, unlike the tie-downs, had been arranged to be released from the cockpit; she dropped them at once and swung right in a slightly overcontrolled but fairly graceful turn. She was trying to find the narrow line between maximum glide range and stall attitude as she headed for the possible source of lift. They had no airspeed instrument; their inertial trackers were useless for any such problem, of course, without independent wind information. *Almost* useless; they did show local vertical, since Habranha's radius, rotation, and even its orbital parameters had been set into them.

The glider recovered easily from stalls, it turned out, and the pilot lost control only twice. Fortunately, wings stalled before control surfaces. This was rather surprising, considering the history of the latter as hydrofoils, but neither of the crew thought of that.

They still had reserve altitude when they felt an upward surge. Janice glanced over her shoulder, and each could see a grin of triumph through the partner's face protector. The woman concentrated on a gentle turn that kept them in the updraft, using her trackers after the raft faded from view in haze below them. At four kilometers' altitude they ceased to climb; the current was just able to support them. She straightened out in the planned direction—headings were not quite all equivalent. All points on The Iris's near edge were about equidistant from the substellar pole, but the raft was much closer to one side of The Cataract than the other. There was, however, no way to tell where another updraft might be found, and this was the more immediate problem. Janice was pretty certain now of the ideal glide attitude, and maintained it with the aid of the vertical-component tracker since no horizon was visible.

The other component readings suggested for some time that wind was helping them on their way, as The Box had predicted. Below about two and a half kilometers added turbulence heralded the end of this status and their true descent angle steepened, though the glider's ideal attitude did not of course change. Just below one kilometer the ocean surface became visible once more, and both Erthumoi began to search it earnestly for signs of another rising current.

Several spouts showed up almost at once, clustered rather closely together for reasons known only to chaos; no others could be seen within the ten- or fifteen-kilometer range that the slight haze permitted to Erthumoi vision.

Whirlpools would be smaller and harder to see, of course. The flyers had the obvious choice of a straight-line glide that would cover more ocean, get them farther on their way, and in theory give them a better chance of finding whatever lifters there might be, or circling to remain within gliding distance of the spouts in case no whirlpools could be found and the more dangerous alternative had to be used. Hugh said nothing when his wife banked the glider into a gentle turn that kept them circling the spouts. He would have made the same choice. They seemed risky, but at least they were definitely there.

Two hundred meters above the raging surface Janice glanced back at her husband once more. He shrugged. She nodded, and started another slow turn in toward the nearest column of ammonia-rich spray.

The glider was already shuddering in turbulence, and maintaining a steady descent was not really possible. She did not, of course, head straight into the misty pillar but a few dozen meters to its left. They should still be nearly a hundred meters above the waves when they came level with it, and ought to be feeling lift before then.

They did, but under the right wing only. The glider went into a nearly vertical bank to the left and started a steep diving turn in that direction. Hugh's training normally kept him from being a control-grabber, but this time he helped; between them they leveled out at thirty or forty meters. The man released his bars with a major effort of self-control, and Janice promptly and deliberately nosed down again to gain speed and banked back toward the spout—straight toward it. This time the nose felt the lift first, but she forced it down firmly. Hugh nodded silently, not looking at the chop ten meters below. Only when Janice felt strong general lift did she turn once more to bring them side-on to the spout.

Now the difference between the two sides was not so great and she was able to maintain control, and even to hold the inner wing—the left one this time—down so they remained in a slow turn and stayed inside the lift region. They were climbing again, far faster than before; Hugh felt uneasy as he saw the wings bending visibly.

Not bending, flapping. A little yield was normal for any structural material and the woody stems they had used for the frame were extremely springy, but this shouldn't be happening. A steady updraft might have bent them during the initial acceleration, but once they were lifting steadily—

They *weren't* lifting steadily, of course. Habranha's chaos was manifesting itself again. The glider was jerking and twisting, pitching and banking and yawing in gaseous eddies quite undetectable until one was in them and, Hugh

guessed, quite beyond the power of even The Box to resolve into a predictable pattern had it been with them.

"Cut out of this!" he cried to Janice.

"We need more altitude. We have less than a kilo so
far. We've *got* to get higher!"

"We need wings and tail more. We've got enough to
give us some gliding range. We can look for a safer
updraft."

"But at this height the main wind is still toward The
Cataract."

"We can live with that. We were expecting lots of
climb-and-glide cycles before we got anywhere near where
we wanted."

"But that first one—"

"Don't let one piece of luck spoil you. Get out while
we have wings!" Tense as he was, Hugh made no attempt
to seize the controls; he was a recreational flyer, not a
professional, but too good a pilot for that. A vehicle—any
vehicle, land, ocean, air, or space—must be controlled
either by a single entity or by a completely cooperative
and informed team.

If there are two or more experts aboard, the one actually
taking a turn at the controls is responsible.

If there are *no* experts aboard, of course—

Hugh controlled himself just the same.

Whether Janice decided to follow her husband's half-
panicky advice or was simply overpowered by turbulence
that might just as easily have driven them more deeply
into the spout she never said, and Hugh didn't ask, but
things gradually quieted down. The bouncing grew less
violent, and it became possible to maintain something like
flight attitude and even a vague direction with the aid of
the trackers. There was still no horizon; visibility had become much worse and the usual thunder louder and more
frequent, though lightning even now could never be seen
as more than a sourceless flicker in the haze. The wings
and tail ceased to flutter seriously, as did Hugh's nerves.

Janice, however, was bothered. "We're not climbing."

Her husband checked his own tracker. "Sure we are. A meter every fifteen seconds or so."

"That's nothing. We got over three meters a second out of that first lifter and something like five times that from the spout while we were in it."

"Be calm. We're going up, and heading the right way—you're not circling."

"That's the trouble. This updraft has to stop soon, or rather we're bound to fly out of it, and I don't know which way to turn to get back in."

"Back the way we came, of course."

"Not if I can help it. The idea is to get to The Iris where we can find someone to help Thrasher and Splasher."

"Come on." Hugh let his impatience show. "You're letting yourself get spoiled again. Even I don't expect to make it in one straight leg. Gliders don't work that way, and you know it as well as I do."

"I know. But do you really want to fly back into that spout? We won't see it coming, you know—not up here."

"We can stand it for a few seconds. You got out before. You'd better turn back—we're descending now, and you were right about our needing more height."

Janice shrugged, nodded, and put the glider into a shallow right turn. Thirty seconds after completing the half circle their descent stopped. "Not too wild up here," she remarked. "I'll hold for a while, but do a ninety to one side and see if we can climb with ten-minute back-and-forth legs before we get back to where the spout was. You have its tracker readings?"

"Burned on my cortex," Hugh assured her. "I'll give—oh, three kilos' warning? Or would you feel happier with five?"

"One," his wife said firmly. "We want lift. Remember?"

"All right." Hugh tried to conceal his uneasiness and might have succeeded; at least, Janice said nothing more.

The spout, however, did a much better job of concealing the fact that it was not a simple vertical column. That, at least, was what the Erthumoi decided later. They met the wild turbulence long before Hugh's warning was due; Janice instantly started a steep left turn and before completing the intended ninety degrees was into chaos far worse than before.

She tried to reverse the turn, but found her efforts fully occupied simply making the glider fly rather than blow away. Holding her eye on the tracking indicators, she did her best to keep the machine in a slight right bank and with the nose down in what she had decided was best-range glide attitude—this should keep airspeed, and therefore stresses, at a minimum. It did not prevent violent jolts as they struck eddy after eddy with no obvious regularity. Chaos continued to reign, thunder was louder, and twice in the next few minutes lightning flashes were actually visible. They were rising, on the average but not at all regularly. Hugh tried not to look at the slender wings, which were whipping madly again, but to keep his eyes on his trackers or his wife. He felt himself jerked against his safety cord with each flap of the wings, and began to worry about that. Should he hold on to the frame, or Janice? He didn't want to distract her, useless as her flying efforts might be, but if her safety line went—

He reached around her, as unobtrusively as he could, using the piece of cord he had employed on himself just before the launch, and secured her suit to the seat with part of it. Then he cut off the unused couple of meters and employed it to do the same for his own. The turbulence seemed to be easing—but how often could they repeat this sort of thing, and for how long could they keep it up? How long would it take them to get out of The Cataract? One more climb and glide, or a dozen? The area of high evaporation was irregular in shape, as he remembered—he had seen it from space, of course, when they were first approaching the planet that all Erthumoi nicknamed Eyeball at first sight, and the irregularity would be in time as well. For that matter, the shortest direction out might not be the same any more; his arrival had been months ago, and The Cataract probably changed its shape

significantly in hours. They had known when they started
the flight that the raft was not exactly under the sun, and
had headed away from that pole and tried to keep the
average heading unchanged. The trackers indicated that
they had been only partly successful. They could still only
do their best.

Just fly. Hold your heading on the long glides. Get all
the altitude you can, glide as far as you can, find a lifter
if possible, and repeat.

An abrupt upward jolt, more violent than anything they
had felt so far, brought Hugh's mind back to real time.
He looked at the wings with a sinking sensation that had
nothing to do with real motion as they bowed upward for
more than two meters at the tips, wrinkling the covering
fabric—briefly, the man felt thankful they had not covered
the bottom; then, still intact, they whipped back to and
past their normal shape, prolonging for a moment the upward ride of the fuselage.

And at the top of that ride Janice, seat and all, left the
glider. For a moment she hung above it and Hugh reached
for her, but he was not quick enough and would probably
not have been strong enough. With the aircraft's center of
gravity shifting suddenly backward it pitched upward and
its wings took a deeper bite of the air. This brought the
fuselage up toward the errant pilot and for a moment she
seemed about to return to her proper place; but drag had
increased even more than lift. She struck the body well
ahead of the cockpit, slid off after a futile attempt to reach
through the polymer sheeting and grasp a longeron, and
fell—not rapidly, on Habranha, but she fell. Her right
hand caught a wing rigging line, and the glider went into
a vertical bank. Before Hugh could react, Janice deliberately let go.

The man slid his seat forward without hesitation; like
his wife, he had spent much time thinking about possible
emergency actions with their untested craft, and many of
these had involved balance. He seized Janice's controls,
no longer able to reach his own, and without the slightest

concern for air speed or structural strength brought the nose down as far as it would go.

This was not a vertical dive or anything like it, and he had to bank into a tight spiral to bring his wife back into view from under the nose. He was losing altitude, of course, but not nearly as fast as she was, since they were both still in the updraft but the glider was far more affected by it.

For a desperate, unreasoning moment Hugh wondered whether it would do any good to try to hack the wings off with his knife to make his fall faster. Memory of the toughness of the woodlike material they had used for framework, a toughness so well displayed by the wings in the last few minutes, made him decide against it even before he thought of what the fall would be like after getting one wing off but before disposing of the other. After a fleeting and futile thought about the convenience of explosive bolts for quick disassembly, he brought his mind firmly back to reality.

He would have to keep her in sight, obviously. There was sunlight enough, hazy as the sky was; it was little over a kilometer to the surface; Jan's suit would certainly float; it was simply a question of not losing track of her, and landing—no, "ditching" was the word, wasn't it?—as close to her as possible.

And then they could call the Cephallonians. The one glide they had made could not have taken them out of The Box's model range, surely. Of course, part of it had been made with a tail wind of unknown speed—don't be silly, Cedar. You don't need dead reckoning; the trackers will tell you. But you can't look at them just now; you can't take your eyes off Janice. She's starting to blend in a little too well with the haze. But you were reading them often enough a few minutes ago; what did they say?

Hugh couldn't remember. Too much else had happened in recent moments to monopolize his attention. He'd have to worry about calling the swimmers after he'd landed and picked up his wife—where was she? He squinted, and shook his head. There were several specks in his field of vision, most of them moving erratically, and he couldn't be sure which if any was Janice's suit. It had blended in with the background, as it had been threatening to do for seconds—

He couldn't go straight down. The glider wouldn't enter a vertical dive. He tried once more, with his own body as far forward as he could get it, but the broad wings had too much drag and were too far above the center of gravity, and the elevators didn't have enough area.

But there was another way. He had heard of it, though he had never flown anything unstable enough to experience it. He brought the nose up, and for the first time hoped that the glider's long wings were *not* absolutely warp free.

They weren't. The right one stalled out first, and a moment later the glider was in an almost flat spin as nearly straight downward as the local winds allowed. Actually, it was hard to tell by eye that he was descending at all. The spin was slow, thanks to the lightness and span of the aircraft, but it was still hard to fix the eye on any reference point in the haze. Certainly not on his wife.

The tracker insisted that he was going down, however, though probably a lot more slowly than she. He could only guess at the terminal velocity of a human body in Habranhan gravity and air, but the guess was many times higher than the tracker's quarter-meter-per-second reading. This did increase somewhat during the next minute; either the lifting current was not vertical, as he had already guessed, and the fall was taking him out of it, or the turbulence was doing its usual statistical job of working the glider into a quieter area. He hoped it was the former, which would give him a much better chance of hitting the ocean somewhere near Janice.

The water was not encouraging when it became visible. It still showed the mad choppiness of The Cataract area. Spotting a nearly submerged human form in the waves, spray, foam, and seaweed would be hard enough on the way down, and hopeless when being tossed around among them himself. Janice could be floating fifty meters away and easily be missed. Even if he did see her, moving the glider over for a rescue would be impractical. There was nothing to serve as a paddle, she would probably be unable to hear his calls over the roar of wind and wave and thunder, the fuselage floated high at the mercy of the wind, and if he left the craft to swim over to her it would probably be impossible to get back. No, he could use a safety line, since there was plenty of rope; but he would still have to see her first.

He certainly failed to do that before settling with surprising gentleness onto the waves.

The good part was the tracker claim that he was only about twenty-two kilometers from the raft. The single real glide they had made had been good, but not outstanding; it would have taken them a long, long time to reach The Iris that way.

The Box should be able to hear a call for help. Maybe Janice, who must have hit the water first, had already reported and the Cephallonians were now en route.

Even if she had he should also check in, of course. He unclipped the transducer from his suit, reached over the side to hold it under water, and reported the incident and his tracker location, finishing with a heartfelt query about his wife. There was plenty of time for the whole message before the first words could reach the raft, and he waited patiently for an answer. The possibility that he might not be heard was something he would face later if he had to.

The Box was typically terse.

"The Cephallonians are on their way. I can detect Janice with confidence, but not the glider. When they reach your area, you will have to talk steadily so that they can home on your sound."

"Then you can't tell me how close I am to her." Hugh was less patient with the inevitable pause this time, though he knew what the answer had to be.

"No. I was able to associate her original call with a regular set of echoes from local wave sounds, and maintain an image. The submerged part of the sailplane reflects very little sound, and most of that downward, I expect. If you would care to get out and immerse yourself, talking all the time, and of course fastening yourself securely to the aircraft, I can probably resolve the problem.''

Hugh hesitated for only a moment. A five-hundred-kilometer water depth is, objectively, no worse to an Erthuma than fifty meters, just as a fifty-story fall is no worse than one of five. The trouble is that few Erthumoi are very objective even when scientifically educated. He spent several minutes doing careful things with rope, then eased himself out of the cockpit and let himself into the sea, holding on firmly to a wing in spite of his trust in the cord.

"All right, I'm submerged," he reported, and began his favorite party showoff activity, reciting fragments of poetry in ancient English. The Box wouldn't care what he said as long as it got a continuous signal. He was declaiming, with gestures of his free hand, "These are Clan Alpine's warriors true, and Saxon, I am Roderic Dhu!" when the calm response reached him.

"You're almost a kilometer closer to me than Janice, and getting closer at about two meters a second, presumably because of wind. Current should be affecting you both more or less equally on long-time average. There seems to be no emergency. The Cephallonians will reach you first but I would suggest that they go on and bring Janice back to the glider. I assume you will want it towed back here. I do not suppose you will want to repeat this attempt, but the structure represents much labor and material and some of it might be converted to other uses.''

Hugh said nothing. The Box was basically right, of course, but relief about his wife's safety and the experience of what was essentially another anticlimax had shut down for the moment both his enthusiasm and his imagination. Having the heroic rescuers leave the raft and the helpless rescued return was getting to be a little too routine. He had, of course, been perfectly right about the flying project, but it is small comfort for a pessimist to be right. Hugh got no satisfaction out of saying, "I told you so," especially to his wife. He would be very happy to tell how wrong he had been to Janice, the Cephallonians, and the assembled study authorities at Pwanpwan, once they reached the place.

He shifted to old Welsh songs, which called for more attention and allowed less freedom to brood in spite of their usual subject matter, and kept broadcasting. Halfway through "Llwyn On," Thrasher—Hugh could tell the two apart at sight—surfaced beside him.

"Shall I stay with you while Splash picks up Janice, or go along with her? You seem safe enough."

"Sure, go along. Do I need to keep singing? You can see me on your own sonar now, can't you?"

"We can, but your signal helps. Besides, the music is nice. See you in a few minutes." The swimmer vanished with no more splash than could be blamed on the choppy waves. Hugh, not used to having his voice praised and not entirely sure of Thrasher's sincerity—Cephallonians sometimes carried courtesy to the same extreme as many Erthumoi—shifted to "Ar Hyd y Nos." He knew only two verses of this and went on to comic songs in his own language. After all, Janice would be close enough to hear him shortly.

Even with no trouble it took the rescuers several minutes to travel over a kilometer, get the woman into one of their packs, and swim back. Several more were spent deciding that the Erthumoi would return in the glider rather than be carried, arranging tow lines, and getting under way. There was little talk at first en route. Both human beings were discouraged, and now that the tension of the flight itself was over, they realized how tired they were. While each wanted to cheer the other up, neither could think of anything very cheerful to say.

They watched, silently at first, the rhythmic dolphin-style motion of the Cephallonians, and Hugh soon began to compare the vector problems of swimming with those

f glider flight. Janice tried to sound interested as he began
o talk about this and brighten up somewhat, but she found
t hard to be sincere, much less enthusiastic.

The tow was rougher than the flight, of course. Not
only was the surface choppy, but every few seconds one
wing tip or the other would either dip into the sea or be
caught by a wave, adding a jerky yaw to the pitching
discomfort. The Cephallonians had started out trying to do
he trip quickly—after all, the glider *was* decently stream-
ined and drew practically no water—but gave up in a
minute or two. They could stand the jerks on the tow lines
hemselves, but Thrasher was beginning to worry about
pulling the frame apart. That, at least, was what he said;
Janice muttered to her husband, "Kindhearted old fish,
isn't he? I wish he could forget about my stomach."

Hugh raised an eyebrow. "Don't *you* wish you could?"

"It's all right with the diving juice gone. And no comments, please."

Hugh had not planned any, and kept his face as expres-
sionless as possible, since that part of his suit was transparent. Vectors were much more fun than arguments.

And much more inspirational, he was beginning to realize, where practical plans were concerned. The glider experiment had not been a total success, but it had certainly
not been a waste of time. The sailplane had been doing
just what was asked of it, combining a vector directed
away from where they wanted to go with one at right
angles, working in a little basic Newton, and producing a
resultant headed—yes. Even the labor and material that
had gone into the aircraft itself should be useful—

The man's carefully blank expression was gradually
melting into a smile. Janice, seated ahead of him and
watching the waves and the Cephallonians, as well as the
change of tow line slack from moment to moment, did
not notice.

Hugh probably wouldn't have heard her if she had seen
his face and asked him about it. By the time his expression
reached grin level he was setting up nice, detailed, quanti-

tative problems for The Box. Really detailed. There would
even be a use for a thruster, as long as it were reliably
turned off. That distracted him briefly; just what had gone
wrong with the units Janice had employed on the sub?
Why had they chosen to go wide open? They *had* turned
off for her; did that mean it would be all right to use one
of those four for his new idea, or would it be safer to
take another? Or should something entirely different be
improvised? He couldn't think offhand of anything else on
the raft that would serve the purpose, but that didn't mean
there *wasn't* anything.

But that was a minor detail. He forced himself firmly
back to the number of questions that only The Box could
handle in reasonable time. By the time they reached the
raft, Hugh Cedar was completely happy again and went
straight to The Box.

Janice understood the questions, of course, which she
would have heard clearly enough even if their note re-
cording units had not been interconnected. She was less
happy than Hugh, not because she could see any serious
flaw in her husband's new idea but because she hadn't
been able to see one in any of the others, either. They
had *all* been good ideas, but had simply run into unconsid-
ered aspects of reality.

And there is no way in the universe to be sure when
all the facets of *any* situation have been viewed. Ordinarily, the woman would have been quite calm about this;
it was her normal personality pattern, that of a scientist.
In the last few dozen hours, however—well, Chaos had
not exactly developed a personality in her mind, but she
was beginning to capitalize its name mentally. This was
emphatically not normal Janice Cedar.

She remembered what had happened to Thrasher when
he had passed his depth limit and she had had to use the
conditioned command that Splasher had confided to her in
order to rescue them both. Luckily, there was no such
hypnotic suggestion implanted in her own mind that Hugh
or one of the Cephallonians could use—at least, *she* con-

dered it lucky. Erthuma minds didn't work that way. It
ould be a tempting explanation for the thruster incident,
f course, if one were mystically inclined . . .

Janice brought her thoughts back to the job with a start.
Vhat was happening to her? *Was* she worrying herself out
f sense and sanity? So Cephallonians had safety tech-
iques Erthumoi couldn't use if they wanted to; human
ainds were different. Why should she worry about that?
specially, why should she worry about it *now?* All right,
o she and Hugh would be starting another trip shortly,
nd the swimmers as usual couldn't go along. That was
ll. Don't fuss, woman.

She came back to the real present. There had been no
uestion of Cephallonians coming along. They couldn't.
he problem was, how much of The Box could they take?
he boat wouldn't carry the whole unit. A single module
ould handle the running calculations, but more would be
eeded to talk properly to the living crew and tell them
hat action the numbers demanded. The Box had no sub-
ctive disapproval, dislike, or fear of being taken apart,
ut even it wasn't quite sure how much of itself would be
equired for the journey and how much might be needed
y the Cephallonians. There was no obvious reason why
ey would need any of it, as far as safety was concerned,
ut the swimmers naturally hoped to continue at least some
f the planned study work. They were thinking beings;
imply waiting to starve if their friends failed to reach
elp was no part of their plans. For one thing, someone—
ephallonian or Box—might come up with an explanation
f the thruster failure, and it *might* become possible to
end out something piloted only by another module. The
ox was not hopeful and the Cephallonians, who dis-
rusted artificial intelligence on principle, disliked the idea,
ut the possibility existed and feelings might change if a
ermenter died.

The glider had been modified, though not as radically
s might have been expected. The right wing had been
mputated two meters from the fuselage, now once more

a hull. The fabric from the severed portion now covered the other surface of the stub. Hugh's original plan of mounting the wings to rotate on a single lateral spar had turned out fortunate; only minor changes in the rigging were necessary to make it practical now. One of the thrusters that had misbehaved for Janice was lashed firmly to the end of the shortened wing, after having the power line from its fuser disconnected so that nothing could possibly turn it on—all hoped.

After much discussion, most of the rest of the raft's sheeting was cannibalized to use as a covering for the bottom of the left wing; Hugh made an impassioned argument on the importance of symmetry and won without support from The Box, which was quite ready to allow for odd shapes in its calculations. The original cockpit was covered and a new one arranged so that the crew would be located both before and behind the left wing. Lines were rigged to let the wings be rotated on their central spars by the crew.

And, finally, a four-module section of The Box was firmly lashed into the front cockpit, and Hugh's sun tracker plugged into it.

The whole craft was easy to carry on Habranha, though walking was far from comfortable on the heaving raft. The Erthumoi got it over to the tank that had been vacated by the Cephallonians for the moment—if for some reason it didn't float, there was no need for a major salvage job over five hundred kilometers of water. The thruster proved heavy enough to do what Hugh had hoped; the stub of the right wing hung as nearly straight down and the intact left one pointed as nearly straight up as wind allowed. The new cockpits were now on top and the waterline of the floating hull safely below their edge. Hugh had had the foresight to improvise a bailer from scraps of wing covering but still felt uneasy about the roughness of the sea. There was a little sheeting left on the raft; after some thought, and rather more argument, he used this to seal off the interior ahead of and behind the crew stations. He hoped he had done a good job, since the new partitions would obviously prevent bailing even more effectively than they were likely to stop inward leakage. The Cephallonians weren't greatly bothered about the loss of the fabric; too little was left in any case to make the tank much of a shelter for them.

The Erthumoi boarded, Janice in front as before. Wind pressure was holding them against one side of the tank; Thrasher activated several thrusters and turned the raft so the open end was downwind, and the boat drifted quickly away.

The Module began ordering its crew to pivot first one wing and then the other as it computed the air and water currents from the tracker readings. The Erthumoi were not too surprised to find themselves moving across the wind— after all, they did not know the current direction. They did, however, see the waves, and Hugh quickly turned the hull so that these came bow on. There was no point in asking for a bailing job before it was necessary. The Module didn't seem bothered, and their actual direction appeared little affected after the wings were turned once more to offset the change in hull heading.

For a quarter of an hour they maneuvered at seeming random, though the raft quickly disappeared in the distance. Then they approached a spout, and Hugh grew tense. He mentioned it to The Module, which had no sensory information but the trackers.

"I inferred that," was the answer. "I am using the current toward it. We will pass it on the right, and gain more than a kilometer toward The Iris. The technique is very simple, but whichever of you is handling the air wing will have to be ready to respond quickly to orders. The water wing I can predict more readily." Hugh said no more.

"Air wing thirty-five degrees to the right." Janice obeyed. "Overcontrolled. Two degrees left."

"I can only guess at degrees," the woman pointed out.

"Calibrate. Make some sort of marks on the control cords."

"Of course."

"Water wing, eleven degrees right."

"Tell me when I've reached it," replied Hugh.

"Close. Closer. Stop. Keep the hull at its present heading, whoever is handling the rudder. Are we dangerously close to the spout?"

"About a hundred and fifty meters from the nearest spray," Janice replied.

"Good. Hold all settings." There was a pause of over a minute.

"Hull heading six degrees left, air wing six degrees right, water wing three degrees right." It took perhaps a minute and three or four corrections to establish the new setup, and by this time both living crew members were almost relaxed. They were starting to feel comfortable with the orders, and even with the results; Janice, watching her own trackers, reported that they were actually working their way more or less steadily along a fixed line from the raft. Hugh had to take her word for it, since his own inertial equipment was now part of The Module.

In any case, he was having to spend much of his time bailing. The glider had ridden very high on the water and had shipped very little spray; with the weight of the thruster forcing the stub of the right wing to act as a keel, however, this was now less true. He hoped fervently that nothing was getting through the bulkheads he had improvised at either end of the cockpit. He told himself repeatedly that the Cephallonian adhesive was supposed to be very good, but did not say this aloud. Janice could be objective at inconvenient times.

Occasionally the gain in distance was really impressive, as vectors combined to whip them around one side or the other of a spout. At other times human patience would wear thin as they crept one meter along the Iris-ward radius out of twenty or thirty along their current sub-Grendel circumference. Sometimes, even with The Module directing, they actually lost distance for a while. Neither was sure whether this was because there existed no useful vector solution at the moment or because one or both of them had been too slow following orders. Only The Module could keep real-time track of the constantly changing water and air currents, and only The Module could solve their angle problems quickly enough. By unspoken common consent, they did not ask their electronic companion who or what should be blamed, and it did not volunteer information.

They had to sleep, of course. Janice allowed her husband to take the first watch, and carefully refrained from checking the time it started, so she didn't know how long he let her slumber. She had hoped to give him a full ten hours when his turn came, but a complication emerged.

"Our drag component seems to be increasing," The Module remarked six hours or so into Hugh's sleep. "We originally averaged nearly six meters real advance toward The Iris for each hundred of actual travel through the water. This has dropped over the last four hours to about three per hundred." The woman thought briefly of taking care of the matter herself, since the cause seemed pretty obvious, but allowed common sense to override personal pride and awakened her husband. He, after hearing the report and agreeing with her, rigged another safety line to his suit and went over the side—Janice did not argue for the privilege—to spend several minutes removing a ten-meter-long banner of weed trailing from the bottom wing and the thruster. Much of it was charged, but his suit protected him, though flashes were visible from the surface even in daylight and caused Janice some uneasiness. He climbed back aboard, and insisted that he couldn't get back to sleep.

By then the spouts were noticeably less frequent and the air clearer. Grendel could occasionally be seen, though still apparently almost overhead. It was obvious even without tracker data that they were working their way out of The Cataract into clear Pupil. This was the good part. Less comforting was the realization that they were now far beyond the range of the part of The Box that had been left on the raft, and that if any serious trouble developed there was no way the Cephallonians could know about it or find them.

But even Janice had now shed the depression following the failed glider flight and was looking ahead optimistically. The boat was not leaking detectably, the bailing had been able to keep up with water slopping into the cockpit—Hugh insisted that the exercise was doing him good— and it was even possible that in another few hours they might be visible from orbit, though neither of them considered that a chance worth counting on.

Wave and wind were much less chaotic; sometimes half an hour would pass between orders from The Module and two or three times one or another of the Erthumoi had been able to see for themselves slight departures from a fixed angle between their path and the now long and regular waves, and to make a correction without orders.

"You know," Hugh remarked at one point, "this could almost be a sport. We should try it when we get home."

Janice pursed her lips doubtfully for a few seconds, then shook her head negatively.

"I don't think anything needing robot assistance could really be regarded as a game," she pointed out. "A sport is supposed to show your personal skill, isn't it?"

Hugh shrugged. "I guess so. Just a thought."

"Hull heading slightly left, no change in water wing, air wing two degrees right," came the commanding voice. "Slightly" had come to mean "as little as human senses will permit," and implied that several attempts would be needed before the electronic intelligence would be satisfied, so Hugh's full attention wandered from the conversation.

Janice took time to eat, and spent a little more wondering whether their partial recyclers of their suits and the "cheese" they had brought with them would actually get them to The Iris. She was not worried, of course, just planning. They were likely to be seen by a native well before reaching the ring continent in any case—though whether the Habra would be interested was quite another matter. Aliens were no longer much of a novelty on the planet, they had both observed.

On the other hand, it seemed possible that the vehicle they were riding might collect a crowd.

Janice began glancing hopefully at the sky every few minutes.

The routine was getting too boring to be a sport, even Hugh admitted.

"Air wing two degrees right." Ten minutes' silence.

"Hull heading one degree right." More silence.

"Hull heading slightly left." This was at least more interesting, since it took more time and attention to satisfy The Module.

"Drag getting too great. Clean the water wing again." Janice insisted on taking her turn at this, which was a harder job than it might have been; they had agreed not to use their knives, partly because of the risk of losing them irretrievably and partly to avoid chance of damage to the covering fabric. The weed had little mechanical strength as a rule, though sometimes a strand or two of the stuff they had used to build the hull frame would be involved. Several times, as a result, the knife discussion was reopened; saving time in clearing the growths *might* be worthwhile, since they always lost distance—blowing downwind and drifting down current back toward The Cataract—while someone was doing the job. The Module always advised against it, however, since there was no way to tell in advance what sort of material would have to be faced, a preliminary check would be time-consuming, and loss of a knife would be permanent.

So boredom became the order of life, while Grendel shifted very slowly downward in the sky. Erthumoi are

extremely bad at judging vertical angles and they had no
measuring devices for such quantities, so knowing that
they only had to bring the star down to about seventy-five
degrees above the horizon was little help.

More meaningful facts were that the near edge of Iris
was about six hundred eighty kilometers from the center
of The Cataract, that they had started some thirty kilometers from the center, and that the trackers claimed
that they had made nearly a hundred kilometers radially
while traveling nearly two thousand through water in a
widening spiral around the heat pole. They had not kept
very careful track of time; on Habranha there were no
nights to serve as punctuation, its orbit was circular
enough to make one part of the roughly three-week year
just like another, and while Grendel's companion sun
could be seen easily enough in the daylight sky if one
looked for it and would with a little mental arithmetic
provide a "yearly" calendar, neither had bothered.
They had been roughly four hundred hours on the journey; their food was still adequate, and the Cephallonians
should still be safe.

But there was quite a distance yet to go, whether one
thought of ideal vector or through the water.

The sky was clear, now; they were in plain Pupil and
out of The Cataract. The water too was clear except for
life. The next major change would be near the end of
the voyage, when silt from the melting Iris would start
to discolor the ocean. The natives salvaged what silicate they could, of course, but rivers in the melting ice
stole a good deal of the finer material in spite of their
efforts.

There was no sense looking for this for a long time yet,
but both Erthumoi did glance at the sea more frequently
than common sense dictated. Whenever one of them went
over the side to clear weed he or she found it increasingly
hard to feel sure that the water wasn't just *a little* murkier
than last time . . .

It occurred to Hugh, after another couple of hundred

hours, that they might not have to go even that close to The Iris; there would be salvaging subs trawling for silt fairly well out in The Pupil, and fishers even farther, and one of these might easily spot them. If it did, it would certainly investigate. Their craft would certainly be a very peculiar sight to Habranhans either optically—the winged natives could see, of course—or on sonar. There was no point using their transducer to call for help, of course, since the natives sensed radio and would not, unless regularly dealing with aliens, be equipped to receive or transmit sound.

There was no way the Erthumoi could attract native attention. Not deliberately.

They were still nearly four hundred kilometers from the nearest shore of Iris, though they had made several widening spiral journeys around The Cataract as they stole their tiny increments of radial distance from each kilometer of sailing, when the polymer skeleton of a native submarine drew up beside them.

The crew, of course, were all armored and saturated with their own type of diving fluid. Apparently they were not equipped with sound devices, but they looked the aliens over for several minutes, made gestures that the Erthumoi assumed to be the equivalent of friendly waves, and drew away again. They seemed not to recognize the situation as an emergency as Janice and Hugh vigorously waved back.

"Now what?" asked the man as the craft disappeared.

"The wind and current are both weaker, but they both still set toward The Cataract. The choices seem to be to keep on working or give up and drift back where we came from," Janice replied. The man had nothing better to offer, even in his thoughts. The realization of how much better they would have done with a hull that didn't catch wind or current had struck him long ago, but so had the futility of mentioning it.

They continued to follow instructions from The Module but routine changed somewhat for a while. Six more times in the next four hours a submarine appeared near them, remained for a minute or two while its crew, resembling six-winged dragonflies but too heavy in their armor to fly, looked them over, gestured in what appeared to be unsurprised and casual friendship, and went on its way. None of them appeared equipped to communicate with aliens. Both Erthumoi wondered why the first to find them had not broadcast the news, and how long it would take before someone really helpful would show up.

"I suppose," Janice said at last, "that the first one *did* report. Probably no one working in The Pupil expects to run into visitors; these others have been just people who got the word and wanted a look. The help won't get here until news reaches The Iris and someone who knows about our study group."

"Maybe." Hugh was a little doubtful. "Habras aren't usually just curious about aliens; most of them have seen us by now—they fly, remember, and have one worldwide culture. I'd have expected these other subs to have come for some different reason, but I can't guess what it was. I suspect we'll just be waving to them until someone from Inex or higher hears the story and gets here."

"They've all seen *us*, but they haven't seen a boat like this," his wife pointed out. "I'd want to look over something this odd in a lot of detail myself."

"Well, maybe. The vector principle it uses should be obvious enough at a quick look, though. We'll see."

What they saw after the seventh visit was more hours of boredom. There were no more submarines, just travel. There were occasional—very rare, now, as they emerged into the least chaotic area of Habranha's ocean—orders to change a wing setting, but increasingly frequent demands that one of them go overside to clear weed.

This, they knew, would get even worse as they approached the ring continent. Silt from its endlessly melting inner edge enriched the water and supported a gigantic food pyramid. The natives did their best to conserve the silicate, which they brought at great labor and expense from the ocean bottom to fertilize the relatively clean ice of The Iris and let them grow food for themselves; rivers of meltwater flowing into The Pupil encountered beautifully designed and built dams and sediment traps. Still, lots of the fine stuff got away, and the natives had to make the best of it by fishing the teeming waters of the central ocean. Presumably it was fishing submarines that the Erthumoi had seen.

But now these ceased to appear, and hour after hour went by with nothing to relieve the boredom but an occasional trip overside.

Even the thunder of The Cataract was gone, though not the higher-pitched rush of wind and wave, so when the helicopter did come the couple heard its rotor beat long before they saw it. When they did, it was not directly between them and The Iris, and not heading directly toward them.

They waved and even shouted, knowing that both actions were futile against a wave and spray background, and watched with mounting tension as the aircraft went on past.

Then it shifted course roughly toward them. Only roughly; it flew by again. Then it hovered, a kilometer away, and Hugh, rising as nearly to his feet as he dared, caught glimpses between the waves of the upper part of a native submarine below the flyer and heading directly toward *them*.

Then the crew of the helicopter seemed to see their boat, and the machine swelled in their vision. A few seconds later two heavy-duty slings were descending toward the Erthumoi.

Hugh reached for the nearer sling and started to hook it to his suit. A thunderously amplified voice, speaking his own language, stopped him.

"Around your hull! We've got to get that public nuisance out of the water!"

"Why?" asked the man, quite reasonably. Janice went silently overboard with the other sling and began to adjust it.

"Tell you later! Just do it! The Habras are polite people, but in their place I'd be working up an interstellar incident. Get moving!" Hugh was still inclined to stay where he was and try to figure out why his beautiful, well-planned, and successful vector boat was a public nuisance to anyone, but Janice added her voice to the one from above. Thirty seconds later the rotor hum rose in pitch and their hull lifted gently from the surface. The bottom wing followed, trailed by the several meters of weed that had accumulated since they had last cleared it. Habras on the submarine, which had also approached, gestured, and their craft settled out of sight.

The Erthumoi climbed a ladder that had been lowered from a hatch of the flyer, and found themselves surrounded by half a dozen of their own species. Hugh, quite able to put first things first when they were important, reported where, why, and in what condition they had left their Cephallonian companions. The aircraft commander nodded.

"We'll pass that on to the natives. Their subs can probably tow the raft out, and we should certainly let them try first. If they can't make it, someone can design and send in a better raft."

The Cedars nodded. There was little risk of Habranha natives developing an inferiority complex from their alien visitors, both knew, but the policy was basically a good one. It sometimes kept starfarers from getting too arrogant.

"I suppose," the aircraft commander went on, "you've figured out by now why we had to get your boat out of the water." The fellow glared at him, and Hugh had a feeling that he himself should be blushing. A glance at his wife provided no help; she evidently didn't get it either, which was some comfort. The pilot waited only a moment. "That thruster you had on the underwater fin or whatever you call it is made of metal, which is very rare on Habranha. It had gathered weed, much of it highly charged, so it's—"

"It was broadcasting!" Hugh was just enough behind his wife to be slightly out of phase.

"It was, according to the Habras, *howling*. It was making conversation impossible for forty or fifty kilometers around, even under water. What it would have done if it had been producing the same waves above the surface I hate to think, but thank reason for impedance mismatching."

"But why so far? Water doesn't carry low-frequency electromagnetics very well," Hugh objected.

"When the waves stimulate discharge in electrical organisms, simple attenuation formulae don't work," the captain pointed out gently. "But why was the driver mounted so far down? I can see it isn't working now, but when it was, it must have tried to lift your front end right out of the water—or was that the idea?"

Janice smiled. Hugh could get some of his own back, here.

"Oh, no." Her husband shook his head firmly. "The driver was never working at all." Would he explain why? she wondered briefly. Of course not. At least, not completely. No one had figured out yet what had made the thrusters unreliable, unless Thrasher or Splasher had had an inspiration since the Erthumoi had left. Inspirations *did* sometimes happen to people. But Hugh was quite good at covering.

"We were just using it for its weight," he went on. "We didn't have anything else heavy enough that we could afford to risk—nothing at all except our robot and equipment, and we needed weight to keep the wings of our vector boat vertical. If the thruster had been pushing, as you say, we'd have wanted it right up under us. Besides"—he caught Janice's eye briefly—"if we'd been using it that far below the hull we'd have had to rig a line to control it with. Can't you imagine what would have happened when *that* began to pick up weed—at high speed? More drag on the line, more pull on the control; if pull meant more power, then more drag, more speed, more speed, more weed—you've heard of feedback, haven't you?''

Janice kept a straight face, too.

LIQUID ASSETS

REBECCA ORE

KOCH KNEW TIRIFALACK WAS EITHER RICH OR A *fra* user because she had her inner eye partially open. Rich was the better possibility because she was wrapped by an almost invisible special suit to support her against high gravity. A neon tank wrapped around her shoulders. "What can I do for you?" Koch asked the Locrian even though Tirifalack's neutrino message said she'd come to buy art. A Naxian slithered in behind Tirifalack. Outside, a pair of Samians, looking like giant bacon slabs, waited on either side of the door. Samians were very useful as bodyguards. So Tirifalack was rich, although since *fra* was so expensive, she could also be an addict. The Naxian was Tirifalack's truth reader, then.

Tirifalack spoke directly through her simultrans, obviously either wired directly to her verbal centers or a subvocalizer. The speaker was at throat level and almost invisible. "I'm here for discus, koi, or guppies. I'd prefer discus, Singapore bloodlines. I've been to Erth for residual Peruvian Amazonian greens." The accent sounded classic film European, perhaps Garbo, but with something alien enough that Koch understood how many immature males and sterile females this Locrian controlled.

Koch was an art dealer, planning to be honest now after deportation from another system for attempted smuggling, but he knew that some High Asians considered living creatures to be art objects. Herrin was settled by Germans and High Asians. When he came, his handling by customs was quite polite and utterly thorough. He got the suspicion that the original settlers planned to set up a rigorous high-tech nation, modeled after the East Asian Co-Prosperity Sphere of the twentieth century. But Herrin seduced them and turned them into aesthetes with mechanical gardens and farms and high protective tariffs on products coming in and, more especially, art goods and livestock going out. Herrin breeders wrought their greyhounds, their tabby cats, and their fish the old-fashioned way—without gene splicing—and jealously guarded their stock.

"Discus?" Koch knew koi, the colored carp.

"A round flat fish, of water with a conductivity of less than fifty micro-Siemens, brown to highly colored, some solid blue, other like hallucinations of Terran domestic cat skins."

"Arrogant fish," the Naxian said, speaking for the first time. "Boss, he doesn't know what you're talking about. He wonders how to take advantage."

"Mr. Koch, I thought you were an art dealer. Blackwheel, explain to him."

"And if you know that, you know that art objects can't be exported until the tariff is settled. And Herrin livestock breeders are quite possessive."

"An Erthuma tariff," Tirifalack breathed. "And fish may not, perhaps, come under the heading of art."

Getting the fish, Koch thought, wouldn't be as much of a problem as smuggling them out during the tariff blockade. The idea intrigued him.

"Boss," the Naxian, Blackwheel said, "Mr. Koch is intrigued. I will hold you to contract which does not allow me to be put in danger without indemnity."

"First find me the fish," Tirifalack said. "I prefer the cat skin hallucinations, but with broad swirls."

Koch found more discus than he'd ever imagined swam on Herrin, but their owners gave various obscure excuses for not selling—plagues, reputations, perhaps fear that another breeder could use their lineages for advantageous outcrosses. Finally, one Asian breeder suggested Gottke and gave map coordinates. Koch went inland to the quartz sand country where no one farmed except along bull tallow clay veins. The primary goods were glass objects and exotic papers, but the fish were there in a wooden house that looked like a mutant cuckoo clock built on artificial hills made of reinforced concrete and glass. As Koch looked for the helicopter pad he'd been assured existed, he remembered that the original Terrans also used "cuckoo" for "crazy." The landing site was almost obscured by spectra from the glass hills and by the local sand used to temper its cement. Koch wondered if the man who'd built this had some dim tradition of Mad Ludwig's Castle on Old Terra and built the hills, but not out of realistic material, and the castle, but not quite the castle. A man pointed to the ground—yes, flatter, the landing pad. Sand flew off it as Koch landed. He recognized Gottke from the phone.

"So you want to sell my fish to the neon bugs?" Gottke said. "By now customs is much alerted. We have been reclassified as prize DNA stocks. This, of course, means a higher value added tax and prohibition of export. But then, there's always smuggling."

Koch said, "I'm not sure that yours are the fish my client wants."

"I think she has some Peruvian green bloodlines that might ease matters," Gottke said as if Koch hadn't spoken. "I'd thought all the native Terran discus were either gone or under severe protection."

Koch wondered if Herrin had an outpost of the Ecological Police. Naw, he'd have been arrested by now. "My client didn't explain how she got her fish." Koch had smuggled artifacts before, but never restricted DNA in vivo. "But then, why don't you all use recombinant and reconstructive technology?"

"It wouldn't be sporting," Gottke said. "Come with me, please, Mr. Koch."

The fish room was elegant, restrained, but the fish inside the eight-foot-long tanks made up for the restraint around them. Koch didn't know much about fish, but these finned disks in emerald, those in red and blue, this tank full of pure turquoise with high fins were living art. Gottke said, "All parent-raised. I select for other things beside size, color, and finnage."

One fish with a particularly bulbous forehead was playing with a floating ring, tossing it out of the water and watching his other tankmates scurry, unsure whether they were being fed or attacked.

"Discus. The name makes sense."

"I raise the young in water of a hundred fifty micro-Siemens, harden my local water with clam shells. They ship better that way. Can your insect queen client take care of them properly? She's either got to change almost all the water daily or have protein skimmers, ozone purifiers, membrane filters, maybe . . ." Gottke didn't say more, but pulled aside a black plastic panel under one of the giant tanks. Water ran from skimming weirs at the surface of the tank through a fiber filter to a rotating spray bar over red plastic Möbius loops then through what looked like carbon into a well with a pump in it. The pump sent the water through bubbling tubes and then another carbon filter, under pressure this time. From there, another pump carried the water back into the tank, spraying it across the surface.

Gottke said, "The real problem will be shipping, but I must wonder what ozone would do to a Locrian if regular oxygen intoxicates them."

Koch wondered why he hadn't been cut out since Gottke knew a Locrian with Peruvian green discus was his client, but then perhaps Gottke wouldn't have found that any more sporting than using recombinant techniques to improve his stock. "I'll bring my client. She wants her Naxian to examine the fish."

"I've thought about breeding Naxians," Gottke said. "The colors could be improved and I've wondered if they're repressing true ESP genes."

*   *   *

Generally, Koch found most planets had officials who'd help around technicalities like tariffs and embargoes, but he hadn't been on Herrin long enough to locate the discreet people to ask. So, smuggle it was. Considering the odd life support systems necessary for alien comfort, small discus should fit in some bladder or tank.

Gottke didn't want to hear where the fish were going, or how the Locrian would bring in her Peruvian blues. Breaking the government's law was sporting, it seemed.

Koch considered the possibility that Gottke would inform in order to get his fish back, but he figured the Naxian with Tirifalack would be the best judge of that. So he flew back with his client and his client's retinue, calling ahead to ask that the landing pad be cleared and surrounded by something visible against the sand this time.

Tirifalack sniffed neon. Her inner eye was closed. Koch decided his client wasn't a drug user. Blackwheel was curled into a knotted ball and one of the two Samians Koch thought he'd seen earlier had glued itself to a bulkhead and was vibrating slightly. Aliens, Koch thought. He remembered a Crotonite who collected Japanese kites, a wonderful client who didn't care if the kites were reconstructions, so long as the paper was handmade and the designs matched those in his kite reference book. It was always so much better if the creators didn't value the item as much as the collectors.

The Japanese themselves had perfected that scam with Korean kitchen pottery, selecting out a few pieces as examples of perfect unconscious workmanship and turning them into tea ceremony trophies The Koreans couldn't know whether a pot thrown by some farm town potter would be worth a thousand times more than the rest of the day's production or what, so they couldn't dare ask more for the pots.

Koch hoped discus would become a Locrian fad without driving the price of discus higher here than it was. Selected discus with traits only he could see. Oh, dream, he told himself.

The Naxian uncurled and stared at him.

"So, I don't even know that much about discus," Koch told it.

"It/he only reads emotions," Tirifalack said.

"We need to know if Gottke plans to get customs to seize the fish so he can sell them again."

"We know this. Also, is that your plan?"

"I smuggle. I don't cheat my clients."

Blackwheel said, "Not likely that he will in this case, but he'd like to have the advantage."

"Of course. Wouldn't we all," Tirifalack said, the eyelids over her inner eye flickering.

Just after the helicopter landed in a square of potted roses, the Samian unglued itself from the rear bulkhead with a slurp. Koch realized how much he'd been correcting for the Samian's position in the helicopter, how heavy it was.

Gottke smiled as Tirifalack stepped out of the helicopter. Tirifalack opened her inner eye—a blaze of infosuck—then turned to the Naxian who was coming down the helicopter steps in punctuated continuum slithers, tail wrapping around the struts supporting the handrail, then uncurling to allow a little forward motion, then recurling on the next strut down. Koch wondered if he should help it/him.

Blackwheel curled neatly, head centered, and looked at Gottke. It/he rippled psuedopodia at Tirifalack, who closed her eye and said, "Mr. Gottke, I've looked forward to meeting you, but I must breed my Peruvian greens before I have spare genetic material for you."

"Can you raise them where you are?"

"I've had an immature male trained. Ozone killed the first one—an unfortunate addiction."

If excess oxygen made Locrians drunk after some time, then ozone must burn out their brains in close to instant intoxication.

The Samian jumped out and smacked onto the landing pad. Koch wondered if such a weird exit was normal for a Samian. The Naxian turned its/his head toward the animated slab and seemed to smile.

"Can you all follow me comfortably?" Gottke asked. Everyone affirmed he could in various semiotic systems. They followed Gottke between two glass mountains to his cuckoo house with its carved barge boards in the high peaked gables and dormers.

"Hansel and Gretel," Tirifalack said, opening her inner eye again. "The witch's sugar cookie house."

"Black Forest hunting lodge," Gottke replied.

". . . somewhat taken aback," Blackwheel added. Koch realized it/he referred to Gottke's emotional state at being compared to an obscure folkloric witch by an alien several millennia removed from the tale's widest human distribution.

"We've come to see fish," the slab of a Samian said, cutting through the incipient social complexities.

Gottke drove them to the house, to an entrance Koch, on his earlier visit, had not been invited through. Koch smarted under the insult. An art dealer was not a servant, no matter how shady his implied past had to have been to bring him to a high-tariff planet, not to speak of the present outright embargo.

The Naxian's head turned toward Koch, but no one else looked at the dealer as Gottke led them into a parlor where three robot carts had tea, coffee, and little white sandwiches waiting.

"We've come to see the fish," the Samian repeated.

The Naxian slithered up to the Samian and spoke something that seemed to soothe it. Tirifalack opened her inner eye again, briefly, then partially closed it.

"Can you drink our beverages?" Gottke asked.

"No," Tirifalack said.

The carts seemed confused for a second, then they rolled away. "Fish, then, now," Gottke said. Koch wondered how he would protect himself if his fellow Erthuma and the Locrian decided to cut out the middleman. He tried not to think about informing on smugglers until the Naxian looked away.

When they got up to go to the fish rooms, the Naxian slithered beside Koch. "Relax," Blackwheel hissed. "We wouldn't dream of cheating you out of your commission."

That sounded almost more ominous.

The fish room seemed even cleaner, whiter walled, white noise of pumps under the tanks. Tirifalack looked at the dinner-plate-sized adult discus until she found a couple with broader than usual striations. Her inner eye opened. The Naxian crept up the glass and bent its/his head back, belly against the front glass. The fish backed up in the water.

"Hardwiring against aquatic snakes," Blackwheel said. "They are an old pair. The male is getting bored with the female." It/he lowered its/his body and moved away from the tank.

"I'd like to examine their young in a fifteen-cm size and also have my Naxian sex some pairs of young adults with equally promising markings," Tirifalack said.

Gottke walked over to an eight-foot-long rearing tank. "They're mixed with the others, but all these have broad striations."

Tirifalack said, "I'll buy the pair and half the young in this tank, plus six young adults."

"The Naxian can sex discus?" Gottke asked.

"Yes."

"I'd like two breeding units of Naxians, fifty thousand credits or a 1951 restored third generation McCormick grain combine, plus a twenty-five-thousand-credit commission for Mr. Koch for the trade on the combine, fifteen thousand if we just use credits. I'll trade you fish for fish in Peruvian greens when I see them."

Koch said, "I'd be smuggling twice."

Tirifalack said, "We can manage. Then you will know how to smuggle the combine. Smuggling jobs go for fifty credits per ten kilos for professionals."

"Herrin has ferocious security."

"Against a body that can't be x-rayed?"

"It's like a drug," the Samian said just before it broke into a thousand components. They looked like bugs in colors that would make a bacon slab mosaic—reddish, fat-colored, pepper-colored, dark brown—all running up away from one another as the slab slumped into first a cone, then a low heap. The bugs crawled everywhere around the other aliens as if totally fearless about being stepped on.

Koch dabbed his shoe at one that came close. No damage. Did everyone else know Samians could fall apart into thousands of bullet-proof bugs? Koch wondered.

Tirifalack sighed, her eye still wide open. The Naxian said, "We'll need two light, strong frames to put the transport bags in, Mr. Gottke. It would attract less attention if you procured them."

"The core of a shipping container, without the insulation, should do," Gottke said, "if the Samian would be insulation enough."

"Samians," Tirifalack said, snapping her eye shut.

One of Tirifalack's Samians wouldn't be returning, then—at least not in the form it had when it came to Herrin, Koch realized.

Gottke said, "House, what have you on this phenomenon?"

His house, presumably an AI, didn't answer.

"Disrupts AIs and Samians into component systems," Blackwheel said.

Gottke closed his eyes and said, "I don't believe I've read about this Samian trait in the *Six Race Bible*."

The Samian scrambled back into one creature and said, "We play dumb."

Gottke looked over at Koch, who felt the glance obscurely accusing. Of what, he wasn't quite sure. Gottke said, "House, if you're with us, send me manipulators."

"Sir, my clock time is off."

"Yes, you were disrupted. Reset and forget the disruption. Have the manipulators strip the insulation away from two shipping boxes."

The manipulator externals reduced the shipping boxes to their rigid shells. The Samian divided into two masses and flowed around the boxes. "What temperature?"

"Eighty-two degrees Fahrenheit for shipping," Gottke said. "What's a price for a couple of breeding units of Samians?"

"Not available," the Samian said.

Tirifalack said, "Now should we load the fish?" The Samian slumped bits down to expose the shipping boxes' lids.

Gottke said, "Not today. I'll pack the fish tomorrow after they fast."

"Oxygen diffuses though the plastic?" Tirifalack asked.

"No."

Koch wondered what, besides Gottke's lust to have Peruvian green discus, would ensure that those particular fish would go into the shipping containers. Gottke took the boxes and set them down on the floor. The Samian pulled itself together again and rippled. "Can you disassociate like that at will?" Koch asked.

Tirifalack said, "Yes." Perhaps a lie, Koch sensed.

The Naxian raised itself up against the tanks of near-adults and said, "This one, that one, and that one, and that one. Those two flirting."

Gottke came over and netted out the fish the Naxian wanted. They went into an empty tank, small, three feet long. "Tomorrow, then?"

After the helicopter took off, Koch said, "How will you explain the Samians? They must have something that identifies themselves as separate entitites."

"No problem," the Samian said. "We all look alike to you. And we're friendly, jolly, harmless, noncriminal, and too dense. This unit is the two Samians who landed."

It was the greatest smuggling scam Koch had ever heard of—at least, it would be until someone official discovered how it worked. Samians crossing trade barriers thereafter would be dismantled.

The Naxian said, "Perhaps, boss, you should charge for teaching him something useful."

"Two devices, only, in galaxy," the Samian said. "One destroyed by AI Erthuma symbiotic team. Samian and AI Erthuma units not talking official. Great fear. Other unit so small, with a switch a component or pseudopod could move."

The Naxian rippled and exposed a vacuole. Inside the tissue pocket was a tiny circle of something swirling to shift from appearing black to appearing like the inside of a Naxian flesh pocket—a tiny extragalactic invisibility screen. The Naxian extruded a pseudopod through the screen and it vanished, exposing a five-centimeter-long ovoid with a roughened patch on the small top.

"Probably used to sabotage an AI," Tirifalack said. "Or a component being."

Koch knew how dangerous the device would be to Erthumoi as well as Samians. He also knew Tirifalack was offering to make him part of the team. No, Koch had been drafted.

The Naxian made the device invisible, then moved flesh over the vacuole. "Mr. Koch understands," it/he said.

Tirifalack came up in her support suit and took Koch's jaw between her manipulators. "You need us. You have some authentic judgment, but you are an inept smuggler."

Koch remembered thinking that an overpainting could hide a Picasso. X-ray at the spaceport had proved him wrong. "So, I'll stay alive. You'll move the fish out."

"And dead art in," Tirifalack said. "I have enough subsistence that I can afford to be a connoisseur."

"Any way to duplicate that device?" Koch wondered if this were all too good to be true. "No chance we're bugged."

"No," the Naxian said. "No, to both." The Naxian tightened flesh over the ovoid as Koch wandered how he could get his hands on the device. "We'll pick you up tomorrow after lunch."

*　　*　　*

Koch stuck to the second Samian. He wiggled, but the almost magnetic attraction kept him glued to the bacon-colored side. Tirifalack, the Naxian, and the Samian who'd become the outside shipping containers took the keys to Koch's helicopter.

"We're not turning on you," the Naxian told Koch. "We just don't want you to turn on us."

Koch heard the sounds of the helicopter. "Can you disrupt intentionally?" Koch asked his Samian captor.

"Yes/no."

Perhaps it was a stress-triggered reaction. Split and flee. Koch wondered if any other Erthuma knew Samians had possible home planet enemies, hopefully in their past, mean enough and tough enough to make a Samian dissolve in fright. Koch hoped the enemy was as much in the Samian past as spiders were to Erthumoi.

The Samian finally dropped Koch, who sprawled on the floor. "They're back. This unit . . . not fond of disruption, but . . ." The Samian shrugged into thousands of sub-units as the Naxian slithered in.

It/he said, "I'll stay here. You'll stay here, too. Tirifalack'll bring you back a treat."

Koch said, "I need to open my office, keep regular hours."

The Naxian spoke something alien to the bugs. Then it/he said to Koch, "The trip to jump point will take several days. Perhaps it would be best if you do carry on your routine."

Koch said, "And you two?"

The bugs ate a hole between the floor and the corner walls and marched in. The Naxian said, "My visa has been extended. Both Samians left. I will explore further economic and aesthetic possibilities for Tirifalack." As it/ he spoke, the Naxian let the extragalactic artifact camouflage itself in a corner.

Koch grimaced at the damage he'd have to repair, then wondered if his office was bugged by more than Samian components. And did the Naxian know? It/he went home with Koch after hours, but didn't say much.

In the morning, some customers Koch had never seen before asked about nonspacer sophont handicrafts. Koch got rid of them. Perhaps he could smuggle in their goodies in hollowed-out Samians, but he wanted to have Tirifalack clear to hyperspace before he planned anything more illegal. The Naxian went to the wall and listened. It/he said, "I'm having a bad feeling about this," and turned off the extragalactic artifact.

The walls didn't crash outward as a Samian reconstructed itself. Koch asked, "Do the Samian components have to come together now?"

"The unit didn't like being disassociated. We had to pay plenty. It could stay voluntarily disassociated, like the other one, but I don't hear anything. It's not worth it to risk disrupting people's AIs if the Samian snuck away."

"So, we're missing a Samian."

The Naxian hissed and turned the disrupter back to camouflage. It/he said, "I hope I haven't confused someone's AI."

"Perhaps I should close for lunch."

The Naxian said, "I'd like to make a neutrino call, if you wouldn't mind."

"Collect only."

For an instant, the Naxian seemed annoyed, colors shifting in its/his head. Koch realized he wasn't sure any longer whether he'd been dealing with a rich Locrian or some imposter. Surely, the big bug queen had good taste, an expensive exoskeleton, but helicopters didn't rent for that much if you found an owner hurting to make payments.

"Collect, it will be," the Naxian said, as though insulted. Koch wondered how he'd projected emotionally during that pause. The Naxian twisted around onto the top of Koch's desk and extruded pseudopodia. "Pick up the disrupter and bring it over. The Samian couldn't have gotten far without being noticed, but I don't think it's precisely looking forward to explaining this gizmo to Erthumoi.''

"How come you know about it then?"

"I found it," the Naxian said. "Now, bring it to me."

Koch realized he needed to make friends with this Naxian. The Naxian moved pseudopodia into an ancient obscene gesture, so Koch dropped what he was thinking and dipped his hands into the void to pull it, shifting and twisting as the disrupter camouflage tried to match the room it moved through.

"You need to have something about three millimeters long that curls and push through there," the Naxian said. It/he shoved a pseudopod in and turned off the disrupter shield. A somewhat thicker pseudopod popped out on the Naxian's other side and began pushing buttons. "No, we can't do that."

"No?" Koch realized himself that a collect call to Tirifalack's ship would look suspicious, and even worse from his office.

"If the news hasn't gotten out, if the Samian is looking for other Samians."

"You can't read Samians, can you?"

"Not particularly well. That unit did seem nervous, but . . ."

"Maybe it's okay?"

The Naxian said, "You just want to believe that. I think we'd better go see if we can find more Samians before they find us. Put the device back in my vacuole."

Koch did, then asked, "What can we do against them?"

"The device has a lethal setting. At least against AIs. We didn't test it against Samians. You know, if Samians can be programmed to hide things from Naxians . . ." The Naxian shut up.

Koch tried to keep from thinking anything, wished he had a drug that would make him trust. Wished even more that . . . no, don't think about it, he told himself.

"Certainly, it would be simpler if we tried to kill each

other, but I'd prefer to live and you obviously would too. Tirifalack simply provides the means. I hide in her arrogance."

"Your vacuoles?"

"Vacuole. Most Naxians don't have them. Unless you can afford your own hyperspace ship, a partnership between just the two of us wouldn't be profitable."

"A couple of jobs."

"Tirifalack owns two hyperspace ships, now. And she does have excellent taste."

Koch switched on his security devices and the out-to-lunch sign. The Naxian said, "Tirifalack left her helicopter. Let's go play with it."

On board and moving, Blackwheel said, "Those customers were trying to find out why their AI couldn't tap in through your phone."

"Why not?"

"It's too close. I'll turn off the device now while the shop's empty. When we get back, an AI will be screening for phrases, but it seems all Herrin is smuggling these days."

"Because of the embargo?"

"Because of the embargo, it's much more fun. To Erthumoi. Naxians among Naxians just couldn't get away with such stuff. I just love the five other races. Naxians." This Naxian hissed.

"That implies you hate yourself."

"No, I loathe being totally honest and emotionally exposed all the time. I love dishonesty. I personally think that's perfectly natural. You obviously agree."

"So, what are we looking for?"

"What we should look for is a good place to ditch this where nobody can find it and buy tickets off planet."

Unfortunately, the helicopter sank toward what were obviously several Samian units fishing it out of the sky. The Naxian said, "Perhaps if we just give them this." It/he opened the vacuole and dumped the disrupter over the side.

"But . . ." Koch sputtered, thinking of all the millions they could smuggle with the help of these Samians.

"If the device isn't very late extragalactic, we'll find more of them. I know what to look for."

"Debrained ghost ships," Koch said, realizing too late he'd thought out loud.

The helicopter wavered as the Samians figured out what had been dropped out. Blackwheel said, "Broadcast for help. I'd rather work honestly than die."

Koch pushed down the mike button and hailed Herrin police. "This is Augustus Koch with Tirifalack's Naxian assistant, Blackwheel . . ."

The helicopter lurched again. "And Samians are dragging my helicopter out of the sky at coordinates thirty-four degrees, two minutes, four seconds, and sixty degrees, seven minutes, and . . ."

Koch lost the last second in a terror-induced paralysis of his tongue. The Samians had the helicopter.

Blackwheel said, "We've notified the police in case you're thinking of killing us."

"What do you take us for?" one Samian said. "We're Samians. We don't kill."

Koch said, "Neither you nor we want information about the disrupter to get out, do we?"

"We must find reverse mechanism, counteracter," the Samian spokesman said. "Thank you for unit."

Koch wondered how Tirifalack would get her discus out of the Samian bodies. "I have a client," Koch began to say before he realized the Samians could care less about anything more complex than life-or-death matters. "No, intelligences will die if you don't let us borrow the disrupter for a few days."

The Naxian gestured affirmative and chattered at them in alien for several minutes. While one Samian dragged Koch and Blackwheel out of the helicopter, the other Samians locked to each other.

Just as the police helicopter was circling overhead, the Samians said, "Agreed. Call the police."

* * *

Five Samians, Blackwheel, and Koch rendezvoused with Tirifalack's ship five days after the discus were bagged. The device dissolved all the Samians. Tirifalack began drip transfer of the fish to her on-board tanks while Samian sub-units scrambled around to make sure all the intelligent units, even sub-sophonts, were okay.

Blackwheel began to ripple pseudopodia. "I can't read them," it/he told Koch. "I can't quite read them." The sub-units appeared to be collecting more around Black-wheel than around the disrupter.

One sub-unit seemed to have curved a three-millimeter probe. The machine flickered.

A giant Samian formed around Blackwheel. It said, 'The Naxian unit will not die.''

But Blackwheel could scream, muffled to mouse squeaks by oh-too-solid Samian flesh. Koch wondered if he were next to be encapsulated in a Samian, but one Samian said, 'Erthumoi need symbiotic computer connections to leave planets. We don't share environmental needs with Locri-ans, but the device and the Naxian are ours.''

Another unit said, "Of course, we could come back for you, Augustus Koch, or you, Tirifalack, if we discover anyone else, anywhere, has a disrupter. Tirifalack, we will take your fish to Gottke, to avoid bad feelings.''

Two Samians appeared to be linked. Koch speculated one was the Samian unit who'd smuggled the fish. At least, it had been dishonest.

UNNATURAL DIPLOMACY

KAREN HABER

ON THE FOURTH PLANET OF THE THIRD STAR IN A star-misted corner of the Delta system, morning broke in the water-covered Cephallonian retirement colony of Ipsh. And with morning came the inevitable rituals of morning.

Ph'shara and Ph'shant, neighbors for several spans, met early each day in Ph'shara's spacious, iridescent-walled quarters to enjoy the pleasures of debate, discussion, and delicate repast. Ph'shara's food processors were renowned throughout Ipsh and the quality of his conversation was rumored very nearly to approach that of his comestibles.

"You're looking well," Ph'shant said as he emitted rosy bubbles of greeting.

"And you, may I say, look even better today than you did yesterday." Ph'shara's bubbles were bright pink, indicating emanations of courtesy and welcome. "I hope you will join me and perhaps share a few humble refreshments." Ph'shara's sweeping gesture encompassed the low, wide table floating between two silver couches. Its golden surface was covered, as usual, with innumerable small shell-like dishes of food.

"With pleasure." Ph'shant said, and he settled his ponderous body slowly onto a curved, padded couch. Once comfortable, he assumed the appropriate posture for polite conversation, and fastidiously selected a savory morsel

234

hat was wrapped in a wisp of gleaming pink. "Did you ear?"

Ph'shara's bearing indicated surprise. "Are you inquiring about my capability for aural reception?"

"No, no, I'm using the quaint idiom of the Erthumoi to refer to information transmission."

Ph'shara made a gesture of comprehension but his bubbles were tinged with the lime green of annoyance. "You might have stated that plainly."

"Apologies. I beg your pardon. Do you have knowledge of the Summit of the Six Races?"

"Yes. In a fortnight representatives will meet on Lextra to debate the La Se Dan problem."

"On the neutral planet owned by the Samians, so I am given to understand."

"Of course. Who else would choose to run a neutral world? The Samians will avoid every conflict they can. Especially in the interests of trade." Here, Ph'shara paused to ingest a small wriggling creature with many multicolored legs. "I learned from the early newsburst that our ambassador, Ph'shirat, remains undecided upon the summit vote."

Ph'shant emitted lavender bubbles of contemplation. "The La Se Dan seem a potential problem for the Six Races, it's true. But to ask for a vote of isolation as the Naxians recommend seems, well, premature. If the Naxians succeed, this will certainly create enmity in the hearts of the La Se Dans. And even if they *are* isolated, sooner or later they will discover the secrets of hyperdrive independently."

"Most likely true," Ph'shara said.

"Nevertheless, if they are as violent and dangerous as rumor has them I would just as soon shut them out of interstellar trade and commerce."

Ph'shara gave a ponderous shrug that nearly toppled him off his couch and into the food. "I remind you, Ph'shant, that, unfortunately, the La Se Dans reside upon a treasure trove of Hidden Folk artifacts."

"Too much is made of these Hidden Folk objects," Ph'shant said. His bubbles were the icy blue of disdain. "I have managed to spend most of my lifespan in ignorance of them, and would willingly spend the rest of it in like manner if it meant avoiding those unpleasant green-furred folk."

"The Erthumoi do not agree with you."

"No. Their sympathies are with the La Se Dans. Thank goodness they only have one vote in the Summit."

"For now."

The chamber filled with orange bubbles of amusement and both Cephallonians became silent in order that they might concentrate more fully upon the delicate, succulent fare that was floating between them.

A little while later, in the same system, on the neutral planet of Lextra, in that planet's capital city of Menafi, preliminary discussions were under way concerning the impending Summit Conference.

Ctaarh, second consul of the Crotonian Deputation, perched uncomfortably upon the polished black mirwood bench that the Erthuma ambassador, Karim Hoving-Davis, had placed by the red desk in his huge, dark-walled office.

Erthumoi did their best to understand the physical requirements of other species, Ctaarh knew. All the same, the construction of this perch required him to assume a posture that fatigued his forelegs. He would have preferred to stand, regardless of the disarray this would cause in protocol. But the Erthuma ambassador would then have been forced to stand also, and he was so much taller than the Crotonite that eye contact would have been nearly impossible unless Hoving-Davis were to look directly down and Ctaarh, straight up. Obviously, that was out of the question.

The small, gray-feathered diplomat shifted his weight upon the perch and tried to ignore the ache beginning below his knees.

"I thought the Crotonians were opposed to a diplomatic summit." said Hoving-Davis.

"Perhaps you were misinformed." Ctaarh said. "We are willing to meet, although we feel that the La Se Dan issue does not yet require debate. However, we would have been happier with a location more convenient to Crotonis itself."

"I believe this location was selected for its inconvenience to all representatives of the Six Races save for the Samians," said Hoving-Davis. The Erthuma bared his teeth in what Ctaarh had learned was usually, but not always, a gesture of nonaggression. Ctaarh unfurled his wings slightly, then tucked them back to indicate that he, too, was not taking an aggressive stance.

How time-consuming these diplomatic considerations and nuances were! Yet how very crucial.

"If we must meet, let us meet soon," Ctaarh said.

"Agreed," said the Erthuma. He moved a little closer in what Ctaarh had come to recognize as a posture of professional intimacy. The shift made Ctaarh uneasy. He was now so close to the Erthuma that he could almost count the black hairs in the ambassador's beard.

"But tell me," said Hoving-Davis. "Just between us, of course, what is the Crotonian position regarding the Naxian suggestion of isolation?"

Ctaarh frowned. "For the La Se Dans? We are undecided."

"Yes, we know. But could you tell me which way you might be leaning?"

"Historically, isolation rarely works."

"Precisely our point," said Hoving-Davis, and he nodded vigorously.

"However," Ctaarh said, "the La Se Dans seem difficult, potentially dangerous. I fail to see what they could offer us technologically. And their planet does not have rare or even desirable raw materials."

Hoving-Davis lifted his dark, bushy eyebrows until they formed twin arcs high upon his forehead. That signified surprise, thought the Crotonite. Or disdain. Or was it reproof?

"Need I remind you of the Hidden Folk artifacts?" said the Erthuma.

"Of course, of course," said Ctaarh. "We are well aware of them. Therefore, some interaction with the La Se Dans is required, at least until we resolve the secrets of the objects. Or lose interest."

"Not likely."

"No. And if the vote for isolation carries, the La Se Dans are certain to be antagonized. For the Six to recover any further Hidden Folk artifacts from La Se Dan might require the use of force. Which seems inefficient and potentially disruptive."

"Then you'll vote with us against the motion for isolation?" Hoving-Davis asked.

Ctaarh's orange eyes gleamed with satisfaction. This Erthuma ambassador was impetuous. It was a weakness that might be exploited later during more important negotiations. "Did I give you that impression? Your pardon. I did not intend it. No. We do not yet know how we will vote."

"And your personal feelings?"

"Why are those of importance?"

"I'm curious."

"Well," Ctaarh said, "I believe that we cannot isolate the La Se Dans forever. Better the threat you know than the threat you don't."

"Ah, then you would consider yourself to be a cultural relativist?"

"Perhaps a cultural fatalist would be a more accurate term," Ctaarh said. Again the Erthuma's eyebrows rose. "You appear surprised, Ambassador."

Hoving-Davis nodded. "Few members of your embassy would share your opinion. Forgive me for saying this if it offends, Ctaarh, but the Crotonites are well known for their interest in maintaining cultural purity."

"Not all of us are so unrealistic," Ctaarh replied tolerantly. "Any forward-thinking being would realize that the development of stardrive has brought an end to pure culture for any race that has achieved a high level of technological development. Some day we will live in a multicultural Galaxy."

"Quite a radical opinion, that."

Ctaarh resisted the urge to preen. "If I didn't think of myself as a cultural relativist, would I have chosen to accept this position with the Crotonian deputation?" The second consul eyed the tall Erthuma soberly. "Few Crotonites would want this post. Please understand that."

"It's no secret," said Hoving-Davis. "But tell me this, if you don't mind the question. How did you ever manage to retain your wings?"

Ctaarh ignored the shocking discourtesy of the Erthuma's blunt interrogative. He had been trained to expect such insensitivity from the ground dwellers. Calmly he replied, "I am most fortunate. This is a temporary assignment. And my family is quite pr-prominent." Ctaarh stumbled for a moment over the last word. The Erthuma tongue was so difficult to speak. But to expect an Erthuma to speak Crotoni was a hopeless task; and in any case Ctaarh had a keen dislike of hearing his own language barbarically mangled.

"I see," Hoving-Davis said. "Well, I congratulate you on your good fortune, Ctaarh, as well as your enlightened opinions. I trust you will employ the latter at the Summit meeting."

"When possible, yes. In my short career, I have observed that diplomacy must not be rushed."

"Amen. Then I will see you in a few days when we all convene at the Presidium and I welcome my replacement," Hoving-Davis said. "You know, I'll miss this planet. Of course, I'm eager to begin my new assignment in the Greenfall system, but I'm almost sorry to be leaving."

"Yes," Ctaarh said. "I suppose you are. It's actually

quite pleasant, for a Samian world. Nevertheless, I look forward to my return to Pereon in five spans.''

"Well, then, until the Summit." Hoving-Davis stood up and offered a half bow in farewell. Gratefully, Ctaarh unwound himself from his uncomfortable perch and responded in kind to the Erthuma's gesture.

The setting sun cast a greenish glow over the city as Ctaarh hurried homeward. He watched the twin moons rising orange over the spires of Menafi and felt a savage joy at the sight. Try as he might, the Crotonite could not even pretend to be dour. Twice this day alone he had bested the Erthuma ambassador in logic and indisputably proved the natural superiority of the Crotonian brain. So had it gone, all week: small, satisfactory opportunities for correcting the foolish ground crawlers in matters of logic, culture, and even technology. All of which had allowed Ctaarh to provide ample demonstration of Crotonian abilities. Very pleasing. Yes. Ctaarh nodded, savoring some of the best moments yet again. His pleasure was not unlike that which he had often experienced at home on Pereon following a fine smooth flight on a clear morning before his early meal.

Once he was inside the high curving walls of the garden that enclosed his home, Ctaarh gave the Crotonian equivalent of a deep sigh and stretched his wings until the joints cracked. All around the neat yard gray-furred skrill trees undulated in the cool air. The evening crotild was just stirring, opening its purple petals and beginning to croak. He could hear the hoarse peeping of the septibors; the scalim bushes emitted their satisfying ultraviolet glow. It was a little bit of home, this garden of his. He loved it dearly.

Ctaarh stretched one more time and thanked the gods of flight that his diplomatic post was a temporary assignment. No amputation of his wings would be required. At the very thought a shudder ran through his thin-boned frame. To be cast from the sky. What an abomination that was—in the name of diplomacy or not! Infernal diplomacy. Poor Larvis, he thought. The first consul had been inordinately proud of her fine wingspan, and with some justification. But no longer. Small wonder she was difficult to deal with. How could anyone abide such a mutilation? How? How?

Ctaarh's mate, Sylbi, met him at the door. Her bluish feathers were sleekly arranged in the favorite pattern he found most pleasing. She carried a copper bowl of fresh-killed suthilbis meat, and the spice of it permeated the room.

"You will eat?" she said.

"That I will. Gladly."

Ctaarh settled upon the feeding perch as Sylbi hooked the bowl below him. Through the great rounded windows he had a fine view of the downtown spires. Sylbi perched beside him as he ate and stared out at the purpling sky.

They were silent for a time.

"Husband," she said, at last. "You spend too much time with the Erthumoi."

Startled, Ctaarh paused in mid-swallow. "But I have to. It's my job," he told her. "You know what's expected of me here."

"Nevertheless, I'm beginning to believe that you actually enjoy their company."

Ctaarh came close to choking in surprise. Enjoy being with the ground crawlers? Had Sylbi's common sense taken flight?

"What is this foolishness?" he demanded.

"I'm sure of it," Sylbi said. "Why don't you admit it? You enjoy them more than you enjoy our time together."

"Ah. I think I see." He had been warned by senior members of the Diplomacy Guild that spouses who accompanied the Crotonian Deputation might become restive, even resentful of their mates' duties, especially during nesting season. That must be it. "If I could only make you see how wrong you are," he said. "Too much time alone has disturbed your balance. I assure you, I merely wish to do my job well. To represent our people in a proper manner.''

She looked away from him. "It isn't so. I know that. You like the slugs.''

"Erthumoi," Ctaarh said gently. "You mustn't call them insulting names, dearest. Even in privacy like this. And how could I like them? They can't begin to appreciate the simplest aspects of our culture, let alone the fine things that you and I value. Do not confuse business with friendship, I beg you.''

Sylbi did not meet his eyes. "What about that quarrel with Vatiy? You know he was against your joining the diplomatic mission and I don't blame him. Aren't you ashamed? Fighting with your closest nestmate! Turning against your own for the sake of these outsiders.''

Ctaarh gave the Crotonite equivalent of a frown. "My nestmate is extremely unwise. He wishes to hide his eyes from plain facts. We simply can't avoid the other starfolk. Like it or not, we have to deal with them.''

Sylbi sniffed her disagreement.

"One day, Vatiy's short sight will cause him to run into a cliff in the mist," Ctaarh said. "I have warned him of this before. We must move with events. I am first-hatched and forward-thinking. The Erthumoi and the others of the Six are not going to go away. Therefore we need to deal with them in order to keep them at a safe distance. And we can best do that by proving our natural superiority to the land dwellers.''

Sylbi said nothing.

"Foolish one," Ctaarh said. He made a soft clucking sound. "Come here, little bird. Come here.''

She moved closer to him on the perch. He nodded and began to stroke her neck with his beak. Sylbi sighed and made a brooding, contented throbbing deep in her throat.

"That's better," he murmured. "Now let's drop all this absurd chatter.''

But Sylbi had pecked a hole in his confidence, and he preened her absently, wondering all the while whether she could possibly be correct. No. No, it was impossible. Like the Erthumoi? No, no, no. He merely found them peculiar. Fascinating in their strange crudeness, perhaps. Any forward-minded Crotonite could hardly help but share his opinion.

Later, when a much-mollified Sylbi had retired, Ctaarh retained his perch, alternately dozing and pondering the Grand Meeting. Representatives of the Six would be coming to Menafi within the month. Perhaps he should suggest to Sylbi that they hold a small reception? She would bristle at the thought, especially after the last disastrous reception they had held. But it would help provide a positive impression of Crotonian diplomacy and please his superiors. And it would certainly erase the unfortunate memory of their last party. It was important that a progressive Crotonian attitude be perceived by the other ambassadors. Crotonian leadership needed to come to the fore in future dealings among the interstellar races to ensure that Crotonian interests received the consideration they were due.

Thinking this and similar agreeable thoughts, Ctaarh slipped into a doze. And as his sleep grew deeper, he dreamed.

The house was quiet and dark. There was no sound save for an occasional chirp from a night-blooming clotild outside. Inside, all was peaceful. But the quiet was broken by the harsh, insistent buzzing of a wallscreen. And within Ctaarh's dream it seemed to him that he awoke with a start.

A call? At this hour? Stumbling, clumsy with sleep, he reached for the speaker as quickly as he could. If Sylbi were awakened she would be restive for days.

"Yes?"

A Crotonite female, unknown to him, appeared onscreen. She was young and might almost have been attractive, but her greenish-bronze feathers were oddly clipped and arranged in the conventional male fashion. Quite unflattering. She gave him a bold, impertinent appraisal completely inappropriate for one of her age and sex.

"Hello?" she said. To Ctaarh's surprise, she spoke in Erthuma. Her tone was brash but she sounded a bit perplexed.

Ctaarh could scarcely control his impatience. "What do you want?" he snapped. "Do you know what time it is?"

"I'm sorry. What did you say? I'm having trouble understanding you."

Ctaarh switched from Crotoni to Erthuma. "Why are you speaking Erthuma?"

"What else would I speak?"

"Crotoni, of course."

"Crotoni?" Her tone was frankly amused, as though he had suggested something preposterous. "How old-fashioned. Who are you, anyway?"

Ctaarh was taken aback. "You called me. Who are you?"

"My name is Wylla."

"What do you want? It's very late."

"Late? What are you talking about? Why, it's the middle of the morning."

Ctaarh clacked his beak with irritation. "Are you blind? Look outside your window. The moons are almost setting."

The screen began to undulate as though it were made of soft putty. Ctaarh tried to hold it still but somehow he could not get a solid grasp on it.

"The moons?" Wylla said. "I don't see moons. The sun is climbing high above the towers of Menafi. I can see it, casting long shadows over the lawns of the great park."

"I don't have time for this foolishness," Ctaarh said. "Tell me what your business is, if you have any. I don't recognize you nor do I understand what you want. In fact, I'm tempted to report you to the first consul of the Crotonian Deputation for harassing a government representative."

She looked amazed. "First consul?" she said. "What Crotonian Deputation? There hasn't been a Crotonian Deputation here in over a hundred years." She blinked several times. "Isn't this the Center for Multicultural Enrichment?

What I'm trying to do is reschedule my inner-eye study session."

"Multicultural Enrichment?" Ctaarh said. "What center? Where is it?"

Wylla gave a sigh. "Look, I don't know who you are, and this is obviously *not* the Center for Multicultural—"

"No, don't go," Ctaarh begged. "Please. I want to know more. Tell me about this center."

"Well, it's in the middle of Menafi and it's a large, white building with blue windows."

If Ctaarh had had teeth he would have ground them in frustration. "No, not the physical description. What purpose does this center have?"

He listened in confusion and disbelief as she told him about the many events and courses offered at the center, and how the Erthuma and Naxian studies were the most popular classes, almost always overenrolled.

Ctaarh's head swam. Was the girl lying? Why didn't he know about this center? And why was she speaking Erthuma like a native? Nothing made sense.

It became weirder and weirder. She told him about the Eleven starfaring races and the joint agreement among them to adopt Erthuma as the universal language. Of course, that made it easier to do business with the Erthumoi.

Ctaarh shuddered violently. "It's the middle of the night," he said. "I don't understand why you're bothering me. I'm Ctaarh of Pereon, second consul to—"

"Ctaarh?" Wylla's eyes grew wide with some strange emotion, perhaps recognition, perhaps fear. "Ctaarh of Pereon? Is this some kind of joke?"

"You know me?"

"I have to go now."

"Wait—" he cried. But Wylla's image lifted up and peeled right off the screen. It floated before Ctaarh like a leaf in the wind, rocking this way and that. Then it narrowed, stretching into a glowing, bronze-green cord that snaked around the startled Crotonite, pinning his arms and wings back. Slowly it tightened. Ctaarh couldn't breathe. He gasped, struggling against the steely bonds, and staggered off his perch, knocking a holoportrait of Sylbi's parents across the room. Then he awoke.

The room was dark. He could hear Sylbi's steady breath from the corner where her sleep perch stood.

A nightmare. That was all. It had been a nightmare, nothing more.

The girl Wylla, calling him from some impossible future, was a phantom of sleep. All she had said was just babble. The Eleven Races? It was laughable. Erthumoi dominating the starfolk? Even more improbable.

But even as he reassured himself, Ctaarh remembered the words of the Erthuma ambassador: "You're a cultural relativist?"

"Yes," Ctaarh had replied. "Of course I am. Otherwise, why would I have accepted this post?"

Fiercely, Ctaarh whispered to himself, "I *am* a progressive-minded Crotonite. A multicultural universe is inevitable, and it will be for the best." He did not add his deepest thoughts and assumptions: for the best so long as Crotonis is the dominant culture.

He stared out the window at the darkened city. The sky was black, the moons had set, and the stars were cool points of remote light. He felt tremendously alone. Everybody else in the world was asleep. Ctaarh stared a moment longer and shivered. Then he closed the stone shutter with a sharp snap and joined Sylbi on her perch, pressing tight against her smooth blue feathers for warmth.

The next day, Ctaarh awoke groggy and irritable. The air felt thick, the sun hurt his eyes, and the breakfast cazapa meat sat like so much inert metal in his stomach. Twice as he sat rummaging through his papers and dispatches, Sylbi interrupted him to demand if she had done something to displease him.

"Hold your questions," Ctaarh snapped. "Can't you see I'm busy? Diplomacy is a difficult undertaking, you know." And he made a great show of shuffling through the material on his desk until his mate had withdrawn to sulk privately.

Inwardly he seethed. Fragments of that strange, unsettling dream left bright flickering trails through his memory. "Erthumoi will be dominant . . . dominant . . . dominant."

Sylbi returned to interrupt him yet again.

"What is it?" he said.

"A message from the Erthuma Embassy." She dropped it on his desk and without another word turned and left the room.

Ctaarh put the holocard into his reader and the letters came up onscreen glittering in brilliant reds and blues. It was an invitation to a reception to be held the following week in honor of the new Erthuma ambassador, Sarah Fen-James. Ctaarh read the message a second time, extracted it from the reader, and tossed it into the reprocessor. He did not wish to attend Erthuma gatherings. He did not wish to pretend a bonhomie he did not feel for lesser beings. What he wanted was to go home to Pereon and its clear skies, to hunt as the early morning mist melted away. But Pereon was a month's spaceflight away. Ctaarh's assignment here would last another five spans. He was not going to see Pereon's red skies soon.

But perhaps a quick flight, now, yes? Yes, it would clear his head. Exactly what he needed. Despite the fact that he had never in his life taken a flight in mid-morning—and how could he even think of it, when there was work to be done?—he abandoned his duties now as though pursued by swarms of fire moths.

Ctaarh opened the window, climbed up on the broad white stone sill, unfurled his wings, and took to the morning air.

A strong southerly gust sent him soaring high above the tallest spires of the city. Giddily, he swooped around the silver-studded transmitter tower attached to the Presidium, coasting from one swell to another, buoyed up, up, always upward. Strange calls and midnight fears receded in the bright rays of the sun. Ctaarh shed his worries as he glided through the skies over Menafi. It had all been an odd dream, he told himself. Yes, a dream, and the cold, high air would blow it right out of his head.

What did these night thoughts matter? These fears? Crotonis would flourish. Its natural superiority as a culture would be obvious to any who possessed sight.

The city of Menafi sprawled below him in the shape of a broad circle. Graceful avenues lined by strips of gray and yellow vegetation formed the grand spokes of the city, each pointing inward toward the central parkland, the nucleus of Menafi.

Ctaarh amused himself by swooping along each avenue, barely skimming the lofty tops of the haejun trees. The star-shaped leaves ruffled at his swift passage.

An hour in the high air refreshed and heartened him. Slowly Ctaarh circled over the city until he found his own white, domelike residence. From above it resembled an insect's hive encircled by quivering vegetation. The detailed reliefs on the outside of the residence did not become apparent until one had flown much closer to the building. Ctaarh raised one wing, lowered another, and glided downward, making a neat landing right back on the stone sill where he had started.

Sylbi was waiting, trembling, by the window. Ctaarh's heart expanded with love at the sight of her. He had been rude this morning. He would make amends now.

"My dearest," he said.

"Oh, Ctaarh. Where were you? Flying? At this hour?" Sylbi stared at him as though she couldn't believe what she saw. "The first consul called you for and there was nothing I could tell her. She was quite surprised to find that you were out. Oh, how could you do such a thing?"

"The first consul?" Ctaarh's good spirits began to feel considerably less good. "Larvis herself called me?"

"You've never taken a flight during work. It isn't like

you at all." Sylbi peered at him closely. "Are you feeling well? Perhaps you're ill."

He managed an affectionate glance. After all, poor Sylbi had been badly worried. "No. No. I'm fine. I suppose I'd better return Larvis's call right away."

He rang the first consul's number but Larvis was not available and was, in fact, nowhere to be found.

"May my wings wither and fall from my body if I ever again act so injudiciously," Ctaarh said.

Sylbi nodded and her orange eyes glowed with anger. "You spend so much time with the Erthumoi that you neglect your duties," she said.

"Not that again," Ctaarh snapped. "Spare me your ridiculous fantasies. I wasn't with the Erthumoi!"

"No?" Sylbi said. "Then where were you?"

"You wouldn't understand."

"Oh! I don't believe you." She turned her back on him and hurried from the room.

Ctaarh snapped his beak shut on angry words. Again the Erthumoi! They were causing him nothing but trouble. Even a progressive-minded Crotonite like himself could be pushed to the limit by these demanding ground crawlers. And what if his dream had been correct? Would the Erthumoi come to dominate interstellar relations? No doubt they would like to do so. Even now they were most likely plotting to embarrass and cheat their more worthy colleagues. Bah! It was really unendurable to contemplate.

The screen rang.

"Yes?" Ctaarh's voice broke over the word.

"Ah, there you are." It was Larvis. The first consul peered out at him and her amber eyes were alight with displeasure. She was a large, brown-feathered female. The scars of her amputated wings were covered by a red woven sash upon which she displayed her badge of office. "Why haven't you provided me with plans for the welcome of the new Erthuma ambassador?"

"I-I didn't think it was my place."

"Not your place? If not you, who? Are you suggesting that I do your work as well as my own?"

"No, Larvis. Of course not."

"Fine. I'll expect the plans in an hour." Larvis paused. "And Ctaarh, I want all the meat to be cooked this time. No repeats of that last disaster."

Ctaarh found the memory of the food-poisoned Erthumoi lurching toward the door strangely pleasing, but he said nothing of his thoughts. Instead, he nodded.

"And," Larvis said, "there should be information—in Erthuma—concerning the ingredients of the food and the preparation of it. I understand the new ambassador is female. Erthuma females have been rumored to take an interest in such matters."

"It will be done."

"I hope so." Larvis glowered a moment longer, then faded from the screen.

The lanterns hung from the ceiling like spiny yellow stars, twinkling with warmth. The tables lining the carved walls of the embassy were piled high with grilled kufra meat, herbed sharquat kabobs, and a host of other Crotonian delicacies. Beside each platter a holocard offered explanation of the ingredients and their preparation translated into the five other interstellar languages, beginning with Erthuma.

The Crotonian embassy was filled with the noise of diplomatic small talk. Dutifully, Ctaarh moved around the room, nodding at Magarhyb, the Samian third consul.

"Greetings, Ctaarh," boomed the Samian. "A most pleasing party. A pleasure, truly."

"Thank you," Ctaarh said. He privately thought that the ambassador resembled a large slab of red cazapa meat over which someone had thrown a rusted metal blanket. Magarhyb would have provided many meals for a nest of hungry Crotonites.

"How will your ambassador vote at the Summit, do you think?" Magarhyb asked.

Ctaarh shook his head apologetically. "You understand, of course, that I may not reveal that information before the vote." He did not add that Larvis had not bothered to share with him her decision regarding the La Se Dans.

"You know how the Erthumoi will vote, don't you?" said the Samian.

"Of course, who doesn't?"

Philip Woo-Somsk, undersecretary to the Erthuma Embassy, glided by. He carried a tray of drinks and was obviously in a hurry but paused to smile at Ctaarh and Magarhyb. "Hi, guys," he said. "Nice party."

Magarhyb nodded his greetings and Ctaarh nodded as well, pretending good fellowship while he gazed at the Erthuma in amazement: he appeared to have no hair at all anywhere on his dark-brown body. Wasn't he cold?

"Their technological ability is impressive," the Samian said. "In fact, many among us wonder how we managed for so long without the Erthumoi and their cunning toys."

"Yes, how did we manage without them?" Ctaarh said sharply. The Samian ambassador stared at him in evident confusion. "Please excuse me."

As he strode through the crowd Ctaarh saw the sinuous Naxian Ambassador Purple Rhomboid turn its/her golden eye upon him. No, no, that would never do. Quickly, he moved out of range before it/she could use her delicate perceptors to sense the resentment and frustration smoldering in his heart.

"This is wonderful food," said Sarah Fen-James, the new Erthuma ambassador. She towered over the Crotonites. In fact, she seemed nearly as tall as her predecessor, Hoving-Davis. Ctaarh wondered if all Erthumoi suffered such freakish growth. The new ambassador's bright red hair could be seen above the throng from almost any location in the room.

"Please allow us to present you with the recipe," Larvis said, gesturing furiously behind her back toward Ctaarh. He hurried over and placed the holocard in Larvis's hand.

With a flourish, the first consul turned and gave it to the Erthuma.

"Oh, thank you," said the new ambassador. "How thoughtful. And I know my husband will enjoy it. *He's* really the cook, you see. I just help clean up." And Sarah Fen-James made a high-pitched stuttering sound of nonaggression and bared her teeth. Her red-lined mouth was enormous.

Larvis nodded sharply, but her eyes were on Ctaarh and he knew she was angry with him for this faux pas. But how was he to have known that their information had been wrong and that Erthuma males were the ones responsible for meal preparation? Perhaps someone had sabotaged the data that the Crotonian Embassy had received. Yes, that was it. The Erthumoi had purposefully misrepresented themselves in order to cause the Crotonites great embarrassment. Wretched, dishonest slugs. If Ctaarh had possessed teeth he would have bared them as well.

Sarah Fen-James was speaking again. How annoying that high-pitched voice of hers was! "Much thanks for these recipes, Madame Ambassador," she said. "And I see that you've had them translated into Erthuma: another thoughtful touch." She turned to face the crowd. "I'm really grateful that the other members of the Six seem to have such superior language skills. You all really compensate for our severe lack of them."

Ctaarh gnawed at one of his claws in frustration. Couldn't these fools see the cultural imperialism behind this blatant flattery? Were they all so blind? Ctaarh began to hear a buzzing, whining sound. He swatted at the air around his head. Damned Samian flies, they were miserable pests. The buzzing grew louder, and began to sound more like words. Ctaarh looked quickly around him. No one else seemed to hear what he heard. In fact, the voice was familiar, like one out of his dreams. It was Wylla's voice and she was whispering to him alone.

"The Erthumoi will reign first among starfolk," she said. "All the other races will be subservient."

"No," Ctaarh said. "No, no, no!"

"Who are you talking to?"

The second consul spun around to see Larvis glaring at him. She held a container of frothy yellow-green Samian wine in her hand.

"No one." Gods, what had she heard? "I was merely worrying about the food and saying 'Oh, oh, oh.' "

"I see." Larvis shook her head. "You had me worried for a moment." Her voice was a bit slurred and she patted him on the left wing in a conspiratorial manner that was most uncharacteristic. Ctaarh wondered if she had been at the wine before the reception began. "Now, Ctaarh," she said, "I really shouldn't be telling you this. But I have some good news." She took another sip of wine. "Yes, very good news."

Ctaarh stood riveted to the spot, hardly daring to hope. Could it be that he was going to be sent home early for reassignment? His heart thumped heavily in his chest. How happily he would return to Pereon, safe from the obnoxious influence of Erthumoi, Naxians, and others of the Six. He would become a simple hunter and eschew all further thoughts of wretched diplomacy, resign his commission, and retire.

"Yes," Larvis said. "I'm too happy to keep this secret. I've been reassigned to the Crotonian Deputation on LostRoses, effective immediately. You, Ctaarh, will take my place as permanent first consul in Menafi. Congratulations."

Ctaarh didn't hear Larvis's further comments. The sip tube in his hand dropped to the ground. Green wine bubbled out of it, making a puddle at his feet.

It couldn't be true, Ctaarh thought. First consul for life?

Larvis began to say something else, but her words were drowned out by a clicking, metallic noise. Ctaarh knew it was the sound of surgical instruments being readied for him, for the amputation of his wings. The room swam before him as the metallic noises grew louder and louder, louder even than Wylla's whispers of Erthuma supremacy.

"No," he whispered. "I won't do it. I'm going home, to Pereon. Home."

"What did you say?" Larvis asked.

"Home." And he turned toward her with his wings extended in the fully aggressive mode.

It was evening in Ipsh and the town was awash in reddish light. Before the late newsburst, Ph'shara and Ph'shant shared a meal and discussion as was their nightly habit.

"Did you hear that the Crotonian second consul went berserk last evening?" Ph'shant asked.

"No. Not that I'm surprised. They are *so* ill-tempered, those Crotonians," said Ph'shara. "In fact, I have often found their behavior to be just this side of uncivilized."

"Agreed." Both Ph'shant and Ph'shara emitted bubbles of delicate gold indicating the harmony of their opinions, and both helped themselves to another tidbit.

"Please continue," said Ph'shara.

Ph'shant swallowed languidly, savoring the taste. "The Crotonian, I believe his name was Sitarh, attacked the new Erthuma ambassador."

"No!" Ph'shara's bubbles were bright red with disbelief.

"And," Ph'shant said, "when his superior tried to intervene, he turned on her as well."

Ph'shara was wordless. Ph'shant could not recall a similar occurrence and he nearly filled the room with yellow bubbles of pleasure. "Then," he said, "before anyone could move, the crazed Crotonite jumped out the window and flew away. Someone heard him muttering about flying home."

"How odd. And how unrealistic. Was there a reason for his violence?" Ph'shara asked.

"Rumor has it that he had been advanced in his position with the Crotonian Deputation."

"Is that not a cause for celebration? Or have I misunderstood my cultural studies?" Ph'shara paused, and purple bubbles indicated that he was deeply in thought. "No, I'm sure not even the Samians indulge in ritual violence upon the delivery of good news. The Erthumoi had some history of it many cycles ago in their primitive stages. They employed it as a means of community expiation. Also as a control mechanism by their religious/political hierarchy. But I've not heard of recent instances. How very odd. The Crotonians are not noted for this. Not at all.''

"Shocking," Ph'shant said.

"I always did think those bird people were inherently unstable," said Ph'shara. "All that time spent flapping about in the air. It's positively unhealthy."

And both Cephallonians shuddered at the very thought as they helped themselves to another delicacy. The tank filled with bubbles of clear pink orange indicating complacency with perhaps just a soupçon of distaste.

About the Authors

Hal Clement

"Hal Clement" is the name used on the science fiction books and stories written by the gifted Harry Clement Stubbs. A science teacher from Massachusetts, with several degrees from Harvard, he has always brought a strong measure of serious scientific extrapolation to his fiction, which includes such notable novels as *Needle* (1950), *Mission of Gravity* (1954), *Nitrogen Fix* (1980), and *Still River* (1987), among other important works produced in his over forty-year career in science fiction.

George Alec Effinger

George Alec Effinger became a full-time writer in 1971 and has since developed a sizable audience for his frequently humorous, sometimes surreal stories that take typical science fiction conventions and turn them on their heads. Notable novels and story collections include *What Entropy Means to Me* (1972), *Irrational Numbers* (1976), *The Wolves of Memory* (1981), *The Bird of Time* (1985), and the very impressive *When Gravity Fails* (1986). His Maureen Birnbaum stories constitute what is perhaps the funniest series in the field.

Karen Haber

A fast-rising new science fiction writer, Karen Haber has published well-crafted stories in such diverse venues as *The Magazine of Fantasy and Science Fiction*, *The Further Adventures of Batman*, and *Isaac Asimov's Science Fiction Magazine*. Two volumes of her brilliant new series of novels, *Mutant Season* (1990) and *Mutant Prime* (1991), have appeared to date. A talented editor as well as author, she coedits the important *Universe* series of original science fiction anthologies with her husband, Robert Silverberg.

Janet Kagan

Janet Kagan's first novel was the bestselling *Uhura's Song* (1985), which many enthusiasts feel is one of the very best *Star Trek* novels ever written. She followed this with *Hellspark* (1987), a fascinating hard science fiction tale based on linguistics. Her excellent short fiction has appeared in *Pulphouse, Analog,* and especially *Isaac Asimov's Science Fiction Magazine,* where her stories "The Loch Moose Monster" (1989) and "Getting the Bugs Out" (1990) won that magazine's Reader's Choice Awards. Both stories are included in her most recent novel, *Mirabile* (1991).

Rebecca Ore

Rebecca Ore was a journalist, a graduate student, and an editorial assistant at the Science Fiction Book Club before settling down to write science fiction in 1983. Her highly acclaimed Alien Trilogy includes *Becoming Alien* (1988), *Being Alien* (1989), and *Human to Human* (1990), and these novels earned her two nominations for the Philip K. Dick Award. In addition, her excellent short fiction gained her nominations for the John W. Campbell Award for Best New Writer (1987 and 1988). Her most recent novel is the well-reviewed *The Illegal Rebirth of Billy the Kid* (1991).

Robert Silverberg

One of the most esteemed and honored science fiction writers of his generation, Robert Silverberg has been awarded three Hugos and five Nebulas. It is likely that he has produced more noteworthy novels than any other writer in the genre—a few of his best are *Hawksbill Station* (1968), *Tower of Glass* (1970), *The World Inside* (1971), the magnificent *Dying Inside* (1972), *The Stochas-*

tic Man (1975), *Lord Valentine's Castle* (1980), and *Star of Gypsies* (1986). His collaboration with Isaac Asimov, *Nightfall: The Novel*, was one of the most eagerly awaited novels of 1990.

Harry Turtledove

Harry Turtledove combines excellent writing skills with his extensive knowledge of ancient history in such novels as his four-part historical fantasy series (*The Misplaced Legion, An Emperor for the Legion, The Legion of Videssos,* and *Swords of the Legion,* all published in 1987), which received widespread critical acclaim, as did his novels *Agent of Byzantium* (1987), *Noninterference* (1988), and *A Different Flesh* (1989). In addition, he is known as an *Analog*-style writer of hard science fiction short stories. His latest books include *A World of Difference* (1990) and *Krispos Rising* (1991).

Lawrence Watt-Evans

Lawrence Watt-Evans is equally at home with science fiction, fantasy, and horror writing. Since the publication of his first novel, *The Lure of the Basilisk,* in 1980, he has produced some fifteen books, including the bestselling *The Misenchanted Sword* (1985), *Denner's Wreck* (1988), *Nightside City* (1989), and the excellent horror novel *The Nightmare People*. His short story, "Why I Left Harry's All-Night Hamburgers," was nominated for a Nebula and won the Hugo Award in 1988.

BIO OF A SPACE TYRANT
Piers Anthony

"Brilliant...a thoroughly original thinker and storyteller with a unique ability to posit really *alien* alien life, humanize it, and make it come out alive on the page." *The Los Angeles Times*

A COLOSSAL NEW FIVE VOLUME SPACE THRILLER—
BIO OF A SPACE TYRANT
The Epic Adventures and Galactic Conquests of Hope Hubris

VOLUME I: REFUGEE   84194-0/$4.50 US/$5.50 Can
Hubris and his family embark upon an ill-fated voyage through space, searching for sanctuary, after pirates blast them from their home on Callisto.

VOLUME II: MERCENARY   87221-8/$4.50 US/$5.50 Can
Hubris joins the Navy of Jupiter and commands a squadron loyal to the death and sworn to war against the pirate warlords of the Jupiter Ecliptic.

VOLUME III: POLITICIAN   89685-0/$4.50 US/$5.50 Can
Fueled by his own fury, Hubris rose to triumph obliterating his enemies and blazing a path of glory across the face of Jupiter. Military legend...people's champion...promising political candidate...he now awoke to find himself the prisoner of a nightmare that knew no past.

VOLUME IV: EXECUTIVE   89834-9/$4.50 US/$5.50 Can
Destined to become the most hated and feared man of an era, Hope would assume an alternate identify to fulfill his dreams.

VOLUME V: STATESMAN   89835-7/$4.50 US/$5.50 Can
The climactic conclusion of Hubris' epic adventures.